Quill of Blood

Dawn Wortley-Nott

PublishAmerica
Baltimore

ISBN: 1-4241-2552-9
PUBLISHED BY PUBLISHAMERICA, LLLP
www.publishamerica.com
Baltimore

Printed in the United States of America

Chapter 1

Anne Jolliffe's first impression of Brading Haven was a favourable one.

"Not so welcoming when the tide's low," Dan said. "'Least that's what I've been told. Just a stretch of sticky, foul-smelling mud. Tried to reclaim the land some twenty-seven years ago, they did—'twas doomed from the start. There's an old legend what says that if a well be uncovered in Brading Haven, one day the sea'll rise up from it and reclaim the land. They found a well all right, stone cased and all. Proves it'd happened before, see—that hundreds of years ago there was pastures where the sea later held sway."

Anne kissed Dan on the cheek, and the small fishing vessel rolled sideways as she lifted her lavender-coloured petticoat and stepped out onto the quay. Her shoes were of reversed calf with high heels—which gave her confidence as she was really quite small—and she wore greyish-white stockings. Her cloak had fallen open to reveal a fitted bodice and stomacher, and her overskirt was of fine green wool bunched up for freedom of movement.

"You're sure you'll be all right now, Lass?" Dan said, after lifting her luggage out of his boat. "You've been good friends to me—you and your uncle. I feels responsible for you."

"You have done quite enough bringing me right round to Brading. Besides, my father is meeting me..." Anne's voice tailed off. Perhaps she should have said that she *hoped* her father was meeting her, for she had not had a reply to her letter. In fact she had not received a reply to any letter she had written him. Of course her father was not one of life's fortunates whom had been taught to read and write, but she had hoped that he would find someone to read her letters to him; and that he would ask that someone to write a few words for him to send to her in return.

She tried to ignore the growing feelings of apprehension when she found that her father was not there to meet her. She felt so alone as she waited on the quay, and she wondered if she would ever see Dan again. Her uncle had taken him in after finding him injured and homeless; just one of the many victims of the bloody Civil War. Dan had completely recovered and had been able to find work, and he had remained good friends with Anne and her uncle. But Anne knew that he would not be really happy until the troubles of the land were resolved and King Charles was restored to his throne. Anne also knew that she would miss him, but felt that now her aunt and uncle were both dead, her place was with her father.

Sighing and picking up her luggage, she knew there was only one thing to do: she must make her own way to her father's cottage as he obviously had no intention of meeting her.

Struggling along with her belongings, she reached the end of the lane and wondered whether to turn right or left into the street in front of her. She put her luggage down on the road.

A coach drawn by four horses rattled to a standstill and a gentleman stepped down.

"If I may be so bold as to introduce myself: I am Sir John Oglander—can I be of assistance?"

"I'm Anne Jolliffe—Walter Jolliffe's daughter," she said.

"You cannot possibly struggle any further with all that luggage," he said. "I know where your father lives, so will you allow me to take you to his cottage?"

Anne's instincts told her that this upright man, whom she would have thought to be in his early 60s, was a true gentleman and she nodded.

"Thank you, Sir John," she said, and his coachman jumped down to pick up her luggage.

Soon they were on their way and she realized that the road they had turned into was the High Street. They stopped to let a woman cross and Anne listened to the gentle lap of the sea, which, she realized, came right up to the back of the cottages.

Sir John was studying her face.

Her auburn hair was taken up to form a coif on her crown, with a fringe of short curly hair. Side ringlets framed her face in stark contrast with her pale complexion. And if there was any outward sign that all was not well within, it was in the disturbed green eyes that came to rest on the elderly gentleman.

"Do you know anything about our island?" he asked gently.

"Only what my late aunt told me…she lived here years ago," she said.

"Yes, of course…I remember her…and I remember your grandparents, too." He was silent for a few moments before continuing: "Will you be staying long?"

"I hope to live with my father—I have no other family left,"she said.

He smiled. "Well, I am sure you will love it here. The countryside is amongst the greenest in the land, and it is the most beautiful, too. And Brading's town and harbour have such character. You cannot help but wonder what secrets they hold. So much has happened here over the years, with Brading having been such a busy seaport and the people crowding her shores. St Wilfrid sailed up the harbour and may even have established his first church here in the 7th century…my ancestor Richard d'Orglandes arrived over four hundred years later from the Chateau of Orglandes in Normandy. Parts of our present church date back to Norman times."

When they reached the cottages where the coachman brought the horses to a standstill, Sir John said: "There is a market in the town tomorrow. It is centred around the town hall, up by the church."

Anne was surprised at how much she had managed to relax in the company of Sir John, but as she stepped down from the coach her apprehension returned with force now that she was so near to meeting her father. "Thank you, again, Sir John, for saving me from struggling with my luggage…it was so kind of you."

Sir John grinned, his once handsome features still much in evidence. "Oh, but the pleasure was all mine, Miss Jolliffe." He beckoned to his coachman to stay where he was and nimbly lifted her luggage from the coach. She followed him towards the cottage.

Thoughts bombarded her mind: this was the cottage in which she would have lived if her mother had survived her birth. At long last she was going to meet the father that had rejected her. The father that she had always dreamed would be so pleased to see her. Perhaps he had not even received the letter that she had sent to him, telling him that she would be coming to join him on the Wight. She had also told him how much she was looking forward to meeting him, at last. But the letter could quite easily have gone astray, she thought. These were troubled times and anything could have happened to it. She tried to steer her imagination away from the inevitable thought that her father had received her letter, but did not want her with him; that he still hated her just as vehemently as he had hated her on the day that she was born. She tried and failed. She swayed as the suspicion and all the weeks of sorrow and uncertainty culminated in a tidal wave of emotion.

"Are you all right, Miss Jolliffe?" Sir John asked anxiously.

Anne nodded her head, but felt an overwhelming desire to confide in Sir John. She tried to hold back; for she was not in the habit of revealing herself to virtual strangers. But there was something compelling about *this* stranger, which made her yearn to unburden herself to him: "I had hoped my father would meet me," she blurted out, then bit her lip; she did not want Sir John to think she was overreacting. "I wrote to him telling him I was coming…"

Sir John looked at her thoughtfully for a moment, and when he spoke, he seemed to be choosing his words with care: "Your father works long hours on the land…perhaps he was unable to get away."

Anne frowned. It was November and she had waited at the quayside until the light had begun to fade. What could be so urgent that he could not meet his own daughter? she thought. It really was unforgivable of him.

"Or perhaps your father has been at the quay for most of the day, waiting for you…" Sir John said as though reading her mind, but his voice tailed away as she shook her head.

"I told him it would be afternoon because of the tide and…well…there could be another reason why he has not met me. Did you know that my mother died when I was born and my father rejected me?"

Sir John nodded.

"He loved her very much, you see, and hated me for causing her death…and he probably still feels the same way about me."

She felt a sense of relief now that she had voiced the thought that had been worrying her the most. For years Anne had not known of her father's true feelings towards her, though she had always felt that her aunt and uncle were hiding something from her. It was not until she had started talking of visiting him that they had reluctantly told her of his rejection of her. She had cried, but she had been writing him the occasional letter since regular, or more accurately irregular, post had at last made it possible. She had asked him if he still hated her, or if he would like her to visit him, but she had not received any replies and had dropped the idea of travelling to the Island to see him—until her uncle's death, that is.

Sir John was looking at her with compassion. "I did know about your father's feelings towards you when you were born, but I don't know how he feels now. You know, you are quite like your dear mother. I remember her so well as I look at you. She was such a lovely person…how long is it now since she—" he hesitated and Anne answered his unfinished question.

"It's nineteen years since she died."

"Would you like me to stay with you until you have met your father?" Sir John asked kindly.

"Thank you, but no," she said decisively. This was her problem and she must not involve Sir John any further…and anyway, she had already taken up far too much of his time.

Sir John had put her luggage down outside the cottage door and was looking at her uncertainly. "Well, if you're sure…but if ever you need someone to talk to, my home, Nunwell House, is quite easy to find—if you don't mind risking your virtue, that is." There was a twinkle in his eyes as he gestured towards the north-west. "If you need a change of scenery, you can walk in that direction. There are paths through some of my fields near my home. Or you can just walk in my parkland, if you prefer." He turned and made his way back to his coach.

Anne had been acquainted with him for such a short time, yet, strangely, she felt as though she had known him for an age: she was sure that her virtue would be quite safe with him, but she admired his sense of humour. For a moment her will floundered and she was on the verge of calling him back, her decision to handle her own problems momentarily wavering. She pulled herself up sharply and chastised herself silently for her faint-heartedness.

With as much courage as she could muster, she knocked on the cottage door.

After what seemed an interminable wait, without her knock being acknowledged, she knocked again, harder, and the door moved. It was open. She pushed it further open and called out softly: "Father, are you there?" There was no reply, nor sound from within, and she hesitated for a moment before entering the cottage.

The air was dank inside the cottage and the place smelt foetid. With a quirk of nostalgia, Anne thought of her uncle's vicarage and the herbs that had always kept the place smelling fresh.

It was now fairly dark, but there did not seem to be a candle burning in the cottage. There is no one here, she thought, and felt a sense of disappointment mingled with relief. But as her eyes grew accustomed to the dimness, she realized that there was a faint glow of light and a man sitting on a bench. He was bent over a table with his back towards her, and for a moment she was unable to speak, only staring at the hunched figure. Oh, Father, please love me, she cried inside herself.

"Father!" she croaked. It sounded so inadequate and the figure at the table neither spoke nor turned to look at her. As she walked closer she saw that his hair was quite long and straggly, but at some time had been unevenly cut.

She moved round to the side of him and saw that there was a candle on the table, which was almost entirely melted and giving out little light.

Looking down at the man she knew must be her father, she thought he had fallen asleep. On closer inspection, however, she realized that his eyes were open, but virtually hidden by thick lashes. His beard was as unkempt as his hair. She stood, willing him to look up at her; but it was obvious that he had no intention of making things any easier for her.

"Father—please…" there was a desperate note in her voice, "I wrote…I wrote to you and told you that my uncle had died. I told you I was coming…" her voice tailed off hopelessly as a tear trickled down her cheek and landed on the table.

Suddenly her father seemed to flame into life. He lifted his head towards her and her heart began to pound in anticipation as his eyes met hers. But there was a look of such hatred in his that she shuddered, and the last of her hopes that he would have forgotten his grievance against her were finally laid to rest.

His face twisted into a contorted expression. "I dedn't get no letter," he growled, and raising his fist into the air and slamming it down on the table angrily, he declared: "And I hay no daughter!"

Chapter 2

"My wife died and I hayn't got no daughter!" Walter shouted at her after leaving the table. Then he stormed out of the cottage.

Hot tears rolled down Anne's cheeks. Of course she had considered the possibility that her father might react hostilely towards her; but nothing could have prepared her for the depth of the hurt that she was feeling now. It was a hurt that was intensified by grief for the loss of her uncle, and she longed to be back at the vicarage where she had felt safe and secure.

When all her tears were shed, she wiped her eyes and replaced the guttered candle with a fresh one that she found on a shelf.

There was a bed at one side of the cottage, but it only had one blanket, and there was only one pillow on the long bolster at the head. There was nothing that she could borrow without almost certainly inflaming her father's temper.

She took the candle from the table and, holding it aloft, climbed into the attic. She was too weary to care what her father's reaction would be when he found her still in his home. He would have to get used to her being there, anyway, she thought: whether he liked it or not she was his daughter and was here to stay.

She put the candle down on the attic floor and brushed away the nearest cobwebs, which might have otherwise caught light. The flame flickered and then flared brightly for several moments as the disturbed dust burnt with a soft sizzling sound.

This would have been my bedchamber, she thought, if I had lived here all my life. But the only furniture in the attic was a wooden trunk. She went to it and brushed away more webs before opening it and rummaging through its contents, looking for anything that might serve to keep her warm during the chilly night ahead.

A couple of rats scurried across the floor, squeaking protests at having been disturbed. Anne jumped more from surprise than from fear of the creatures; for she had always harboured an unusual sympathy with nature's less desirable creations. But her uncle had begun to suspect that rats were spreading some of the deadliest diseases in his parish, and she cringed at the thought of them running across her face in the night.

She lifted three books out of the trunk and looked at their titles. They were: Aesop's Fables, William Shakespeare's plays and Morte d'Arthur. Instinctively, she knew that they had belonged to her mother—her aunt had told her that her mother had been able to read and write—and she hugged them to her. "Oh, Mother, I wish I had known you," she said softly.

She had brought her Bible and her own much prized copy of Chaucer's Canterbury Tales to the Wight with her, but she would be grateful for a little alternative reading.

She recalled how her uncle had painstakingly taught her to read and write, when she was a small girl. She would always be grateful to him; and she would be thankful for the joys that she experienced and the knowledge that she gained through being able to read the words of others. Pity welled up inside her for her father and everyone like him who missed so much by not being able to read and write.

She sighed with relief: there was a large blanket. It smelt musty and was full of moth holes, and Anne wondered about the bugs lurking in its fibres. There was also a pillow, and it brought her comfort to think that this too must have been her mother's, many years before; but she knew there would be plenty of time for speculation, when she did not feel so tired. She closed the lid of the trunk.

Taking the candle, she went down to collect her Bible and the comb from her luggage. Her hair rags could stay where they were; for she was too tired to bother binding her ringlets around them tonight.

Back in the attic, she unfastened her hair. Then she removed her cloak and used it along with the blanket and the pillow to make a semblance of a bed on the floor. But despite her tiredness, she found it difficult to sleep. Even when she pulled her cloak around her the blanket made her itch, and lying on the floor was so unlike being in her comfortable bed at the vicarage.

Fears filled her mind for her uncertain future: supposing her father refused to acknowledge her as his daughter, or even to treat her with cordiality—what would she do then? His words echoed through her mind: "I hay no daughter…My wife and daughter both died." She turned restlessly and then, when her thoughts turned to the rats scurrying across the floor, braved the itching and buried her head under the blanket.

Walter Jolliffe had already left the cottage when Anne awoke the next morning, and she was not sure if she was sorry or relieved. She knew she must talk to him, plead with him, even, to try and find a little love in his heart for her. But at the same time, she was filled with apprehension at the thought of doing so, fearing that his attitude would remain the same.

She took her moth-eaten blanket outside, along with the one from her father's bed, which was little better. And after shaking them vigorously, she draped them over the fence to air.

Re-entering the cottage, she heard the sound of scurrying feet. Only then did she notice the mouse droppings and crumbs of bread upon the table. And opening the door of the small and only cupboard in the cottage, she found a piece of cheese and a hunk of bread, and these too had been savaged by mice—uph! Surely her father had not intended to eat this if there was any of it left when he returned from the fields, she thought in disgust. She threw it out.

"Good morning," she called over to a woman outside a neighbouring cottage, but shut the door sadly when the woman turned away without acknowledging her.

She cleared the crumbs and droppings from the table. And whilst she wondered how her father could bear to live in such an unwholesome hovel, she had seen it all, many times before, in her uncle's parish.

She also knew that many people lived on little else but cheese and rye bread washed down with a tankard or two of ale. But now she was here to look after her father, she would at least be able to make sure that his food was fresh and give him some variety, depending on what was available on the Wight.

There was a pail and a birch broom in the corner and, after brushing aside the cobwebs that covered them, she lifted the broom and knocked it against the wall. She gasped with surprise at the number of spiders that fell out onto the rush matting.

She used the broom to clear more webs, and then went to sweep the attic, but the dust made her sneeze, thrice. She sighed, knowing that she should have fetched water to sprinkle and stop the dust from rising. She went down, collected the pail and went out to the nearest pump.

On her way, she passed a couple of women, who were standing talking. They eyed her with suspicion and did not respond when she smiled at them.

Four little girls, who, Anne decided, were about six years old, were playing by the pump, and she stopped and listened when they began to sing:

"Dree blinde Mice, Dree blinde Mice,

Dame Iulian, Dame Iulian,

The Miller and his merry wold Wife,

She scrapte her tripe licke thou the knife—" Their voices trickled to a halt when they saw Anne, then they stared at her for a few moments. She smiled and one of them seemed about to smile back, but then another nudged her and all four fled.

"Please don't run away," Anne called after them, but they ignored her plea.

Although she was an outsider, she had not expected these people to be so wary of her. With Brading being a harbour, and its many alehouses having thronged with the seamen drifting to its shores throughout bygone days, she would have expected its people to have had an inbred tolerance towards strangers.

She filled the pail with water, allowing enough to wash pots and pans, finish sweeping, and not least wash her face and hands.

Back inside the cottage, she set aside some of the water for herself, continued sweeping the attic, then washed pots, pans, wooden spoons and bowls and pewter plates. Oh, Father, she thought, I shouldn't think these have been washed since my poor mother passed away!

She freshened herself with the water that she had set aside in an old wooden bowl, together with some soap that she had brought with her from her uncle's home; she had brought it knowing that her father would be unlikely to possess such a luxury.

She was pleased to discover that several herbs had survived the weeds in the overgrown plot of land at the front of the cottage, and she gathered what she needed. Wild flowers, too, were growing amongst the herbs and weeds—some of which she could use.

She hung bunches of herbs around the cottage, including her favourite, lavender. Then she scattered herbs with wild flowers on the floor: some were to freshen the air; some to help keep away the moth and, hopefully, others would repel rats and mice.

She decided to visit the market, which Sir John had told her was there today, up by the town hall. She needed to buy food, and she needed to make herself a cheap mattress to lie on. She had thought of buying a trundle bed, but had decided against it; she did not want to spend too much money…

Her uncle had put some money aside for her, though it had never amounted to much; for he had always been so willing to help those in need. He had never allowed his own family to go without, but there were times when he had given a poor wretch his last farthing. And times when he had saved an unwed mother from a whipping, or from being locked in the stocks, and then let her and her baby stay with them at the vicarage.

When she reached the market, she was surprised to see so many officials in attendance; she had never seen the like in the market at home. If anyone was swindled here, she thought, it certainly would not be due to lack of concern by the town authorities. She watched as provisions were measured by the official yardstick, and by standard measures for the pint, quart and gallon. The butcher was arguing with an official viewer of the butcher's shambles about a cut of meat.

"Stop thief!" shouted a seller as a youth tried to escape with a measure of ale without paying. An official grabbed him by the scruff of the neck and hauled him towards the town hall.

As she wandered round, Anne saw the viewers at the corn market and the cheese and butter market, and many other officials being kept busy along with the sellers.

She bought a cheap rush basket, half a yard of muslin, and enough cloth to make a small flower bag, along with a few other provisions, including 1.lb of mutton scraps, thread and ticking. And she was just about managing to carry the ticking under her arm as she made her way out of the market. She still needed lots of filling for the mattress, but that would have to wait.

"You're 'n overner, aren't you?" the woman's voice broke into her thoughts, and on seeing Anne's puzzled expression she did not wait for a reply: "You're not from hereabouts. Sir John Oglander took you to Walter Jolliffe's cottage, didn't he?" She was squinting at Anne, and Anne could sense some hostility underlying the words.

But she was not going to be intimidated: she had every right to be here. "Yes, Sir John was very kind, and I'm living with Walter Jolliffe because I'm his daughter, Anne Jolliffe."

"Another damn Puritan in the town!"

Anne swung round and stared straight into the eyes of her accuser. She had been on the verge of telling him that she had no idea what he was talking about. She did not know what her father's religious or political beliefs were, but if he was a 'Puritan' it really was nothing to do with her—she had only just arrived.

She knew that the Wight had sided with Parliament since the beginning of the Civil War. But it rather surprised her that her father might be involved in any cause at all. In her uncle's Parish, there appeared to be little interest among land workers as to the feuds of the land.

Her uncle had been registered as a Presbyterian minister, but he had been a very moderate one, and a Christian above all else. He had not believed that sectarian prejudices necessarily made one a better preacher, but he also believed that to question Royal authority was to question all authority, and Anne sometimes found this a little conflicting.

Uncle Silas had been deeply affected by the outbreak of civil war. Every day, during and after the war, he had prayed for peace and for King Charles and the Royalists. But being a sincere Christian, he had also prayed for Parliament and its supporters and the sectaries that had ensued. He had prayed for the Independents or those who were 'Puritan' by one degree or another, including the revolutionary minority that had taken over in some counties. And with the complete breakdown of law and order threatening in many parts of Britain as well as in his own parish, her uncle's health had deteriorated rapidly, in spite of his faith.

But Anne did not correct the stranger; instead, she just stared at him. For he was having a most profound effect upon her. Something in the young man's eyes paralysed her momentarily. She was totally unprepared for the state of emotion that coursed through her body, and a flush came to her cheeks.

The stranger's long hair was fair. His slender nose and full mouth were so perfect, in Anne's mind. And his dark blue eyes, which seemed to bore into her soul, were startling in their intensity. She turned away quickly so that he would not see the confusion in her eyes. No one had ever affected her in such a way before.

You are not normal in the head, Anne, she told herself silently on the way back to the cottage, which she could not yet think of as home. He is a most objectionable young man.

Anne found herself awaiting her father's return with trepidation. But she knew she would have to make him understand that she was here to stay. She also knew that there was nothing she could say to make him love her—or even like her, come to that. But she hoped that he would at least try to show her a little consideration.

She made some nourishing broth, and began to feel impatient as she continued waiting for her father to come home.

Eventually she sighed. She had waited quite long enough. She was hungry. She filled a wooden bowl with the hot, steaming broth, and wondered how long she would have to keep the rest hot without letting it spoil.

Impatience turned to anger, however, when it had been dark for an age and there was still no sign of her father. He knew that she was still in his home. He would have seen her luggage, and he was staying away on purp—

Her thoughts were interrupted by the sound of laughter. The door swung open and Walter entered the cottage. But he was not alone.

The portly gentleman with him looked a little younger, and his thin, dark hair was shorter than her father's. By the candlelight, Anne could just about see that his velvet cloak was red. His breeches looked green, and he was wearing an elaborately brocaded jacket to match. His chubby fingers were adorned with several rings with big stones. The only sombre note of his whole attire was his large, plain, white collar.

He was hanging onto her father's arm and they were laughing and singing. The words of the song brought a flush to Anne's cheeks. This was not the way that she had always imagined or dreamed of her father behaving.

As soon as her father's companion saw Anne, he stopped singing and stood staring at her in open-mouthed admiration. But Anne had already found herself disliking him and did not find his admiration at all flattering.

"I am Sh—Samuel Jarvis, Walter's employer and landlord," he said, moving nearer to her. "Walter's my drinking partner." His speech was slurred and he laughed for no reason. "And wh—who—who are you?" he asked, stepping almost against her. She took a step backwards as he tried to put his arms around her.

"I am Walter's daughter," she replied stiffly.

"Walter—how could you keep her s-secret?" he said, swaying forwards and nearly falling over.

Walter, who was now sitting on the bench by the table, snorted. "She's not my daughter. I don't hay no daughter." Samuel burped and moved closer to Anne, again.

She did not want him so near her, he made her feel as though ants were crawling over her skin, and she turned and moved right away. Why on earth was her father drinking with his employer and landlord, anyway?

Samuel moved back towards her and was ogling her, and she said the first thing that came into her head. "Do you want some broth?"

He was laughing at her as he shook his head. Not surprisingly, her aunt and uncle had not taught her ways of dealing with a drunken father and his equally drunken friend. And she was feeling anxious as she rushed to fetch her father's broth.

Samuel was still staring at her, and as she ladled the broth from the couldron to the bowl, some dribbled down her clothes onto the floor. How she wished that there was a separate kitchen and scullery, like in her uncle's vicarage! She grabbed clean rag, which she had used earlier in the day to wash the pots and pans, and tried to wipe the spills away.

Carrying the bowl to the table and placing it down in front of her father, she expected no thanks; but neither was she prepared for his reaction as he rose unsteadily from the bench with anger blazing in his eyes. For a moment she feared that he would strike her. But fortunately for her, he attacked the bowl of broth instead: with a swoop of his hand and foul words he swept it from the table, causing it to land upside down on the rush matting.

"Get out o' my home," he growled finally. "Do you hear me? Get out!"

Anne fell a step backwards as though she had been dealt a physical blow. Hot tears filled her eyes and sadness overwhelmed her.

Samuel, doubtlessly realizing that her father was unlikely to care what happened to her, lunged at her, pulling her into his arms. His mouth sought hers hungrily and for a few moments she was completely overpowered by his size and strength. She tried to pull away, but he was holding her too tightly. Then the audacity of his assault sent indignation surging through her body. How dare he treat her like a common whore? She forced her arms up between them and with all her might pushed him away from her. "Don't you ever do that again!" The words were barely more than a whisper, but they were expressed with such vehemence that Samuel could be left in no doubt as to their sincerity.

He stumbled. "Damn wench!"

Walter was looking ill-tempered again. Anne wanted to believe he was feeling fatherly instincts towards her and hating Samuel's disrespectful behaviour; but she could not believe it.

Samuel went and filled two tankards with ale, and after thrusting one onto the table in front of Walter, he took a swig from the other and wiped his sleeve across his mouth to remove the froth. Then banging his tankard down on the table and giving Anne a sideways glance, his face broke into a semblance of a smile.

"I like a woman with spirit."

Anne gave him a withering look before turning away sharply and retreating to the attic. She was too hurt to cry as she fingered her bruised lips.

"She's an amazing woman," she heard Samuel say.

Her father snorted. "Girl, not woman."

Samuel began to brag about the land and property that he had gained from the Royalists, whilst her father made the appropriate comments and noises, and when the hurt had subsided a little, Anne began to wonder at this strange friendship. But two things were clear to her: Samuel enjoyed boasting and her father was a good listener. Tears filled her eyes and she wondered how she was going to endure living here.

She found herself recalling everything in Saint Mary's Church on Sunday, but she was not sure with whom she felt most aggrieved: her father or Samuel. She tried to concentrate on the service. But becoming aware of several pairs of eyes upon her, during the sermon, she allowed her mind to wander.

The only friendly gestures were made by Reverend Newland, who shook her hand after the service. And by Sir John Oglander, who winked at her as they were leaving the Church, and again she found herself warming to this charming gentleman. She knew not why, but the strange thought passed through her mind that she could trust him with her life.

Chapter 3

Anne soon learnt to stay out of Walter's way as much as possible; it seemed the only way to avoid his wrath. During the day he worked on the land—except Sunday, that is, now strict observance of the Sabbath was demanded by the 'Puritans'.

When he returned, Anne would put food in front of him and 'thank God' that he did not sweep it to the floor. She would then light a candle to take into the attic, where she would read, at least until her father left for his favourite alehouse.

She liked to prepare for bed before he returned. And if Samuel came home with him, she would muffle the sound of his voice by covering her ears with the old blanket, and a sheet of linen that she had bought by the yard and hemmed.

But now she was surprised to see her father coming through the door in the early afternoon.

"Samuel sent me home…he wants t'talk." His voice was gruff, but Anne was delighted that he was bothering to tell her what was happening.

"I wonder why he wants to talk to you here." On seeing her father's disgruntled expression she hurried on: "Well it must be quite important for him to send you home so early."

Walter snorted and turned his back on her, and disappointment welled up inside her. "Oh, Father…please!" She moved round in front of him. "It's the first time you have bothered to tell me anything and I thought perhaps you were beginning to accept me."

"I had to tell thee…it's thee he's comen here to see." He went and sat down at the table.

"I don't understand."

"He wants to see *you*, not me, girl," Walter said impatiently.

"I understand perfectly what you said. What I don't understand is why he is coming to see me…or why you thought I'd agree to it, come to that."

"You must agree, Samuel wants—"

"What Samuel wants is none of my concern…I'll not be here."

"I demand thee—"

"No, Father! I don't like Samuel…and anyway, I can't think why on earth he'd want to see me…" and then, as if struck by a sudden thought, she added ruefully, "unless, of course, he intends trying to kiss me again!"

"He was drunken when that happened," Walter was holding onto his temper, "and you've only met him once."

Anne took her cloak from a hook on the wall. "I am going for a walk."

"If you dun't stay, he'll be—"

"I'll see you when I return," she interrupted him, throwing her cloak round her shoulders in a gesture of defiance.

"If thee were a youngen I'd give thee a tannen, you! You should obey your father." Anne stared back at him for a moment before leaving the cottage. At least he had acknowledged that he was her next of kin. She had been tempted to yield to him, for she longed to do the right thing in his eyes. But he had given her no reason to believe he had softened towards her, or that he would do so if she obeyed him, and she would not…could not stay.

"He likes thee," Walter called after her and she cringed. She could think of nothing more unpleasant than Samuel liking her and making further unwelcome advances on her every time he drank too much ale.

She passed several women as she walked along the lane, but none of them acknowledged her. Sadness overwhelmed her. She shivered and pulled her cloak about her; but the chill was due more to the unfriendliness of the folk here than lack of warmth from the late November sun. She quickened her pace.

She thought about Sir John Oglander and his kindness towards her, and she considered his suggestion that she should visit him if she needed to talk to someone. He had waved his arm to the north-west, and she turned now and made her way in the direction of his home.

Lifting her petticoats, she climbed over a stile. Dried leaves crunched beneath her feet as she followed the footpath. Sheep were grazing in the fields on one side, and on the other, a few yards from the path, were dense trees. Gradually the beauty and tranquillity lightened her mood; for no one who loved the countryside, the birds and the animals as much as Anne did could continue to remain unaffected by their enchantment. Sir John Oglander was right: this countryside was the greenest she had ever seen.

On reflection, she did not feel that she knew Sir John well enough to knock on his door, but it comforted her knowing that the land was a friendly and welcoming place to be, because Sir John had invited her to walk there.

She followed the path, which was now only bordered by tall grasses, wild plants and spaced out trees. On either side was open parkland.

Stooping down beneath a mighty oak and picking up an acorn, she was vaguely aware of caressing it between her thumbs and forefingers, but her thoughts had drifted back to her father: she doubted that he had meant to acknowledge her as his daughter. She was sure that he still hated her. For if he cared about her at all he would not have tried to force her to stay and face a man who had treated her like a whore…Her mind was so preoccupied with her thoughts that she did not hear the thud of hoofs…

Her eyes opened wide with fear. A horse was galloping straight towards her and was almost upon her. With a desperate effort to move out of its way, she fell sideways to the ground as the dapple-grey horse reared whinnying into the air. She lay terrified as its hoofs came down, missing her by only inches.

From where she lay, she saw only a distorted image of the rider. But it was an image that seemed to be surrounded by a cloud of enmity, which engulfed her for an age. But then the horse was gone as quickly as it had arrived, and Anne was left wondering exactly what it was that she had seen.

Hearing more hoofs, her eyes misted with tears. Oh, no…please…not again! But she could see a shape coming towards her. She knew that it would be futile to try to struggle to her feet and run, so she closed her eyes and prayed. But the sounds of hoofs softened and slowed to a stop. And when she opened her eyes, she found herself looking up into the concerned face of Sir John Oglander.

"Sir John!"

Sir John dismounted and helped her to her feet. "Are you all right, my dear? I saw what happened."

"Y—yes, I think so," she said, pulling her cloak back round her. She was shaken but so relieved to see Sir John again.

"What an unpleasant welcome to Nunwell!" he said.

"It's so nice to see your friendly face," she said meaningfully.

Sir John sighed understandingly. "Did your father not welcome you?"

"My father hates me…most folk ignore me…" She put a hand to her head. She had not meant to sound so full of self-pity.

Sir John smiled. "Your father has been living on his own for a very long time—he will probably need a lot of time to adjust. As regards the other folk, I am sure they don't mean to be unkind. They are just wary of strangers."

"You would expect them to have inherited a tolerance towards strangers…I mean, with Brading Haven having been such a busy seaport."

"Yes," Sir John studied her thoughtfully, "but in recent years many of the Island folk have been abused. When Scottish soldiers were billeted here they raped and pillaged—no-one was safe from them. It has increased people's wariness of all strangers.

"Sometimes I feel that the whole kingdom has become a gloomy place, anyway. The war has seen to that, with brother killing brother and families divided. My brother George died in August. Unlike me, he supported Parliament."

Another horseman arrived and Sir John looked at the rider questioningly.

"Sorry, Sir John, I could hardly see him in the distance, let alone catch him." He dismounted.

Sir John looked at Anne now. "You won't have met Paul Miller." But Anne hardly heard Sir John; for she was staring at Paul. He was the same young man who had accused her of being a 'damn Puritan'.

"Well, well, it's our Puritan Lady," Paul said. There was a hint of sarcasm in his tone and a flicker of hostility in his dark blue eyes.

"I—I am not a Pur—" Anne stopped, flustered again by the sensations aroused in her by Paul's nearness. She forced herself to look away from his eyes, and found herself noticing the way the ends of his fair hair curled under onto his shoulders.

"I suppose you know King Charles is here on the Wight?" Paul's tone sounded hostile now, and Anne shook her head.

"He fled from the fanatics at Hampton Court, and he's now at the mercy of our damn Governor, Robert Hammond!"

Sir John gave him a warning look. "I do think Miss Jolliffe should be spared the oaths."

"Sorry, Miss Jolliffe," Paul said, but Anne did not think he sounded at all sincere.

"Robert Hammond is a kind and honest man," Sir John said, looking at Anne and Paul in turn, letting them know that he was talking to both of them. "He is sympathetic towards the King and—"

"He notified Parliament that the King was on the Wight," Paul interrupted impatiently. "He could have kept quiet."

Sir John sighed. "He's answerable to the Army leaders. They would have eventually found out that the King was here, and what then? How would Hammond's arrest help the King? At least Hammond is sympathetic and can make him as comfortable as possible.

"I must tell you, Paul, that when I visited His Majesty, he praised the way Hammond was treating him." He looked from Paul to Anne.

"Even so, coming to the Wight might be the worst thing the King could have done. I fear for his freedom.

"He told Hammond that he had fled from Hampton Court because of Army extremists and that he was particularly in fear of the Levellers. He had hoped to go to Jersey."

"But Hammond persuaded him to come here instead," Paul said.

"I know, I know…and Hammond was probably made Governor of the Wight to be his keeper as he had met him before. But at least Hammond is his keeper, not some bloodthirsty extremist.

"I was summoned to a meeting in Newport by Hammond, and he said how concerned he was for the King's safety. In fact, he had been in a quandary when he went to the mainland as to whether he should advise the King to come to the Wight, or warn him to keep right away."

Paul looked at him sharply. "But I thought…If Hammond was sent here ready for the King's arrival, why would he turn him away?"

Sir John stroked his beard. "Perhaps Hammond wasn't told why he'd been sent here. But anyway, Hammond promised the King he would do all he could to meet his desires—"

"Except help him to escape the land if it becomes necessary," Paul butted in.

"When the King asked Hammond if he could protect him until he reached an agreement with his Parliament, Hammond answered him by saying that he would do all he could to meet the King's wishes 'in relation to the commands Parliament would give'. It must have been the best Hammond could offer him without going against orders."

"That's not very encouraging," Paul said.

"No," Sir John frowned, "and neither was the gilt inscription on the King's bed at the Plume of Feathers in Cowes, where he spent his first night on the Wight. How I wish that he had come to my home and not stayed there!" He explained to Anne: "The King has his own room in my house where he stayed when he visited me in happier times."

"What was the inscription?" Paul asked.

"Remember thy end."

"Oh, no, how awful!" Anne said.

"Yes, it was most unfortunate in the circumstances. His Majesty believed it to be a bad omen."

Anne had almost forgotten about her own problems while she had been listening to Sir John.

Sir John took his horse's reins and led the animal forward as he said to Anne: "I'll walk with you to the lane to make sure you reach it safely—you have had enough excitement for one day."

Anne was thankful that Sir John did not know just how much excitement. She wished Paul did not affect her so. He was despicable and she had no desire to feel anything but dislike for him.

To Anne's surprise Paul began to walk with them, but looking at Anne, he was quick to make his purpose clear: "I can't bear to leave until I hear what else you know about the King's arrival, Sir John."

"There's not a lot left to tell. The day after the King arrived on our island he was moved to Carisbrooke Castle."

"Does that mean he's a prisoner?" Anne said.

"He still has freedom to leave the castle, and he is waiting for his coach to be shipped over here."

"The Wight is his prison!" Paul said.

"Sadly, Paul is probably right. But on the way to the castle a woman gave him a rose and others told him that most of the Wight now supported him, apart from officials, of course. They even thought Hammond might be talked round if necessary, but I cannot share their optimism, I'm afraid."

"Hammond would never help him escape," Paul said.

Sir John sighed. "Despite not wanting to harm the King, I think he lacks the strength of character to go against those in authority, even if it were for the sake of the King's life.

"I was so anguished by His Majesty's arrival here that I wept." Paul looked shocked by the admission; for it revealed the full extent of Sir John's fears for his King.

"It's a pity you're not still Deputy Governor." Paul looked at Anne and said angrily: "Sir John was stripped of all his public appointments early in the war just for being an honest Royalist and refusing to support Parliament against the King!"

Sir John frowned at him. "The truth is, Miss Jolliffe, I could not allow myself to be reappointed Deputy Lieutenant...and Deputy Governor of the Wight under the new regime, which was against everything I believe in. I doubt if remaining as Deputy Governor would have helped the King much, anyway." He laughed. "I can't imagine them being foolish enough to leave me in charge of him.

"But I have been punished for being an honest Royalist. I have had my home ransacked, paid extortionate fines and been taken prisoner three times. I learnt the hard way to be a little discreet in my opinions." Meaningfully, he looked at Paul. "I only hope others can learn by my mistakes.

"When I was arrested and kept in London for two and a half years, I never dreamed that such heartache would follow.

"I was allowed to live in my son Richard's house for a year. Then I was put under close arrest in a messenger's house in Westminster without being allowed a hearing. Franck—Frances my beloved wife, came to London and begged permission for me to live at my own lodgings at the Seven Stars in the Strand. My poor, poor, darling Franck..." He stopped talking for a few moments as though it hurt too much to go on, but then he continued: "My Franck, overheating her blood in procuring my release, got the smallpox and died. I would rather have remained a prisoner for the rest of my life than have my Franck die. She bore me nine children and was the most wonderful wife a man could ever have," his voice caught in his throat. There was a bleak look in his eyes now and he seemed to be far away for a few moments.

He must have loved his wife dearly, Anne thought, and there was a look of utter respect on Paul's face as he looked at Sir John.

"I am sorry, Sir John...about your wife, I mean," Anne said.

Sir John smiled. "I should not have burdened you with my troubles."

"I am glad you did," Anne said feelingly. "I can understand how you must have felt."

Paul turned on her angrily: "What could you possibly know of what Sir John felt, or of how he has been discredited for being a Royalist?"

"Paul!" Sir John sounded angry, now, but Anne turned and hurried away without waiting to hear what else was said. Paul's words were exactly what she would have expected of him, yet they stung her like wasp venom.

Sir John called her name, but she hardly heard him, so intent was she on holding back her tears until she was some distance away. She was disappointed with herself for letting Paul upset her so: he deserved contempt.

When she could no longer stop the tears from falling, she sat on a tree stump until her eyes cleared. Life was complicated, she thought. There was Samuel, whom she disliked intensely, with his unwanted attention. Yet she would appreciate just one kind word from Paul. She was startled by her own admission. She must be mad to want attention from such a bigot!

Chapter 4

Tom Fletcher was tempted to speak to the girl with the tearful eyes. She was quite pretty, despite her solemn expression, he thought, and he could ask her the way to Nunwell House.

Then he reminded himself that he was not supposed to do anything that might make his encounter with Sir John Oglander seem contrived. And he had been told to avoid talking to anyone, unless strictly necessary, until after the encounter. But Tom did not always obey his master, especially when the order seemed unreasonable.

There were many things that he could say to the damsel without casting suspicions on his reason for being there; and why would she care, anyway? She looked as lonely as he felt, and he wanted to make her smile. But then the girl hurried by without even noticing him and the moment was lost, for he could hardly run after her.

Tom sighed and thought about his assignment; the reason that he had been sent to the Wight. He had arrived on the island that morning and was prepared for a long dreary stay.

"I shall be there, too," Edmund had told him, "and I'll be watching you."

Tom had heard Edmund and his friends referred to as 'Puritans', and although he had been swept along by their beliefs and fought with them in the Civil War, he was confused when he tried to understand what the war had really been about. Some said it was directed against the King's malignant councillors. "It is to bring the monarchy to its just limits," said others. But religion seemed to have become one of its main forces.

He thought it strange that many branded as 'Puritans' observed the Sabbath and were sticklers for discipline, abhorring anything remotely frivolous, while others sought to shake off all lawful authority. And he had difficulty justifying the wealth enjoyed by Edmund with the ideals that he had heard expressed by many enemies of the King for a more equal society.

Sometimes he suspected that Edmund and his friends were just rebels seeking to destroy the King for their own selfish ends, and that they had little loyalty to any cause.

"I believe the King's enemies will soon have total control of the country," Edmund had told Tom, and Tom knew that Edmund intended to be up there with them. He also knew that he dare not fail another assignment. Beads of perspiration formed on his forehead as he recalled his last, failed mission, which had been to steal some important papers from a messenger whilst masquerading as a highwayman. So vivid were his memories that he almost felt that he was back there:

Tom knew how magnificent he looked in his highwayman's guise. He was not handsome, but the highwayman's mask allowed him to feel as splendid as he desired, and it excited him. Maybe this was his true calling in life. It would be such a rewarding occupation and he would be free of Edmund forever.

He saw the messenger approaching and rode out onto the highway. "Deliver your money and papers to me," he demanded. But after pulling on his reins for his horse to stop, the young messenger just folded his arms and looked at Tom's pistol, a half smile on his face.

When he spoke, it was in a mockingly cool voice: "Are you trying to rob me, you oaf. Should you not be telling me to stand and deliver?" He raised an eyebrow and Tom's eyes widened in alarm. This was not how it was meant to be. His left hand was resting on his breeches and he clenched the cloth, not knowing what to do next, and before he was able to regather his wits the messenger lunged forward and pulled him from his horse. His black hat fell off, and the messenger pulled the mask from his face. In the scuffle that ensued, Tom received bruises and cuts, and he heard the crack of a firearm as he fled...

Edmund had been livid to hear that Tom had not succeeded in his errand. "You are failing our cause," he had cried, striking him with his whip and catching him across the shoulder. A few inches higher and Tom's face might have been disfigured for the rest of his life.

How he had hated Edmund at that moment! Sometimes Tom admired his determination, sometimes despised his cruelty. For Edmund always did what he wanted, regardless of whom might get hurt. Sometimes Tom longed to be more like him; but at other times he feared the motivation that seemed to drive him to evils beyond the necessity of whatever he was doing.

But now Tom saw two figures ahead. A little nearer and he saw that one was probably slightly older than his own 18 years and was of fairly slim build with fair hair, while the other looked about sixty.

As Tom studied the elder of the two, he wondered if this was the knight whom he was on his way to see. He noted his maroon cloak, which was of excellent quality, and although he seemed to be chastising the younger man, he had strong but kind features and was well built, but not fat. Tom considered the description that he had been given and believed this must indeed be Sir John Oglander.

This was better than he had expected: he did not even have to await his chance. Perhaps it was an omen that his fortune was changing for the better.

But Tom knew that he would have to tread carefully. He had been warned that Sir John had been Lieutenant-Governor of Portsmouth, Deputy Lieutenant/Governor of the Isle of Wight, and even Sheriff of Hampshire and would not be easily deceived.

"Excuse me," Tom said, fixing Sir John with his deep dark brown eyes. "Do please excuse me for the intrusion. I am Tom—Tom Fletcher. Please, I desperately need somewhere to rest my body, and I also need to earn my keep. Can you help me?"

Sir John introduced himself and Paul, and then stroked his chin. "I don't kno—"

And Tom, fearful that he had used the wrong approach, continued:

"I have been travelling for months, sir. Pushed from village to town, begging for work or scraps of bread, sleeping rough and arrested as a vagrant. I have been refused alms, and I spent my last farthing on a pint of ale, Sir John—fearing it would be my last, you understand. Finally I came to this island." He ran a hand through his almost black, lustreless hair.

"Your family?" Sir John said.

"They are all dead, sir. My father and brother were both lost with the King's infantry at Naseby, while I stayed with my mother and sister, Lucy, in Stow-on-the-Wold, and I decided to do my part by helping work the land, but enemies set our home alight and I was the only surviv—"

"Did you know these enemies?" Sir John interrupted.

"No, Sir John, but they wore the Parliamentary Army uniform. Neighbours were too frightened to help us until these men were well out of their sight. By that time it was too late for my mother and sister…" He paused, shaking his head. "No one could have survived that furnace.

"It happened in the early hours of the morning. I can vaguely remember waking, though now it seems like a bad dream…a nightmare. My head was throbbing and the smoke was so thick I could scarcely breathe, sir, then nothing. I shall be forever in the debt of the neighbour who pulled me to safety."

He searched Sir John's face for signs that his tale was having the desired effect but was unable to determine anything from his expression.

"I had trouble with my breathing for a long time after the fire," he continued, "and the neighbour who saved me nursed me until I was strong again. I stayed in his home even after I went back to helping on the land."

"You went back to work?"

"Oh, yes, Sir John. I lost everything in that fire. But living so near to where my mother and sister had died tormented me so.

"Eventually, I realized I would have to get as far away from there as possible."

Sir John sighed. "I dare say we can find you a place to sleep and work. But it's only temporary, mind you, until you can find something else."

"Oh, thank you—thank you so much, sir. You won't regret it, I promise you."

"I sincerely hope not," Sir John said, and Tom was disappointed that he sounded so uncertain.

Anne had been trying to push Paul's biting words out of her mind as she hurried back to her father's cottage. She still thought of it as her father's cottage, not her home. There was little, as yet, to endear her to the place, but it would be so different if her father loved her.

Glancing over the thatch and local stone with detachment, she wondered if it would be better if she left, perhaps tomorrow, or the next day. But deep down inside herself, she knew that she would stay; for her father was still her father in spite of everything, and he was her only living relative, as far as she knew.

A horse snorted and Anne saw that a brown stallion was tethered to her father's fence. Oh, no! It must be Samuel's. She had so hoped that he would have left by now. She did not relish the thought of having to fend off his unwelcome advances; but neither did she feel like walking any further.

Once inside the cottage, however, she began to think that her worries had been needless. Samuel treated her with the utmost courtesy. He jumped from his seat. "My dear," he said. Then, taking one of her hands, he kissed her palm and led her to his chair. His hair looked as though it had just been groomed, and he smelt quite fresh compared with the last time they had met. "Please do sit down." He stood gallantly by the side of the chair, and when she sat, he looked down at her with gentleness and respect. And although she could not like him, she told herself that she should treat him with civility so long as he remained courteous towards her. He was her father's friend, after all, and her efforts might help to—

Samuel broke into her thoughts, "I'm sorry for any misunderstanding last time we met." His apology sounded false, as though he was not really sorry at all; or perhaps it was just that he was not in the habit of apologizing.

"I should have realized you were well bred and treated you

accordingly, but I had been drinking." Anne's frown was caused not so much by what he said as by the way that he said it: as if his drunken state absolved him from blame for his behaviour, but she decided to let it pass.

He took her hand in his and caressed her wrist gently with his thumb. "I wonder…" he said, rather awkwardly, she thought, for the likes of him, "would you do me the honour of coming to a bull baiting with me tomorrow?"

She stared back at him for a moment, in alarm, before pulling her hand free of his. "No—No…I'm sorry." She wondered why she was apologizing.

"I don't mean a local baiting but a splendid—"

"No!"

"But why? I promise not to try to kiss you or—"

"I don't want to go with you…why would I? And anyway, I hate bull baiting."

"Most people enjoy watching a baiting," Samuel said.

"Then ask one of them to go with you." Anne failed to keep her voice steady. "I thought your Puritan friends were against everything people enjoyed, anyway." She did not wait for Samuel to reply as she moved towards the door. "It's freezing in here. I must fetch some wood." Her father had allowed the fire to burn away to nothing, and she needed to relight it.

"If thee hadn't disobeyed me and had stayed home, thee could hav kept fire in. It's ben cold in here all afternoon," Walter said. Anne ignored him and went outside where there was a pile of logs, twigs and other kindling. She picked up four logs and a bunch of twigs and kindling and took them back inside, and whilst she busied herself relighting the fire, Samuel talked.

"My dear Anne, you talk of my *Puritan friends.* I wonder how little you really know. Strict disciplinary actions are as much Presbyterian as—"

"My uncle was a Presbyterian Minister," she interrupted, "and he was a very moderate and very kind man." She sat back on her heels

36

and looked round at Samuel. "But he believed some of the more austere Presbyterians had toppled over into Puritanism."

Samuel roared with laughter. "Is that so?" He pressed the tips of his fingers together and raised his head as though smelling the air, then with a chuckle he continued: "It's interesting to hear your uncle's theory, but if all those who want any reform of the Church are Puritans the whole Kingdom must be Puritan.

"People who support the English Church support its split from the Roman Catholic Church." He smiled down at her and she turned her head away to busy herself with the fire. "Yet all these years later godly reformation has not been completely accomplished, nor has the English Church been purified of Roman Catholic popery."

"But plenty is being done now to ban everything people love, including Christmas celebrations and the theatre," Anne said.

Samuel was quiet for several moments and she wondered if he was lost for words, though she doubted it, then he continued: "Well, I don't think we need concern ourselves as far as this bull bating is concerned."

Oh no! Anne thought. She had so hoped that he would drop the subject of the baiting.

"Hammond has given the five guineas for a bull to be baited at Newport," Samuel continued, "and the Mayor has agreed to decorate his dog with ribbons and let it be first dog with the bull. I have it on very good authority that the Corporation only agreed to be in state after a lot of persuasion—I must admit I've heard rumours that baiting will be banned by Mayor's Day, which is why they want to have an extra special baiting now."

Anne stood up and brushed the bits from her clothes, then she moved away from the crackling fire.

"Most girls in your position would think it a great honour to accompany such an affluent gentleman as myself," Samuel said, spreading his fingers and looking down at his rings. Then he lifted his head and looked at Anne hopefully.

How clearly she remembered him telling her father how he had gained his wealth! She felt irritated by his arrogance. "I would not go anywhere with you even if someone offered me a guinee to do so...and as for bull baiting, I could name at least one person who is far more deserving of being baited…" her voiced tailed off as Samuel's face crumpled with amusement, and then he roared with laughter again.

"My, my, she is quite a little shrew." His shoulders heaved with mirth. "Oh, Anne, my darling!" he breathed, when his laughter had abated.

"I am not your darling…and you insult me by laughing at me. I—"

"No insult was intended," Samuel interrupted. "I have the greatest regard for you, my dear. Perhaps you would rather wait and attend a more local baiting—if another is allowed."

"Samuel's trying to court thee, you, so—"

"What?" Anne silenced her father and stared at him in disbelief. "You cannot mean it…How could you even consider such a thing?"

"Samuel's not poor and'es risen—"

"Rising on money and property he has stolen from Royalists!" Now her previous thoughts of trying to be civil towards Samuel were forgotten.

Samuel's face was reddening. "You dare pass judgements? You know nothing of how it was." He was quiet for a few moments, then he continued: "There was a war. Royalists were our enemies…still are…even over here, where there were no battles and people came to escape the fighting.

"But everyone should have the same chances, both in the Church and—"

"Are you a very religious man, Mr Jarvis?" Anne asked. It would greatly surprise her if he could truthfully answer 'yes'. "People do call you a Puritan, but I find it difficult to believe."

"I can't help what people call me. But in the first place the Civil War was not even about religion, but more to do with reducing the Monarchy's power. I admit I'm not always as religious as some of God's flock, but he has blessed me with good fortune for supporting his true followers." He has an answer for everything, she thought.

"Is that what you really believe?"

"I'm explaining it in simple terms, there is so much more to understand."

Anne raised her head defiantly. "While there is no need whatsoever to explain anything to me in simple terms, I can't believe that God would reward you. As for courting me, why, you are old enough to be my father."

"Then you must be very young." Samuel's voice had a sardonic edge to it. "I'm barely 29." Anne gasped in astonishment. She had believed him to be much, much older.

"Well, that is quite old to someone of my age." Her voice sounded strangled. She turned to her father. "But why, Father? Why do you want Samuel to court me? Do you hate me that much?" He looked away without answering. "Why father? I want to know…please tell me."

He looked back. "You know I don't want thee here, but Samuel wants to marry thee…and you shall wed 'en."

"If you'd always been a father to me, I might feel obliged to marry someone you chose, but you have never been a proper father. My aunt and uncle always said they would let me decide for myself whether to accept a proposal. I want to marry someone who really loves me and whom I can love in return."

Walter snorted. "I s'pose your aunt filled your head full o' fancy notions. Love won't feed and clothe thee. Be thankful…you've nothing to offer, but Samuel's willing to take thee without—"

"You make it sound like charity," Anne interrupted indignantly.

"Don't be woollen-headed, girl!" Walter was getting angrier by the minute and his face was turning red. "Thee shall be wed!" Anne turned and fled to the attic.

"I won't marry him," she said softly, sinking to the floor and burying her head in her hands. "I won't…I won't!"

Chapter 5

It was during Anne's next visit to the market place that a youth rode his horse into the crowd. There were screams from women and children, and shouts of abuse from the men.

"He should be put in the stocks," a woman shouted, after the men had had their say; she was hugging her frightened child to her.

The youth brought his horse to a standstill and Anne saw that one of his arms was injured: in the natural opening at the front of the sleeve of his doublet his shirt was slashed and blood was seeping from a wound. Dismounting, he winced with pain as he stumbled and almost fell.

Their anger vented, the people moved away, leaving a clearing so that the youth and his horse stood alone.

Sadly, Anne looked around the mingling crowd: no one seemed concerned that he was wounded. Of course he had frightened them; riding his horse into the midst of them might have made them insensitive to his plight, or perhaps it was the 'Roundheads' they feared and did not want to get involved. But then she saw a woman pushing her way through the crowd.

When the woman reached the youth she gave the wound a brief examination. Anne moved forward to join her, and she saw that the woman was quite young and delicately pretty. She had a pale complexion, and wispy fair hair that was complemented by her bonnet.

"Can I help?" Anne said. The young woman shook her head in reply, then bending down she tore a strip from one of her petticoats.

"It's quite old and worn thin at the hem, otherwise I would not have been able to tear it," she explained on seeing Anne's look of surprise, then she hurried to the water pump by the side of the road and soaked the piece of cloth. On her return, she squeezed out the cloth and gently dabbed at the wound and congealing blood on the youth's arm.

Anne saw now that the youth was about the same age as herself. He was not particularly tall, but his eyes made her shudder as something stirred in her mind: a memory or similarity. It troubled her deeply, then she remembered the horse that had reared into the air, missing her by inches, and the rider whose evil she had sensed. Could it be…No, she did not think so; although she had only glimsed the rider that had almost run her down, she felt sure that he had been much older. It must be the similarity in the way that she had first encountered these two riders that had sent her imagination reeling.

"It's only a surface wound," the young woman was saying. "How did it happen?"

"A maniac on a horse asked me how I felt about the King being imprisoned in Carisbrooke Castle." He stopped talking for a moment and looked around him, and Anne was surprised when he continued without lowering his voice: "When I said I hoped he would escape and punish all those responsible for him being imprisoned he thrust his sword at me. If I had not moved quickly he could have killed me. Oh…my name is Tom, by the way. Tom Fletch—" he stopped, and Anne wondered if he was having second thoughts about announcing his name to the crowd. "I work for Sir John Oglander. He took pity on me," and then as though suddenly remembering his manners, "but I have not thanked you, er…Miss…"

Anne thought it very strange that he had continued talking in such a loud voice; he must know that he could be arrested. She thought of Sir John Oglander, and how his wife had died because he had been imprisoned in London for speaking freely against the King's enemies.

If people were listening, however, it was with only a passive interest. Except for Samuel, that is, who was pushing people out of his way and hurrying towards them. And the young woman, who had been about to tell Tom her name, remained silent. Anne so hoped that Samuel was not about to make trouble for the boy.

But it was the young woman he reached out for and shook by the shoulders. "Damn you, Mary, helping a Royalist and tearing your petticoats to—" he broke off as he noticed Anne and his face softened. "Anne," he said affectionately, "I would like you to meet my twin sister, Mary."

Anne swallowed in surprise. Whatever she had expected it had not been this. Mary seemed so gentle and kind and, unlike Samuel, she had such a young appearance. How could they be twins? But of course not all twins were alike, she realized. How strange that some were born as from the same mould, while others could be from different families.

Mary pushed her hair back from her shoulders, but wisps of her fine fair locks escaped to form soft curls against her face. More wisps of curl lay on her forehead, and her pretty blue dress with its black velvet bars and bows and its lace collar suited her so.

After witnessing Samuel's imperious behaviour towards Mary, Anne would not have been at all surprised if his sister had been bullied into a more drab mode of dress; even though Samuel had obviously made little effort to moderate his own appearance to that of a Puritan zealot.

Mary smiled at Anne before tearing another strip of lilac material from the petticoat to bind the wound that she had been tending.

But Samuel, placated by Anne's presence, merely raised his eyes to the heavens at Mary's action. "The war has ended but do these people accept the peace?" There was only a trace of agitation in his voice. "And my sister tends the enemy."

Anne stopped herself from telling him that he had contradicted himself. "Maybe she is trying to accept the peace," she said instead. But Samuel drew himself up to his full height and continued as though she had not spoken, and she wondered if he had even heard her.

"God knows when the foolishness will cease! The King lost the war, so why is Parliament trying to humour him and reach an agreement? And Cromwell and his blessed son in law, Ireton, seem to have influenced Lord-General Fairfax to delay bringing him to justice, still willing to reach an agreement under their terms. But is the King grateful? No, he is not. He is completely unreasonable."

"He is the King. Losing a war cannot change that, and their terms will take away his power."

"He dismissed his Parliament three times and insisted on ruling alone."

"My uncle said he was not breaking any laws by ruling alone when his Parliament failed to support him. He had to do what seemed best at the time. No one but God has the right to take his power from him." She had begun talking in a low voice, but it had risen a little with emotion. Samuel motioned her to stop, but her face flushed as she continued: "We already have insight as to what can happen when the King's enemies gain power over him."

"Sh— for mercy's sake keep your voice down! You clearly know little of the true state of things," Samuel said.

"Little of the way you see them...and I was not talking very loud," she finished in little more than a whisper.

"I see things the way they are, my dear. But I really don't think you should be filling your pretty little head with gentlemen's affairs."

"I am quite capable of understanding affairs, Samuel, whether or not they are gentlemen's." Samuel's outburst of laughter made her frown.

"I have never met a woman like you before. You fascinate me."

Tom took his horse by the reins and bade them good day.

"I know not why you laugh at me," Anne said, but her tone was flat, for something was puzzling her: when Tom had turned to leave, Samuel had nodded in his direction. It was only a slight nod; but a nod nonetheless. And although Samuel had chastised Mary for tearing her petticoat to tend the wound of a Royalist, he had uttered not a word of reproach directly to Tom. She had expected him to chastise the younger man, at least, for so loudly proclaiming his support for the King. It seemed strange...no, it *was* strange.

She supposed Sir John would be proud to have Tom working for him when he heard about the incident, and she wondered if she should warn Sir John of her suspicions. But what were her suspicions? She really did not know, and right now, all she wanted to do was leave the market place and the noise…go back to the cottage and busy herself.

"Wait!" She turned to find Mary hurrying after her. "Samuel has talked about you a lot. Please visit us at Leeward House."

"No!" Anne said, and Mary looked as though she was going to burst into tears.

"Please come…I get so lonely."

Anne hesitated, but then the thought of Samuel trying to court her in his home strengthened her resolve. "No, I don't think so," she answered ungraciously. She felt a twinge of guilt as she walked away. For she had no cause to be unkind to Mary, and besides, she liked the girl, well *woman* really—she still found it difficult to believe Mary was the same age as Samuel.

"Your presence has been requested at the home o' Samuel and Mary Jarvis, and you must accept graciously," Walter said slowly, and it was obvious to Anne that Samuel Jarvis had tried to make him remember exactly what to say.

"How honourable you are, Father," Anne said ruefully, but her tone failed to raise a response. She had longed for her father to treat her as a daughter. Longed for him to take a little interest in her, but not to have him force her into the arms of a man like Samuel Jarvis and, anyway, he still treated her with indifference the rest of the time.

"You'll disappoint Mary—she's not had an easy life."

"I am not surprised…living with Samuel."

"Don't be pudden headed, you! I'll tell'ee for why. She were orphaned when her mother died and dedn't hay no kin like your aunt and uncle."

Anne felt trapped. She already regretted upsetting Mary in the market place, three days before. She did not want to hurt her again. In fact, her father's words made her feel ashamed, even though she knew it was exactly what, incited by Samuel, he had intended.

She sighed. "All right, I shall accept the invitation, but only for Mary's sake—I still don't like Samuel…and I don't trust him."

Walter snorted but looked contented as he lapsed back into his own thoughts.

Anne could not help being impressed by Leeward House, and not least by its trimmings. There were several pieces of lace adorning the furniture and Anne fingered one. The design was far more intricate than any she had attempted. "This is beautiful, Mary. They all are. Did you make them yourself?"

"Thank you—yes I did." Mary blushed. "My mother taught me. I still miss her after all these years. She died when we were 13 years old."

"Tell me about her," Anne said.

"Oh, she was pretty and kind and never got angry. She was so patient and always seemed cheerful. Though there were times when she looked as if she had been crying when our father was alive. He was not very nice to her sometimes. But she would spend hours teaching me all she knew."

"I never knew my mother," Anne said.

"Oh! I am sorry…it must be much worse for you. At least I have my memories."

Anne smiled. "I have wonderful memories of my aunt and uncle, but I would love to have known my mother."

Samuel was as attentive as ever, and they sat in the drawing room. Mary played tunes on the spinet, and servants poured mulled wine.

"My mother would sing when she played. It is the one thing she was never able to teach me—I just could not keep in tune," Mary said, laughing.

Anne could not help marvelling at the luxury around her: beautiful chairs; one big chair even had side rests for arms and the back and seat were upholstered in tough material, dyed red to match the red velvet curtains. Elaborate embroideries and a tapestry adorned the walls, and silk drapes—she had never seen the like.

"This embroidery is wonderful. Is it your own work, too?"

Mary nodded. "It takes an age to complete one, but would you like me to do a small one for you?"

"Oh, Mary, I would love that. Thank you." Anne thought how out of place it would look in her father's cottage, but at least it would bring a little colour into their lives.

The evening passed very quickly. Anne found her fondness for Mary growing, which made her feel less antagonistic towards Samuel: he was Mary's twin after all, so really could not be that bad, she reasoned.

She was surprised that her visit was so pleasant, and as though some unspoken agreement had been made between Samuel and herself, no mention was made of their conflicting views on King and Country.

Anne declined Samuel's offer to take her home, however, for the thought of riding pillion on his horse, near him, repelled her.

"I cannot possibly let you walk home alone...I will walk with you."

"No, please...I want to be alone." She needed to be alone to consider how she would answer her father if he questioned her about her visit. She did not want to give him the slightest impression that she was now less adverse to marrying Samuel.

"Then take Rosebud, she is a gentle horse. I don't like the thought of a young lady walking home in the dark, alone. I would not let Mary—"

"Thank you, but no, I need to walk."

Mary joined in now, as though sensing the depth of Anne's desire to walk home on her own: "If Anne takes the south path through our orchard and past Paul Miller's cottage, she will not have so far to go when she reaches the road. And the moon's bright enough for me to watch her part of the way from an upstairs window." As she spoke her voice developed an enthusiastic, almost childlike quality.

Anne fought to keep her face from showing emotion at the mention of Paul Miller. So he lived in a cottage on Samuel's land.

Samuel laughed. "All right, I admit defeat. But do be careful, my darling."

Anne bit back the words 'I am not your darling', for she did not want to spoil what had been an enjoyable visit. Instead, she kissed Mary on the cheek. "Thank you so much...I've really enjoyed it, Mary."

Mary hugged her. "Do take care, Anne. I must go upstairs, now, to the window." She lifted her petticoats and hurried away.

It was a dry, pleasant evening; just right for making her way home slowy, thinking about her visit and her father as she walked. She turned and waved a couple of times before she reached the orchard, initially searching the windows until she saw Mary's hand waving back at her.

When she neared Paul Miller's cottage, which was the smallest clay cottage that she had ever seen, and little more than a hut, she unwittingly increased her pace. She was aware that her heartbeat had quickened, however, but was uncertain if it was in the hope of seeing Paul or in a desire to avoid him.

"So you have been to Leeward House." Paul was standing in the shadows, holding his saddle.

"You startled me."

"How fortunate for you that you were only startled! I believe my father was murdered by the wicked fiend you have just been visiting." Shock made Anne gulp, and she stood staring at Paul wide eyed.

"Did you know that Leeward House should have belonged to me? No, I can see you did not—well, beware Puritan Lady, your Samuel has taking ways!" he said pointedly.

"He's not my Samuel," Anne protested. "I really went to see Mary."

"Oh, yes," he said, and she knew from his tone that he did not believe her. "Mary's mother was a Lady who married beneath her class. She married a commoner who was attracted by her inheritance, and when her family forbade her to see him she eloped and married him anyway." He was quiet for a few moments, and when he continued he seemed deep in thought and as though he had forgotten to whom he was talking: "Not that it did the rogue any good. His wife was disinherited and they received not a penny.

"He probably thought his in-laws would eventually relent and accept him, but they never did. They knew what a worthless scoundrel he was. Folk say Mary has inherited all the grace and virtues of her mother," he looked at Anne now as though suddenly becoming painfully aware of her presence, "but Samuel takes after his father. He wants wealth, position, even though he appears to need the company of his father's class too. He has my home and my fortune."

"I—I don't understand."

"Leeward House belonged to my father and I lived there with him.

Your dear Samuel cheated him out of his land and his home, and then when he thought my father was going to try to recover it, he killed him, or so I believe. But there is no way I can prove it, nor can I disprove that he won Leeward House from my father by fair means. This tiny cottage is all I have left." Anne was alarmed by the look of hatred on his face and the vehemence in his voice as he said: "Now you want to share in my lost fortune, too!"

Chapter 6

Anne did not sleep well that night. Paul's cruel accusations had distressed her so much that she lay going over them in her mind for what seemed like half the night.

But after considering all things, including the unlikelihood of an apology from Paul when he realized that he was wrong about her, she thought he was probably wrong about Samuel killing his father. How could dear, sweet Mary be twin to a murderer?

"How did Samuel gain possession of Leeward House?" she asked her father without preamble, the following morning. He looked startled and she did not think he was going to answer her. "Please...I need to know."

"You'll hay to ask Samuel, then, won't'ee," he mumbled through a mouthful of bread and cheese. She was too troubled to eat anything herself.

She sighed. "I should have known it would be a waste of time asking you."

"Your hair," Walter growled disapprovingly. "Your mother would ne'er hay looked like 'ee...she brushed her hair virst thing every mornen...except last." He stared ahead of him unseeingly, and Anne realized that he meant the last morning before her mother died.

"Yes, father," she said gently. At least he had noticed her and aknowledged her as his wife's daughter, but she had seen so much pain in his eyes while he was talking about her mother. She wondered if he had kept the pain locked up inside him all these years. "I am sorry, Father…" She stood for a moment not knowing what else to say. She was not even sure if she was apologizing for making him sad or for coming down with her hair still in rags; she had dressed, but she had not yet removed the strips of rag around which she bound the hair that formed her side ringlets. She stood looking at her father, knowing that whatever else she said might be wrong and make him feel worse. She turned and left him alone.

Back in the attic, she undid one of the knotted rags and carefully pulled it out of the ringlet. She did the same with the others. Then she began to neaten the ringlets by combing them, one at a time, around the forefinger of her left hand, pulling her finger down through the ringlet as she combed it.

Her father had said she would have to ask Samuel about the accusations Paul had made against him: perhaps he was right. His response would probably tell her enough to put her mind at rest, though he would almost certainly be angry, but what else could she do?

When her father had left the cottage, she picked up his plate and cleared away the crumbs that had fallen onto the ale stained table. Then she cleared away the ash from yesterday's fire and went to fetch logs and wood from outside, ready for later. Finally, she grabbed her cloak and left the cottage. It was still quite early in the morning to visit Leeward House, but she thought she would be more likely to find Samuel at home now, than if she went later.

"I knew you would keep your promise to come and see me again," Mary clasped her hands together, excitedly, "but I didn't think it would be quite so soon."

"Well, I…yes, of course I wanted to come and visit you again…but I wondered if it would be possible to speak to Samuel…"

"Oh! He's not here. How I wish he was here so you could see him! I know he adores you."

"No, Mary, this is something unpleasant I need to talk to him about." She wondering if Mary would be able to tell her what she wanted to know. Perhaps this was a blessing sent to save her from having to ask

Samuel. "When I left here last night, Paul Miller stopped me and told me that Leeward House should have been his...and he accused me of being after his lost fortune."

"Oh, how dreadful for you! Leeward House did belong to Paul Miller's father, but Samuel won it quite fairly when his father owed him lots of money."

"What happened to his father?"

"He died. Some people blamed Samuel, and Paul Miller even accused him of murdering him, but Samuel didn't really have anything to do with it—the constables were satisfied that he had died of natural causes."

"Thank goodness!" Anne said.

"How I wish Puritans didn't try to stop all Christmas celebrations!" Anne said, when she met Mary in the market place a couple of days later. "Oh! I forgot—your brother..."

Mary laughed. "He loves the celebrations as much as anyone...and he says lots of people still intend celebrating like they did last year."

"With my father behaving as he does I feel as though I have no family to celebrate with, anyway."

"Oh, Anne, I am sorry...but you must come to Leeward House and be treated like part of our family...but why wait until Christmas? Visit us whenever you want to be with friends. Please say you will. I often feel so lonely."

"Well..." Anne hesitated, but knew that it would be foolish to spurn the invitation: she felt lonely, too, and liked Mary. In fact, she would love to visit her at Leeward House and be friends. And as long as Samuel continued to behave respectfully towards her, she had no reason to stay away. She could always leave, anyway, if Samuel annoyed her. "Yes, thank you, I should like to visit you."

Mary slung her arms around Anne's neck. "Oh! Thank you. Thank you!"

And so Anne began making regular visits to Leeward House. Sometimes she would sit with Mary, talking and sewing, and at other times listen to her playing the spinet. And through their friendship she found herself becoming more benevolent towards Samuel.

A couple of days before Christmas, Anne and Mary went to a farmhouse, taking with them a small amount of money. A whisper had reached them that the Mumming Pageant of Saint George was taking place there; while officials had been led to believe it would be performed on twelfth night at the other side of town.

The money was to give to the 'Chrissmus Bwoys', who were local labourers, turned mummers. Some lingered in the farmhouse porch. They were dressed in decorated costumes—mostly in keeping with the characters they represented.

The audience grew bigger as the play began. Those arriving on horseback left their mounts in a part of the farm specially set aside for that purpose, and everyone was in a jovial mood as the character known as Poor and Mean stepped forward. He was dressed in tatters decorated with streamers, and he was carrying a tankard in one hand and a lute in the other. He put the lute down and held the tankard in the air before he began to speak:

"Here be I—Poor and Mean, Edden't this the worst eye you hav'ever seen?" He pointed to his blackened eye, and the audience responded with a medley of answers and laughter.

"I've jest vout a battle and escaped from gaol,

And now I drinks a jug o' Sir John's Chrissmus ale." He drank from the tankard, smacked his lips and wiped his sleeved arm across his mouth.

"Move all thy horses and move thy waggons,

Vor after me there comes zome viery dragons!" There were gasps, especially from the younger members of the audience, who looked around them talking excitedly. When they had quietened down again, Poor and Mean continued:

"I come vull butt 'n' han't got long to stay,

But I'll play the lute and zing in rhyme

Avore I goos away,

Zo gracious volk, gimme room, I zay,

All on this Chrissmus time." And he called for Saint George to clear the way. Then he put his tankard on the ground and rested his foot on it while he played and sang a short Christmas ballard.

"The mummers are so brave," Mary said. She looked around as though fearing there might be someone in their midst who would cause them grief. "Officials arrived last year and arrested three mummers before they had had time to start the play. Now some say it's being banned all over the land."

The Noble Captain stepped forward:

"My naame it es the Noble Captain

And thou might a heerd I am zo boold.

In France I fout wi' the King o' Spain,

And now I be here to vight Saint George again."

On feeling her skirt being pulled, Anne looked down and found a pretty little face staring up at her. "Are there really any dragons coming?" the little girl asked. "And will they eat me?"

Anne smiled and hugged the child to her. "No, of course not," she said. "There are not really any dragons." The child pulled away from her and disappeared into the crowd.

Mary laughed. "I hope she doesn't have a nightmare tonight."

The Valiant Soldier had entered the scene. He was dressed in an old red uniform and a helmet and, like most of the characters, his clothes were decorated with brightly coloured tinsel and ribbon. And now it was his turn to speak:

"Here be I—the Valiant Sojer,

"Oliver Cromwell es my naame."

"Dressed like that?" someone called out and there were roars of laughter, followed by timid ones before the Soldier continued:

"I brought Royalists to gurt slaughter,

They zay 'twas how I gained my fame."

"Oh, thou cursed and cruel Puritan!" the Noble Captain said. Gasps could be heard coming from the audience, and many people were looking around them as though fearing reprisals from 'Roundheads' or their followers.

The Valiant Soldier spoke again:

"Ded ye call me cursed and cruel?

Pull out thy zword 'n' vight,
Or begone you dirty rascal,
King Charles es in the castle,
A prisoner in the Wait."
The Noble Captain put his hand on the decorated hilt of his sword and said:
"What prattlen tongue es this I hears?
Be silent or I wull cut off yer ears."
Both characters pulled out their swords and the Valiant Soldier answered the Noble captain:
"I wull swing my zword and cut off yer hand!"
He then crossed swords with the Captain and they fought. Some of the audience jeered, while others made noises of encouragement before John Bull entered with a club and struck down both men's swords.
"Here be I—wold John Bull…" He continued his rhyme and invited the Turkish Knight to clear the way. The Turkish Knight entered, splendidly attired in green with a silk turban, followed by Saint George.
"Here comes I—wold Saint George;
I wull vight the viery dragons,
But virst I'll dice the Turkish Knight
And throw 'en on the waggons." There were more roars of encouragement from the crowd, and the Turkish Knight and Saint George both drew their swords and fought. More words followed while swords and right hands were pushed together, then Saint George forced the Turkish Knight to the ground. A child could be heard crying and the doctor was asked to come in haste, for the Turkish Knight lay dying and upsetting the children. There was great merriment and laughter.
"They seem to have left out the three Christmas characters arrested last year," Mary said, as a doctor joined the scene.
"I be Doctor Hokum, I treats hurts and diseases:
Palsy and gout—measles 'n' wheezes,
If I puts my 'Chrissmus potion' upon his chin,
He'll kick and rise to vight agin." He dropped a drop of the potion onto the face of the Turkish Knight, who opened his eyes and struggled to arise.

Just as the Noble Captain began to confront Saint George the sound of a pistol firing made many of the audience surge towards the small open gateway. Some folk stood their ground, thinking it was all part of the play. But then, realizing their mistake, they too tried to reach the gate. Horses that had been ridden to the pageant were forgotten as everyone pushed against those in front.

"Anne!" Mary screamed out. She had not moved as others surged past her, but Anne had been swept along by the crowd.

"What on earth is happening?" Sir John Oglander asked. He had his horse in tow. "I meant to be here earlier but was detained."

"Somebody fired a pistol to disperse the crowd, but they panicked. Anne's in there, somewhere. Oh, please help her, Sir John, she'll be trampled to death!"

Sir John mounted his horse and called out across the crowd, "It is all right. There is no need to panic. There is nothing to be afraid of." But the crowd just ignored him and continued to push. One or two men had managed to scramble over a wall that separated the farmyard from a field of sheep, but many people were being crushed against the wall. Children were screaming.

Mary began to cry. Sir John moved his horse and gently but firmly forced his way into the crowd, talking to everyone as he went, calming them.

The mass began to disperse, but people were left lying on the ground. Sir John dismounted and checked two of them. He looked towards Mary and shook his head—they had both been trampled to death. Several soldiers had arrived and they began checking the bodies, too.

Most of the audience had now gone, leaving only the casualties and those comforting injured friends or relatives, and those weeping for the dead.

Sir John beckoned to Mary to join him as he went and fell to his knees by Anne's side.

"Thank God! She is alive," he said.

* * * *

"I've brought you some warm milk. We have been so worried about you. It was lucky you didn't fall down sooner like some of the others," Mary told Anne. "I was so frightened. I remembered you telling me about that evil horseman, and I thought it must have been an omen, warning you that you were going to die."

Anne smiled despite the pains. "Oh, Mary, of course it wasn't. It was just a coincidence." Anne was in bed in a room at Leeward House. Mary had pulled back the heavy blue velvet drapes and was sitting on the bed.

"You were unconscious for five days," Mary said. "Of course I told your father what had happened to you, when I collected the things you might need."

"Has...has he been here...visiting me, I mean?" Mary shook her head.

How nice it would have been if he had, Anne thought.

"Sir John rescued you from the crowd and then fetched a doctor, who said there was nothing to do except wait for your injuries to heal and hope you recovered," Mary said, and Anne remembered back to when she had had the strangest feeling that she could trust Sir John with her life.

But she felt worried. The doctor must have cost Sir John such a lot of money. "Did they arrest anyone in connection with the play?"

"No. It seems they were really looking for Paul Miller. They were saying it was God's will that led them to the farm where the mummers were performing, and they fired the pistol to stop the play. They found Paul at his cottage, later, and took him away."

"Took him away?" Anne repeated weakly.

"Yes. The wrong people overheard his sentiments concerning the King and his enemies. Oh Anne! You have gone very pale. Are you in a lot of pain?"

"I am all right, in fact I really think I should be making an effort to get out of bed. Perhaps I ought to be going back—"

"No, it's too soon...and Samuel will be angry with me for not stopping you from leaving your bed. Please stay there...please..."

"Very well," Anne said. At least she was made to feel welcome here, which was more than could be said for living in her father's cottage, and this bed was so comfortable. "Did you embroider this beautiful quilt?" She stroked her hand across it.

"Yes, I did," Mary said.

Anne looked around the room. The curtains were the same blue velvet as the bed drapes, and a small fire was burning in the grate. She yawned. "I do feel tired…how can I feel so tired when I have been sleeping for so long?"

"Samuel says you should stay in bed for at least another week, maybe two."

"I don't think that will be necessary," Anne said, closing her eyes.

"The doctor told Sir John it might be longer."

But it was exactly two weeks before Anne was able to go down the stairs with Mary's help. And then the next time Sir John came to ask after her, Mary invited him in, but he looked dubious.

Mary laughed. "Samuel won't be back for an age. I know Anne would love to see you." So he followed Mary into the parlour where Anne was sitting near a blazing log fire, sewing.

"It's wonderful to see how well you are recovering." He held out his hand to her—and when she took it, he squeezed her fingers gently.

"Thank you for saving my life, Sir John," she said, before their hands parted. She wanted to question him about Paul, but controlled the urge lest she should appear more concerned than would be expected of her. "Please tell me about the King and how he is faring," she said instead.

Sir John sighed. "Sadly, he has been made a close prisoner because he could not agree to Parliament's proposals…they are preposterous, Anne. But I don't think he will be freed unless he agrees to all the changes in the Church and the loss of most of his royal power.

"People gathered in Newport demanding his release when they heard what had happened. Now one man is being accused of inciting them and has been charged with treason."

Anne looked puzzled. "How can it be treason when he was trying to help the King?"

"It isn't. The King's enemies are the ones who are guilty of treason.

And by betraying their king they are betraying their country, too. But the gathering has hastened the arrival of extra troops, and more ships have been sent here."

"Surely someone will be able to help the King."

Sir John shook his head in despair. "He has been talking with the commissioners of the Scottish Parliament, who are against the proposals, but I cannot tell you about it—I have been sworn to secrecy. But he surrendered to the Scots at Newark in May of '46 only to have them hand him over to our Parliament nine months later."

Anne hoped that the Scots would help the King, this time, but decided that it was time to change the subject: "Mary told me about Paul Miller being arrested," she fought to keep her emotions calm as she said his name.

"Alas, he has been taken to London and there is nothing I can do about it. I no longer have any influence, but at least he has no wife to go pleading for him and getting the smallpox for her trouble."

Anne gasped as she looked towards the door and saw Samuel entering the room, his face red with anger.

"What the hell are you doing in my home?"

"Take care of yourself, Anne," Sir John said, before turning to Samuel. "I am just leaving."

"You shouldn't be here in the first place."

"I—I invited him in to see Anne," Mary said. "I didn't think you would be back so soon."

"So this is what my twin does whilst I am out...invites Royalists into my parlour and thinks it's all right so long as I know nothing about it!"

"Please don't be angry with Mary," Anne said. "I wanted to talk to Sir John."

For a moment Samuel continued to look angry, but then his eyes rested upon Anne and his expression softened. Sir John had been standing in the doorway, but when he saw Samuel's face relax, he left.

"Oh, Anne," Samuel said, "why do you want to see Sir John when you have me? I can tell you anything you wish to know...and unlike Sir John's corrupted Royalist rendition it would be the pure and simple truth." He bent forward and took one of Anne's hands in his own. "Such beautiful hands." He raised one to his lips and kissed it. "Is there anything you need, my dear?"

"No, thank you. Both you and Mary are being most kind to me."

"We both love you." He smiled, and Anne hoped that he would not start annoying her now that she was recoving from her injuries. But then she reminded herself that he had been treating her with respect before she had been injured; there was no reason why that should change, now.

"Samuel is so fond of you," Mary said when he had left the room.

"And I'm quite fond of both of you," Anne said, but then she wondered if it had been a foolish thing to say; for she suspected that Mary would need little encouragement to start imagining that she was more than just well-disposed towards Samuel, so she added: "especially you."

The time passed so quickly for Anne, during the weeks she stayed at Leeward House, and Samuel continued to be a perfect gentleman; even if at times he kept his lips upon her hand longer than she felt was necessary. But there was the far more arduous matter of Paul being at the mercy of the Roundheads for her to think about, and she prayed that he would soon be allowed to return home to the Wight.

"I should be going back to my father's cottage—I have convalesced long enough," she said half-heartedly a few days before Easter, but she was easily persuaded to stay at Leeward House a little longer.

So her first venture outside since the pageant was not to go back to her father's cottage, but to go to the market with Mary. With Easter approaching they needed to buy extra flour for the Goodies to make into loaves of bread for the poor.

"If the Goodies can carry the flour round the town, it's only right that I should carry the extra flour home and not leave the servants to do it," Mary said. They both laughed, but shared the load.

And after the Goodies had called on Good Friday, Mary said: "Those bags must be so heavy for those old women to carry when they're getting full. I'm always tempted to help."

Anne laughed. "You might start a new tradition…I wonder what the old Goodies would call you?"

But the next day, Anne's 'convalescence' at Leeward House came to an abrupt end, not long after Samuel bounced into her bedchamber.

"Samuel…I could have been…you never just enter a lady's bedchamber without knocking or asking if it is all right."

Samuel ignored her protest. "I have brought your father to see you. He's in the parlour."

"Oh…thank you!" Anne smiled and decided to forgive Samuel for invading her privacy on this occasion. She followed him down to the parlour.

"Father, I'm so pleased to see you. Thank you for coming."

Her father just grunted and looked awkward. "'Twas Samuel's idea."

"Oh, Father, it would have meant so much to me if you had thought of it yourself."

"I hay ben on my own since…since—" he could not finish the sentence. His face hardened and he turned and left, and Anne was left staring after him.

Samuel had been standing just inside the door, but now he moved towards her. "It would please your father greatly if you consented to be my wife…I had hoped he would talk to you about it while he was here…it is what we planned."

"What? You mean you brought my father here to try and talk me into marrying you? And…and I thought you brought him here to please me."

"He could make you marry me, but I said I wanted to persuade you in my own way…because I care about you."

"You more likely both realized I would refuse to be forced into marrying you. Anyway, it is obviously time I left here." She hurried out of the room with Samuel hurrying after her.

"There's no need to run away just because I mentioned marriage," he said.

"I am not running away. I am quite well now, and I am grateful to you and Mary for all you have done for me, but it would be improper for me to stay here a moment longer."

"Please don't go," Mary pleaded, but this time Anne did not weaken.

"I must," she replied simply, then collected her possessions plus one fish of a brace that Mary had given her tearfully.

"Please take both," Mary said, wiping her eyes with the back of her hand.

"No, it's kind of you, but I'll just take the one...I doubt if my father has bought much fresh food while he's been on his own. Thank you both for your hospitality." She kissed Mary on the cheek and hugged her briefly. "Thank you for everything, Mary."

They were standing in the hall, and Anne hardly glanced at Samuel, who was standing with his arms folded a few feet away, watching her.

"I'll visit you tomorrow," she called back when she turned to wave to Mary and saw her sorrowful expression.

When she arrived back at her father's cottage, it seemed smaller than before. She removed her cloak, then prepared and lit the fire. And while it was difficult not to compare living here with her stay at Leeward House, she knew that Mary's company was what she would miss most; they had grown so close that they were like sisters.

How right she had been to think that her father might forget to buy fresh food: there was only stale bread and cheese again. He probably did not care what he ate, so long as he was rid of her. And while she did not really mind clearing up after him, today she found it wearying, knowing that Samuel had been talking with him, again, about his desire to marry her.

When she had prepared and lit the fire, she fetched the copy of Aesop's Fables from the attic and sat at the table with it open in front of her. She stared down at the pages, but was unable to absorb the words; for her mind was preoccupied with thoughts about the wretched, unkind man that just happened to be her father.

Perhaps it was her Bible she should be reading, she thought. Honour thy father...She sighed and, pushing the book aside, sat with her head in her hands, her elbows resting on the table. She let her head relax to one side, so that one hand and arm took all its weight, and closed her eyes. Her troubled thoughts gradually left her, and she drifted into such a peaceful frame of mind that she did not want to move, in fact, she felt more like falling asleep…

She yawned and rose to prepare and cook the fish, feeling as though she had briefly slept.

She was removing the cauldron from the fire when her father arrived home. She greeted him cheerfully, but then turned away, not wanting to see his displeasure at finding her back in his home. But at least he did not shout at her, and they sat and ate the fish together.

"I must talk wi' thee," her father said.

"No…please…I mean not if it has anything to do with marrying Samuel. I have already told you I'm not interested…but we can talk about anything else."

"Others wuld be grateful vor what Samuel has to offer…and they'd be afeared o' goen agin their fathers."

"But you have never been a proper father to me, have you? You don't even like me…so how can you justify trying to force me into an unsuitable marriage?" Walter grunted and Anne could almost feel his rising impatience, so she left him sitting there and went into the attic.

"Don't let me hear no more o' this…others'd welcome the chance to wed 'en," he called after her.

Maybe some girls in her position would be only too willing to marry Samuel, she thought. Some girls might even find him charming, and he could be so attentive. He had a beautiful home. And who could wish for a nicer sister-in-law than Mary? But for her, without love, this would not be enough.

* * * *

After Paul was released from prison and arrived back on the Wight, Sir John called a secret meeting at his home to continue making plans to help the King escape.

"He should not have any problems when he climbs out of his window. The inner courtyard is not patrolled at night," Firebrace, a servant of the King, said. "He will be provided with a rope on the day of the escape, so when the time comes he can lower himself down into the courtyard." He stopped talking and waited for Sir John to take over.

"He will then cross the courtyard and climb to the battlements on the south to distance himself from the officers' quarters, by way of the curtain wall," Sir John said. "And another rope, with a stick across the bottom for the King to sit on, will be used to lower him down to the top of the grass bank. There will be helpers along the escape route."

"How tall is that wall?" Paul said.

"About 15 feet. There is also a drop of about nine feet at the fortifications beyond."

"I can help him down there," said one of Sir John's guests.

"And I," said another.

Paul recognized the two gentlemen as Richard Osborne, now one of the King's servants, and Edward Worsley, but it had been suggested that names should not be used. Paul recognized another man in the room as Sir John's son, William; but for fear of eavesdroppers, and also as practise for the escape itself, everyone was to remain anonymous.

"The King is naturally very anxious to escape as soon as possible, and has started walking round the castle again to look at his escape route," Sir John said. "He said that he has regained some of his dignity already just by knowing he will soon be free. And he feels more in control than he has felt for a long time."

Everyone at the meeting knew that the escape was to take place on a Monday, but no one spoke the date aloud.

Sir John expressed his main worry concerning the escape: "If the space in the window proves to be too small for the King to climb through—"

"He knows how much we both want to remove the bar," Firebrace interrupted, "but he says tampering with it previous to the escape could arouse suspicion. He has tried putting his head through the window and he is sure that he will be able to squeeze through it when the time comes." And Sir John had to be content with that.

The King's servant made his way into the courtyard at Carisbrooke Castle. He realized the enormity of what he was about to do. Soon his king, sincere, honest, brave and well meaning, would be free to lead his cavaliers again, and to talk to people who would listen. Not only was he assisting in the escape of his king, but he was helping to determine the future of his beloved country.

There was a candle still burning in the King's bedchamber window; most other windows were now dark. The servant stood, watching and waiting. The courtyard appeared to be deserted. He could hear loud, ranctious laughter coming from the guardrooms in the gatehouse and thought it probable that the guards had already begun swigging their ale.

He took a stone from a small velvet bag, which was attached to his wrist. And gripping the stone in the palm of his hand he waited for the King's light to be snuffed out.

How he yearned to see his king free and ruling again! He knew that he had inherited problems and ill-advice along with his adviser Buckingham, while discontentment had already been simmering across the land. But cruel folk had been quick to blame the young, inexperienced king. And when Parliament had grown difficult and opposed the King, he had, sensibly, the servant thought, exercised his right to rule alone. And the servant knew that ship money, which the King had had to extend over the country, had been a modest sum, with judges ruling in his favour. But the cursed revolutionaries had made sure that the rumours concerning these and other matters grew worse, discrediting the King and making it easier to turn everything else that he did against him…

The light in the King's bedchamber was extinguished, and the servant said a silent prayer before throwing the stone into the darkness towards the place where the light had been. Hearing the stone tinkle against the glass he closed his eyes. "Thank you," he whispered. "Thank you, God."

He hardly dared breathe as he waited patiently. He thought he heard the window opening, and he waited and waited. The King must be climbing down the rope, now, he thought and prayed silently for his safe delivery upon the ground.

But then he heard groans and became fearful that his king was hurt or had become ill. Perhaps he had fallen or been caught trying to climb out of the window. He wanted to call out to his king to ask him what was wrong, but he dare not. He wrung his hands in frustration. Oh, please be all right! he prayed silently.

After what seemed like eternity, a candle was lit in the King's bedchamber and placed in the window. This was the sign that they had all agreed upon for 'danger and abandon' and it confirmed his fears that something had gone wrong.

His emotions were in a turmoil as he left the courtyard and made his way back along the escape route. He took three more stones from the velvet bag and threw them ahead of him into the darkness, one at the time. He had no way of knowing what had happened back at the castle and he wanted to warn the others to go home at once.

Chapter 7

Sir John's sadness was reflected in the faces of the other Royalists seated before him. Most of them already knew that the space in the window of the castle, through which the King had tried to climb, had proved to be too small.

"I cannot describe the anguish I have felt since Monday night," Sir John said. "And when I visited His Majesty yesterday I found him even more melancholy than I had expected. Getting stuck in the window was such a humiliating way of finding out that he should have let Firebrace remove the bar…and his ankle was swollen and painful from twisting it landing awkwardly back inside the room." There were murmurs of sympathy for the King, and Sir John waited for them to fade away.

How he wished that he did not have to continue! But he knew he must: "Sadly, the King is being ridiculed." Horrified sounds went round the room and Sir John's voice was filled with emotion as he said: "And someone took it upon themselves to tell him how his enemies were jesting and making rhymes about Charlie the fool getting stuck in the window." Talking about it hurt him so much that he felt a tightening in his chest.

There was an uproar in the room and a Royalist in a reddish-brown doublet jumped to his feet and drew his sword. "We will kill the bastards!"

"No we will not," Sir John said. "That would not help anyone, least of all the King."

"How did his enemies find out?" another Royalist asked above the noise.

"I think at least one of the King's confidants must be an informer."

"We should kill him," the Royalist in the reddish-brown doublet insisted and voices chorused in agreement.

"And bring more wrath upon His Majesty's head? Besides, we have no idea who the informer is."

"Surely you cannot think any of us betrayed—"

"No—no," Sir John interrupted, wanting to explain the situation without leaving the others suspecting that he mistrusted them in any way, "it could be someone from inside the castle.

"The King is beginning to realize what a very dangerous position he is in." Sir John knew that he was now considering the possibility that Parliament could govern without him indefinitely. And to add to his gloom rumours now led him to believe that he would never gain control over the New Model Army.

"Is it true that servants have been dismissed from the King's service?" a guest at the back of the room wanted to know.

Sir John sighed. "Yes, I am afraid it is." He knew that Firebrace was amongst them. "The informer knew names of servants involved on Monday night…the information is reported to have come from the governing committee at Derby House, but too late to stop the King's encounter with the window."

"Why did the information come from Derby House if there's an informer in the castle, sir?"

"And why was Hammond not told before the attempt?" Sir John looked from one to the other of the men asking the questions.

"Maybe he was," he said. "I have been wondering the same things myself, and there is one possibility we have to consider. It might seem unlikely, but knowing how reluctant Hammond was to be the King's gaoler, I cannot help wondering if he dismissed the warning as another rumour in order to let the King escape." There were sounds of surprise from several visitors, and Sir John waited for raised voices to grow quiet again. "So the informer contacted Derby House, knowing that the governing committee would force Hammond to take action.

"Hammond showed complete intolerance towards those that the committee notified him were involved in Monday night's events, and he has been growing increasingly impatient with the King. This could be to vindicate himself." Sir John frowned and looked towards the window. The corner of his left eye had caught a movement outside it. He excused himself and marched from the room and from the house.

Rounding the corner of the building he found Tom Fletcher coming towards him. "What are you doing here?"

Tom sounded calm and unwavering as he handed Sir John a medallion on a chain: "I found this in the stable and thought it might be yours."

"No, Tom, it's not mine…I have never seen it before, and I would rather you did not creep around outside my house."

"Yes, sir…sorry sir," Tom said and, taking the medallion from Sir John's outstretched hand, turned and walked away. Sir John watched him for a few moments before returning to the house and asking the servants to provide him and his Royalist guests with ale. Then he rejoined his guests and arranged another meeting to make further plans to help their king elude his gaolers.

"We should not keep him waiting long. He is anxious to escape as soon as possible. But I will advise him not to trust any of his remaining servants—at least for the time being."

Sir John was concerned about the number of people involved in their talks. And he shared his forebodings with Paul when the others had left: "I don't want to cast doubts on any of them. I know they are all loyal to our king and want to help him escape, but it only needs a few careless words and I fear it will just be another wasted effort."

"Sir John, could we not make our own plans without telling them? I know it sounds ignoble, but we could remind ourselves it's for our king's sake if we feel bad about deceiving them."

Sir John fingered his beard. "Mmm."

"We could do it with Tom Fletcher's help."

Sir John let out a soft, one noted whistle. "Tom Fletcher…I don't think I trust him enough."

It was true that through her friendship with Mary Anne had begun to treat Samuel as a friend, too: she knew that being Mary's friend meant it was impossible to exclude him from her life. And most of the time he was so charming and undemanding that she grew quite fond of him in a brotherly way, despite being aware of a darker side to his nature. But during her last three visits to Leeward House, he had annoyed her by begging her to marry him.

Today he had obviously been waiting for her, and he started pleading with her almost as soon as she stepped inside the house: "I know I upset you on Saturday by what you referred to as 'pestering you' but how else is a man to persuade the woman he loves to marry him? Please tell me you will at least think about accepting my proposal."

"No! You know very well I am just a friend to Mary…and a friend to you too, but nothing more." She removed her wet cloak and Samuel called for a servant to take it from her. Although it was spring it was cold, and it hardly ever seemed to stop raining.

"You look as lovely as ever, my dear," he said.

"Have I not been the perfect gentleman and shown you every courtesy?" he continued as they went into the parlour. He put out a hand to touch her arm, but then withdrew it as though fearing she might bite him if he made contact with it.

"Yes, Samuel, you have been the perfect gentleman and I cannot fault your behaviour. You know I wouldn't continue to visit your home otherwise."

"Then why do you not accept my proposal of marriage? What do you want me to do?" Rather clumsily, he went down on one knee. "Just tell me and it shall be done." Now he had no qualms about touching her as he raised her hand to his lips.

Anne sighed. How she wished that he would not go on so! "Stop trying to woo me—that's what I want you to do for me. Yes, you can be charming and respectful, and I am sure that there is a girl…or woman somewhere who will adore you, but I don't love you and never will."

During his previous proposals, she had almost felt as though she was humouring a child. Yet only yesterday she had been shocked to find herself thinking that quite rational girls found happiness with worse men than Samuel. Knowing that he was twin to such a lovely person had helped her to look for the good in him. And even with Mary's friendship, she felt so lonely at times and yearned for affection through some closer relationship.

But now his overtures made her feel impatient and she decided to change the subject: "How is the new Governor and keeper of Carisbrooke Castle faring? He must have been in charge for…six months now?"

"It's over eight months," Samuel said irritably. He was obviously displeased that she had turned the conversation away from his feelings for her, and he did not answer her enquiry as to how Hammond was coping.

"Robert Hammond is a good man, is he not?" she persisted, anxious to keep the conversation on a more impersonal note, but without giving Samuel reason to argue; Robert Hammond was a Roundhead and so on his side.

"Well I suppose he must be, for the Army to leave him in charge of the King," he said even more irritably, and she wondered why Mary was taking so long to join them. She did not like being left alone with Samuel for so long.

But then he continued more benevolently: "The Royalists are revolting and causing another war over the Solent. I can't see an end to it until they bring the King to trial and do something about him."

Anne wondered whom Samuel meant by *they* and what exactly he wanted them to do about the King.

But then he said: "It will only be a matter of time before Oglander is arrested again. Do you know where that rogue Paul Miller spent part of the winter?" Anne felt herself colouring at the mention of Paul's name. She turned away, praying that Samuel had not noticed, and she was relieved when he continued without waiting for an answer. "In prison, that's where. He was arrested and taken to London for voicing his opinions as to what should be done with the King's enemies."

"Yes, I know," Anne said simply. But she was dismayed that Samuel believed Sir John would be arrested again. She had feared another arrest, but none came, so she had regarded the whisperings concerning his involvement with an escape as no more than rumours. Now Samuel had reawakened her fears. Mary joined them at that moment and the conversation turned to lighter matters.

But Anne was left with an uneasy feeling in the pit of her stomach, and she wanted to talk to Sir John about her fears. She could not sit indulging in unimportant chatter, knowing that Sir John might be in danger. She must go and warn him. She rose abruptly. "I am sorry, but I have just remembered…an important errand." She kissed Mary on the cheek, and then hurried from Leeward House. Mary called after her, but she was too worried to hear.

She shivered with apprehension at what Samuel had told her, but when she continued feeling cold all the way to Nunwell House, she knew that it was her own fault for leaving Leeward House without her cloak. The rain was now so light that she hardly noticed it.

At Nunwell House, she was told by a servant that Sir John was working somewhere outside. "He's a proficient farmer, you know, and believes in putting his ability to use," the servant added. Anne found Sir John working quite near the house, and he greeted her with a smile.

"Oh, Sir John, I'm so glad I've found you. I have been so worried about something Samuel said."

"Get your breath back first. You look chilled. Come into the house and tell me." He began walking towards the house and she followed him.

"I was so worried, when Samuel said it would only be a matter of time before you were arrested again."

He smiled. "I think Samuel is just voicing his wishes aloud." Once inside the house, he opened the door of a spacious room. "Sit in here while I go and ask for some mulled wine to be prepared for us."

Anne was about to tell him that it was not necessary to go to such trouble on her behalf, but he had gone and she glanced around her. The room was comfortable, but more frugally furnished than any room in Samuel and Mary's home. It was unpretentious, but that did not mean it was dull—and she liked it.

Sir John returned and he sat down and smiled at her. "Anne…if the

Roundheads were going to arrest me, I think they would do so at once, not talk to Samuel about it first. But thank you for telling me…did he say anything else?"

"Yes. He said he wished they would hurry and do something about the King."

"He didn't say what he meant by *something*?"

"No, but he meant something sinister, because he said he hoped the King would soon be brought to trial." She was quiet for a few moments. "He also said there is another war over the water."

Sir John sighed. "Unfortunately, word reached Westminster that the Scots were raising an army to help the King and it has caused a terrible breach between the moderates and their radical allies, especially in our New Model army. And at a Windsor prayer meeting, army officers said they had been wrong to try and make peace with the King and that they hoped to bring him to final account after this new war."

"Oh, no!" Anne said.

"But the moderates still hope to reach an agreement with him and the Commons had a majority vote in favour of making peace with him."

"That's good…is it not?" Anne said.

Sir John sighed. "I wish I could say 'yes'. It would be good if the Army wasn't becoming so strong. It's doubtful if Cromwell and his blessed son-in-law, Ireton, will be able to stop it from dominating the land—that is if they even try. Some think Cromwell will be the one who will harm the King eventually, despite holding back now.

"But I believe more people than ever want the King restored to power. They realize what terrible alternatives could befall us if our army continues without guidance from him. And many people, including the Scots, are demanding its disbandment."

Spring gave way to summer with little change in the weather. The Island lay shrouded in grey mist and rain: "As if in sympathy with the King," Anne heard it said.

However, Anne had other reasons to be miserable. Not long after Paul's return to the Island, she had seen him with a beautiful young woman whom she recognized from the market place. And when she saw the way the young woman was looking at Paul, she felt as though a sword twisted in her heart:

It had been a sunny afternoon and Anne had asked Mary to take a walk with her, and it was while she was shutting a gate across a road, which divided one property from the next, that she saw them together.

"Who is that girl?" she asked Mary, trying not to sound too earnest.

"Her name is Christina. She is very beautiful, is she not?"

Oh, yes…how I wish I was as beautiful! Anne thought, but she knew that God must have had His reasons for not making her so…and he would surely frown upon her envy…

Mary had not waited for an answer, however. "She has no real family. A local man, Gregory Stay—the youngest son of a Newtown Nobleman—and his wife, whom had not been blessed with any children of their own, raised her after she was found abandoned as a baby…lots of people said she had been left by gypsies, though none were seen. Paul was very protective towards her when they were children." Anne had hardly heard Mary's last words as Christina put her arms around Paul. "Ooh, I wonder if they will get married!"

Anne had turned away not wanting Mary to see her anguish.

And so, from that moment, Anne often wondered if they were together…

Today was just like any other day. It was drizzling with rain and Anne was about to turn and leave the market when she saw Paul. Her body jerked in recognition and her eyes lingered on his face, then they wandered from his slender nose to the fair tendrils of golden hair curling into his neck and onto his jerkin. But then he reached Christina and put an arm round her shoulders.

There was too much noise in the market for Anne to hear what Paul said, but she saw the devotion on Christina's face as she looked at him, and then saw the love in her eyes as she kissed him on the cheek.

Anne witnessed Christina's display of affection towards Paul with an intensity of pain that alarmed her. For it made her acknowledge the depths of her own feelings for him. She wished that she had stayed in the cottage, or gone for a walk…been anywhere but here in the market to see them together.

She felt Christina's eyes on her and saw Paul's scorn as he looked in her direction, nevertheless she moved towards him when he summoned her over. He grudgingly introduced her to Christina with a vague gesture of his hand and walked away.

Christina glowered at her, and there was fire in her beautiful, sultry, dark-brown eyes. She was wearing a red velvet dress, which complemented her long black ringlets, and she flaunted her shapely figure with her hands on her hips, and her eyes were narrowed as she said: "Paul is mine. You'll never take him from me…so don't even try."

Anne felt as though all her blood was rushing to her face. Christina must have seen her watching Paul; perhaps she had even seen desire or passion in her eyes that she had not meant to reveal.

Christina's lips had adopted a sullen pout, as if daring Anne to defy her, and she continued: "Anyway, do you really think he could love *you*?" Her eyes travelled over Anne. "You saw the way he put his arm round me—a weak gesture considering what he does when we are alone together." Her lips curled into a sensuous smile. She slowly slid her hand down over the silk bodice that covered her breasts, and then continued sliding it part of the way down the middle of her petticoats and Anne, with a heavy heart, was left in no doubt as to her meaning. She turned and hurried away in desperation. For she knew that Paul would never return her feelings; not even if he stopped hating her so. Christina had confirmed more than her worst fears that they were courting: they were lovers. Her anguish was almost too much to bear.

"What on earth is the matter, Anne?" Samuel grabbed her by the arm. "You look so very melancholy, my dear."

"Go away," she said, but he stood looking at her, then his face broke into a smile.

"Despite your sadness, you look enchanting…if only you would consent to be my wife," he said, and she wondered if he had been watching her and seen everything, and was taking advantage of her vulnerability. Even if he had been unable to hear what was said, he might have a shrewd idea of what was happening, after seeing Christina's expressions and her own embarrassment and anguish.

"I love you, Anne, and I want you to share my life, my name and my wealth. I will make you so very happy." And then, so quietly that she could only just hear the words, he said: "You will soon forget Paul—he is not the one for you." Anne moved away from him, intending to leave the market, not wanting to hear any more. She knew that she would never be able to stop loving Paul, let alone forget him.

Samuel moved after her and pulled her round to face him. "Do you understand what you're throwing away if you continue with this foolishness? You know Paul doesn't want you. He has Christina." Anne desperately needed to get away from him, but he put his arm around her and continued gently: "You have to forget this silly, foolish fancy. Oh, Anne, I know the market is no place for a proposal, but please—please marry me." He spoke loudly and earnestly, and a couple of children standing close to them turned to look at them and giggled. "I am sorry about Paul. His being besotted by another, I mean. Did you never see him with Christina before he was arrested? No, I can see you did not. You can see how much they are...well...you know what I mean. They have known each other for most of their lives, but since Paul returned from prison...well...believe me they—" They were in the way of stalls and were being jostled along. And Samuel was trying to guide her to where there were fewer people, and his voice jolted and hesitated as he was nudged in the back. "Believe me they really are—"

"Stop it! Go away. Leave me alone." His arm fell from her.

"Please, Anne—"

"For goodness sake! Leave me alone...I—I don't feel—"

"Are you ill?" He looked concerned. "You should have stayed with us longer to convalesce. You seem to have forgotten how ill you were. You nearly died. Let me help—"

"No, I am not ill. I just need some peace...away from you. Leave me alone and I shall be all right."

"Then just say 'yes', or I'll stand on a cart, so the crowds can see me, and I'll declare my undying love out loud."

"No...please..."

"Then say you will marry me. Please…I beg of you with all my heart!" She tried to walk away but he grabbed her arm. "Say you'll marry me and I'll let you go."

"Oh, for God's sake! I…if it makes you stop pestering me…I'll consider it…yes, I'll definitely consider it. Now leave me alone." He released her arm and she sighed with relief and walked away. She would go back to the cottage and lie down for a while. And another day, she would tell the wretched man that she had considered his proposal and decided against it. But how would she make him accept that her answer was for once and for all? Perhaps she should write him a letter in firm, carefully chosen words; he could not argue with a letter.

Samuel bounced round in front of her. "Oh, no, stop following me. What now? Why are you so excited?" she asked wearily.

"Oh, you will never regret it, I promise." He was ecstatic and barely able to constrain himself as he hopped from one foot to the other.

"Regret what?"

"Marrying me, of course," he said, laughing. "What do you think?"

"But, S-Samuel, I have only agreed to—"

"You have agreed to be my wife," he said loudly and she was stunned into a brief silence. How could he have misunderstood her so? She was clasping her hands together tightly, her nails biting into her flesh. Samuel pulled her hands apart and kissed both palms.

"S-Samuel I have not said I'll—" But he was already pushing his way through to where Mary stood pondering over some yarns; Anne had not even realized that she was with him.

"Mary, come and hear the good news." He took hold of her by the shoulders and hustled her along. "Anne has consented to be my wife…is that not wonderful?" Samuel's words were loud and urgent as though he feared that at any moment she would deny it completely.

Of course she would deny it! This was ludicrous. "No, I have not agreed to marry you." But Samuel and Mary were talking excitedly and not listening, then Mary slung her arms round Anne's neck and kissed her. This could not be happening. It must be a nightmare.

"Oh, I am so happy," Mary said, as she let go of Anne, "so very, very happy. I was hoping it would happen. I shall so love having you as my sister-in-law. Would you like me to help you make a special dress?" she asked eagerly, but when Anne failed to respond, she looked uncertain. "I'm sorry if I am taking things for granted and you already have a favourite dress you wish to wear…"

Anne shook her head, again. "No, Mary—"

"You don't seem very happy for someone who has just accepted a proposal of marriage." Mary looked concerned and continued in an almost childlike voice: "I would be so excited…oh, Anne, I am excited—for you…and it will be so wonderful for me, just like having a real sister!"

Anne closed her eyes for a moment. She had to make it clear at once that she had not consented to be Samuel's wife; make it clear that there had been a terribly misunderstanding. "Oh, Mary, I am so sorry, but—" Samuel grabbed Anne by the arm and pulled her away.

"Stop grabbing my arm. I need to tell you both—"

"Look, I am taking you without wealth and your father will benefit from the marriage—I promised him. But he will suffer dearly if you go back on your word, and think how heartbroken Mary will be. You have just seen how excited and happy she is—it's the most wonderful thing that has ever happened to her. It will destroy her if you change your mind now. She is not strong."

So her father wanted her to marry Samuel for his own personal gain: how dare he? He had never been a father to her in any real sense of the word and now he was selling her!

She thought of how her aunt and parson uncle had promised her that she would be allowed to marry someone of her own choosing. She wondered if her uncle had worried about her future when his health was failing. He would have prayed for her, of course, but she doubted that it would have been enough to reassure him. She remembered witnessing his despair when he heard that feuds and troubles were prevalent throughout the land despite all the prayers of so many.

"Anne…please," Samuel's voice broke into her thoughts, but it was kinder now, pleading even and Anne stared at him.

"You seem to have left me little choice," she said, shakily. She was too shattered to feel angry with him or her father for bargaining with her future. She surprised herself by not apportioning equal blame on Samuel, anyway; for since she had met Paul she had been learning about the agony of desire. At least Samuel had made a promise to her father in exchange for her hand in marriage because of his love for her. At least in days and weeks to come, that knowledge would be some consolation to her.

"Oh, Anne," Samuel said, "shall we find your father and tell him the good news?"

"No...I mean I would rather tell him myself...alone."

"We must be married as soon as possible—we have my home, so what is there to wait for?"

What indeed, Anne thought, and returning to Mary, she said: "I really would like you to help me with a dress—two dresses, one for you." Her mind seemed numbed against the anguish and pain caused by the pressures bestowed upon her that morning, but her spirit was also subdued.

Seeing Mary's face aglow with pleasure, she forced a smile to add conviction to her words. She hugged Mary and walked away.

"Where are you going?" Samuel called after her, sounding worried.

"To tell my father, of course." She was glad that he did not insist on accompanying her, and before she went to find her father, she just walked, turning everything over in her mind: her unrequited love, her father's betrayal and Samuel's cunning; for she no longer believed that Samuel had misunderstood her.

But then she reminded herself that when they were married, she would have a husband that loved her, a lovely home...and she would have the sweetest sister-in-law in the world—all she had to do, now, was convince herself that it was enough.

She found her father felling a tree and she stood, watching him until he saw her. He looked away without acknowledging her, and she waited for the tree to fall before she moved closer and said: "You will no doubt be relieved to know I am going to marry Samuel."

"So you've found sense." He scoffed: "Love!"

"How could you, Father?" There was no anger in her voice. "Some fathers might genuinely believe they have arranged a marriage for the good of their daughters, even when the couple are as ill-matched as Samuel and me, but you didn't believe it was for my good when you decided to sell me to Samuel, did you? As for love—you loved my mother."

She sighed when he did not answer. Deep down inside her was a forlorn hope that he would regret the arrangement and help to release her from her betrothal. But a little spirit returned to her voice as she continued: "You don't care about my happiness at all, only the benefits you can reap from me. I have given up hope that you will ever love me, but I had hoped for a little fatherly concern." A look fleeted across Walter's face and Anne wanted to believe it was shame. "What is it that Samuel has offered you? I have an aching curiosity to know. I suppose as your landlord and employer he can offer you quite a lot. I would love to know what you thought I was worth."

"Go away...I'm working." Anne knew he had no intention of answering her question; for his tone forbade any argument and he had turned his back on her. She was really not that interested to know what he thought she was worth, anyway, despite what she had told him—in fact, she found the whole subject distasteful.

That night, Anne's sleep was fraught with fitful dreams and images, and she was filled with terror when she saw the stranger with the dapple-grey horse watching her. He was surrounded by an aura that was even more menacing than before. The horse reared into the air, and its whinnying was unlike any that she had ever heard. Mist thickened around her and she could no longer see the horse or its rider. Then she was standing at the altar, about to be married. But the altar was ablaze, and when her bridegroom turned he had no face.

Chapter 8

"The King is bowling on the new green with Robert Hammond and Major Oliver," Sir John was told on reaching Carisbrooke Castle for his weekly visit. Major Oliver was the Lieutenant-General Oliver Cromwell's nephew.

The previous week, the King's mood had lightened considerably when he had taken Sir John to the green and shown him that it was almost finished.

Sir John had previously been concerned that his king was not getting enough exercise and fresh air: he had taken to sitting in his room, writing page upon page…of whatever it was that he was writing. "I will allow you to read it when it is finished," he had told Sir John. "I have put lots of tttime and effort into it." And then, as though talking to himself, he had said: "Time is something I have plenty of here."

But now the sky had darkened with storm clouds and Sir John hoped that they would pass over without stopping the King's game.

There was a clap of thunder as Sir John reached the green beyond the curtain wall but inside the outer defences. He sighed as large raindrops began to fall. There was a flash of lightning, soon followed by more thunder.

"Rain, rain, rain," King Charles said loudly and marched from the green, his fawn suede boots partially darkened by mud and squelching in the already wet ground.

"Is the weather always so wet on your island?" he said on reaching Sir John.

"No, Your Majesty, I have never seen the like."

King Charles laughed. "Cromwell's nephew and Hammond and are such fools who have no idea how to bowl properly and I tttold them so." He seemed high in spirit today. "I had three fools bowling, yesterday." He spoke loudly and Sir John looked over to where Hammond was frowning in their direction.

Sir John knew that the King's remarks were the only way he had of easing the humiliation he must be feeling at being held prisoner. But Hammond was becoming even more impatient with him, and Sir John hoped that he would not begin withdrawing what might be regarded by some as the King's privileges.

There was more lightning followed almost immediately by an explosive crash that reverberated around the dark clouds. "We had better return to the castle before the heavens rupture," Hammond said to nobody in particular.

Sir John kept pace with his king, who was striding ahead of the younger men.

"Would you like me to leave, Sire?" Sir John said when they reached the castle.

"Certainly not—I want to talk to you. I would tell you if I wanted you to go." The rain chose that moment to turn torrential, and King Charles laughed with amusement as they went inside the castle; for Hammond and Cromwell's nephew were some way behind and getting soaked.

"How are plans for my escape progressing?" King Charles asked Sir John as soon as they were in his room and the door was shut. And without waiting for Sir John to answer, he continued: "Of course it is more likely I shall be allowed to go to my Parliament to discuss the ccconcessions."

"I hope so, Sire." Oh, how Sir John hoped so!

King Charles removed his hat and cloak, then waited for Sir John to do likewise.

"I have so much to tell Your Majesty, if I might?"

"Of course. Tttell me everything you know."

"Well, there are already so many involved in your escape…if I may advise Your Majesty," King Charles nodded his consent, "not to trust anyone inside the castle except Osborne." Richard Osborne was the King's Gentleman Usher and had long since proved himself worthy of the King's trust.

"I always value your opinion above all others, Sir John, and of course you are right that I should be mindful in whom I put my ttrust. But there is at least one other still in the castle who would never betray me. Now tttell me more about my escape and your own week."

Sir John did as he was told. "I've held two meetings at my home since—" he stopped short of mentioning that fateful Monday night. "The second meeting was to begin making fresh plans for your escape."

"Well, come along then. What did you decide?"

Sir John outlined the plot, then cautiously led his summary back to the King not trusting anyone in the castle except Osborne.

"I would ttttrust one other man with my life," King Charles replied with a hand gesture that told Sir John that the matter was closed. "Now stop worrying about me and tell me what has been happening to you."

Sir John related the events of his week, while King Charles sat quietly, smiling from time to time. He laughed when Sir John told him about a new servant girl who dropped a plate full of food at Nunwell House.

"She was so apologetic and contrite, I had to reassure her three times lest her torment caused her to drop another!" Sir John laughed, too, but not unkindly. "While I cannot suffer fools gladly, I could well understand the girl's uneasiness on her first day." But even as he laughed, he knew that he would never stop worrying about his king until he was completely out of danger.

"I thought Hammond might think any plans to help the King escape were abandoned when Fibrace and the others were banished from the Castle," Paul said.

Sir John frowned. "Apparently not. Hammond has details of the escape plot."

Paul's eyes strayed away from Sir John to an oil painting in a heavy gold frame that was hanging on the wall of the hall in which they were standing. It was the portrait of a young woman, but Paul's attention did not appear to be focussed upon it.

"What are you thinking?" Sir John said, and Paul looked back at him. "You seemed far away."

"It's just that…well…I was wondering if there *was* anyone at the meeting who might deliberately betray the King."

"They are probably all amongst the King's most faithful subjects, though we both know the risks in involving so many. But I still suspect there is a traitor inside the castle, and Hammond is hardly likely to have banished him with Fibrace and the others, is he?"

"And the letter from Derby House warning Hammond to be on his guard that he told the King about?"

"The King has only Hammond's word for that. If it did come from Derby House, then it must be as we said before, to make sure that Hammond takes notice, but anyway I think the King unwittingly confides in someone who is passing information directly to Hammond."

"And, of course, saying it comes from Derby House makes it seem less likely to have come from the traitor in the castle…" Paul said slowly, as though thinking aloud.

"…and the King continues to trust the traitor," Sir John finished for him.

"Is Hammond really that devious?"

"Maybe…maybe not. He could be following orders. But either way, I doubt if he has a choice—if he wants to keep his position, that is."

"But that means the King will never escape." Paul sounded vexed.

"I have warned him not to trust anyone in the castle except Osborne, but he insists on including at least one other—one whom he insists he can trust with his life. How I pray that he is right!"

"But what if he's wrong?"

Sir John stroked his beard. "I am considering your idea of making our own plans without telling anyone. But it might be better not to think that far ahead at the moment. Everyone is putting so much effort into this."

"I know, but—"

"We need to concentrate on the moment, Paul. The sooner our king is free the better, and no plan is infallible—not even our own."

Paul looked ready to argue, but then he shrugged his shoulders. "Do we know for certain now when to be at the castle?" Delays had been caused by Hammond rearranging guards' duties.

"It will be Sunday, if all is well."

* * * *

Paul's horse scraped at the ground with one of its front hoofs, and Paul hastened to reassure it with a pat. "All right, boy."

"We seem to have—" An owl chose that moment to screech overhead, and Paul stopped and cursed before continuing: "We seem to have been here a hell of a long time…it must be well past midnight."

To Sir John the waiting seemed interminable. He wanted to hear his king's voice and know that he was free at last, or at least free of the castle's outer defences. They were at the east side of the castle with a party of fellow Royalists, awaiting the King's arrival.

"Quiet!" a voice said in earnest, but just loud enough for the others to hear. Everyone stopped talking and listened to the sound of feet approaching their hiding place. Sir John held his breath—if it was the King…and, of course, Worsley and Worsley's friend, why were they walking?

"It's only an animal foraging," a deflated voice said and Sir John breathed out. Groans of disappointment could be heard. But at least it had not been the enemy.

"I knew it wasn't them," someone called out. "They would not be on foot."

There was another screech and voices were raised. "Blasted owl!"

"Shoosh, you idiot! Do you want us to be captured by the Roundheads?"

They were too restless to be quiet, now.

Paul groaned. "We seem to have been here so long."

"Here they come!" the words were repeated over and over by the Royalists lest any of them had not heard. Their voices were urgent and their restlessness gave way to excitement. It was impossible to see the riders. Sir John prayed it was the King; not least because the men were making so much noise.

But the excitement waned into uneasiness. "...only two horsemen," the words resounded back and forth.

Only two horsemen...Sir John closed his eyes and bowed his head in prayer. "Please let one of them be our king." Almost before the prayer had left his lips, he heard the devastating news that Worsley and his trusted friend were alone.

"Where is our king?" several of the party demanded to know.

"Still at the castle. We—" Worsley's voice was submerged in angry voices.

"You should not have left without him," Paul called into the darkness.

"Paul, wait and hear what he has to say for himself," Sir John said.

"Someone blundered...there was nothing we could do," Worsley's voice caught in his throat.

Sir John felt angry, too, but not with Worsley. "Is it possible that someone from the castle could have betrayed the King?" he said.

"Yes, it is possible, but there is no time to explain. We must go. There are troopers behind us. Hammond set an ambush," Worsley said.

"If only the King had not been so trusting," Sir John said with anguish.

"Go home...quickly," Worsley said as he began to move away. "No one knows there were so many involved. They only saw two of us."

"*I* know they're involved," the cold voice sent a shiver up Sir John's spine. In the darkness, no one had seen the lone trooper arrive ahead of the others. "It's too late to go anywhere. Stay exactly where you are. I have a firearm."

"What will happen to us?" one of the Royalists said.

"Maximum punishment for helping the King escape," the trooper said.

"Helping the King escape? Well, where is he then? He's not here, and as far as we know he is still back in the castle," the Royalist replied.

"Has anyone here helped the King escape, tonight?" The Royalists made sounds of denial.

"Keep your bleating for your executioner," the trooper said.

"The trooper is standing too far away for us to see his face in the darkness…" Paul began in a low voice.

"So how could he see us well enough to identify us?" Sir John said. "Quick, before he moves any closer…are you ready?" Without answering, Paul followed his lead and they turned and led their horses out of the pit. The trooper fired and there was a cracking sound in the trees in front of them.

"What the—?" Paul began in alarm, "that could have been one of us."

"We must hurry before he reloads," Sir John said. "At least his empty firearm has given the others a chance to follow us." He waited while Paul regained control of his horse, which had reared whinnying into the air. "No need to ask what has upset him."

The others joined them. "It sounds as though more troopers are ahead of us," Paul said. "What are we going to do now?"

"It seems we have no option but to fight and hope that we can get away without being recognized. It grieves me that the only escape we shall be involved in tonight is our own." Even as Sir John finished speaking the troopers were moving in on them, and the Royalists drew their swords ready to defend themselves.

Sir John could see that they were greatly outnumbered as the troopers surrounded them and he prayed for help.

"Look out S—!" Paul stopped.

For one awful moment Sir John thought Paul was going to reveal his name. But he had no time to recover from the moment as he threw himself sideways to avoid the trooper's sword. He struggled against losing his grip on the saddle and managed to pull himself upright and regain his balance—I am getting much too old for this, he thought, breathing heavily. But the attack had been so forceful that his assailant had fallen heavily from his horse and lay whimpering on the ground in pain.

Several men had either dismounted or been pulled from their horses and were fighting on foot. Sir John went to help a Royalist whose arm was pouring with blood, while Paul kicked out at a trooper to save himself from being pulled from his horse.

The Royalists tried to hide their faces with their cloaks, but it proved impossible to keep them covered all the time. Sir John prayed that no one had any outstanding features, making him distinguishable even in the darkness.

They were lucky to escape the ambush with only two Royalists wounded.

"It could have been a lot worse, especially if the sky had been clear and the moon full," Paul said, and there was a murmur of agreement.

Their relief was short lived, however, as the troopers thundered after them, firing into the darkness. One man was hit and fell from his horse, but there was nothing that Sir John or any of the others could do to help him.

Sir John was worried about the two injured men, somewhere behind: it was miles to the boat that could save them, and he doubted if either man would manage to stay ahead of the pursuers for long.

Paul was keeping as near to Sir John as possible, and they were ahead of the others, now.

"We must gain ground," Sir John said.

"Hurry!" Paul shouted back at the others, and all the Royalists, except the two injured men, had gained ground by the time they reached Wootton Park. They dismounted and stood for a few moments, praying for their missing men to appear.

"We can't wait any longer," someone said. "I can hear the troopers' horses!" They went towards the boat, which was waiting for them as arranged.

"Is the King with you?" the boat's master called to them.

"Alas, no—"

"Then I can't take any of you," the master interrupted before Sir John had a chance to explain.

There were cries of dismay from the Royalists and they begged the master to change his mind.

"Please!" voices rang out.

"Don't leave us here—there are troopers after us!"

"You expect me to risk my life helping you?"

"You promised!"

"No, I promised to help the King escape, not you."

The Royalists' pleas were replaced by angry accusations and jibes, but the boat was already retreating.

"Maybe he would have refused to take the King if he'd realized the troopers were close behind," Paul said, and Sir John agreed.

"What on earth are are we going to do, now?" someone said.

"I care not," said another, "since my king is still a prisoner."

"We must care," Sir John said, dismounting, "or how will we live to fight for our King another day? Quickly! Leave your horses and into the woods." He was hurrying towards the trees as he spoke.

"Shoosh. Make as little sound as possible," he said when they were all in the woods.

"What good is this? They will just hunt for us until they find us," one Royalist said and others agreed with him.

"Silence!" Sir John's stern command had the desired effect and the party fell silent. "You will lead them right to us if you don't keep quiet."

The sound of hoofs grew nearer, then quietened and died as the troopers rode onto the beach and brought their horses to a standstill. "Stop in the name of Thomas Fairfax," their leader shouted, but no one came into the woods.

Sir John knew that the trooper must be calling after the boat. He closed his eyes for a moment and thanked God for giving him the insight to make his fellow Royalist leave their horses and hide.

There were yells and shouts of abuse, and then shots rang out in the darkness.

"What the—?"

"Be quiet," Sir John said. "They think we're on the boat."

Some of the troopers had dismounted to urinate, and some were still swearing as they remounted and rode away in the opposite direction. But the Royalists remained hidden until the sound of hoofs could no longer be heard on the distant stones.

"I thought we were all as good as dead," Paul said.

Sir John was not surprised to find his horse had gone along with most of the others. Two lay dead on the ground. "It was the horses they were shooting at, not us."

"But why shoot at the horses if they thought we were on the boat?" Paul said.

"Vengeance…depravity…who can say what is in the minds of the King's enemies at such a time?" Sir John said.

"I don't think I can return home," someone said. "A trooper was staring right at me."

"I dare not return home," said another. "My assailant knew my name."

"You can stay in the woods until I find a boat to take you away from the Island," Worsley said. "I will bring you food at night. I have relatives not so far away whom I can stay with."

"I wonder if it's safe for Paul and me to return home," Sir John said.

"If you don't they will guess you were involved."

"But if we're seen walking home at this hour, they will *know* we were involved and will guess that the rest of you are still on the Island, too. They will probably come here looking for you," Sir John said.

"That is a chance we must take," Worsley said. "It will only complicate matters more if you stay here." And so Sir John and Paul, along with six other members of their party, began their long trudge home.

Chapter 9

"So, you are betrothed to Samuel Jarvis!" Paul's voice matched the expression of contempt on his face.

"Oh! What…what are you doing jumping out at me like that?" Anne's voice trembled. "It's the second time…"

"I didn't jump out at you like anything. If you had been looking where you were going you would have seen me." Anne was struggling to regain her composure. But the turbulence within her was due more to finding herself suddenly so near to Paul than from being startled by him.

She had been on her way to Nunwell House to tell Sir John that she was marrying Samuel. Like Paul, he probably already knew, but Sir John treated her like a friend, and friends deserved to be told about something so important, personally. She sighed, wondering how many people Samuel had told, while others would have eagerly listened to the gossip. Not that it really mattered: everyone would know soon, anyway.

"I wasn't at all surprised to hear you were marrying Samuel. I said you were after my lost fortune, and this proves I was right."

"What? It wasn't…isn't like that. Samuel would not stop begging me…and then—"

"You accepted because of the goodness in your heart," he said sarcastically. A tear slipped down Anne's face, but she was determined not to let more follow.

She tried to match his sarcastic tone, "Of course not," but failed by sounding defensive instead. She gripped the back of one hand in the palm of the other, still battling with her emotions. "You have never given me a chance to explain anything. Why are you always so objectionable? Despite what you might think, I have done nothing wrong."

"You deserve Samuel Jarvis," Paul spat. "I hope you both rot!" He marched away and Anne was no longer able to stop the tears from running down her cheeks. She turned back towards home. She no longer felt like talking to anyone—not even to Sir John. She knew deep down inside her that she had been clinging to a notion that Sir John would know how to release her from her betrothal without hurting anyone, which, of course, was nonsense; no one could do that.

Maybe her marriage to Samuel was for the best, anyway. At least he would cuddle her and comfort her…and make her feel wanted. Everyone must feel melancholy at times and need to be comforted and loved.

All three Royalist casualties of the King's aborted escape attempt were dead. Sir John and Paul left St Mary's Church with the other mourners and, standing in the graveyard, listened to Reverend Bushnell's words as each coffin was lowered into the ground.

With a heavy heart, Sir John knew that every mourner there was painfully aware that the three men had died for nothing.

When the funeral was over and mourners began to leave, Sir John and Paul left the graveyard in silence. But once outside, Sir John turned to Paul. "There is something I have to tell you," his voice sounded strained, "but please try not to get too angry. Smith's wife asked me to look at her husband's body before the coffins were nailed down. I was shocked by what I saw. Smith was less likely to have died from his wound than from being shot in the back. The troopers showed no mercy."

"Cowards! Shooting a man in the back," Paul said angrily.

"All the Army would say is that he was a traitor who was getting away."

"He was already injured and hardly likely to get far or resist arrest if they gave chase."

"Yes, but unfortunately none of us is in a position to say so without admitting we were there…though I doubt if the troopers would be charged with anything, anyway." He knew that the New Model Army in its present form was unlikely to punish its men for killing active Royalists. And extremist influence and sheer arrogance was likely to have strengthened high ranking officers' conviction that it was above reprimand from any outside authority.

"The guilty troopers were probably reassured that they would be protected by the Army when the bodies were returned," Sir John said. He knew that the troopers had dropped the three Royalists unceremoniously outside their families' doors and ridden away.

In respect for the dead Royalists Sir John and Paul parted and went home. But first Sir John told Paul to meet him at the stables the following morning.

When Paul arrived at the stables, the next day, two horses were saddled and waiting. But a slight nod was the only acknowledgement that he gave the young lad before taking the reins from him and leading the horses out into the weak sunshine. Sir John joined him, but neither man spoke until they were mounted and well away from the stables.

"Our friends have left Wootton by boat," Sir John said at last.

"Thank goodness!" Paul looked relieved.

"But it seems our horses are still roaming loose in the woods," Sir John continued. "So long as we are careful, I see no reason why we should not find them and bring them back before the Roundheads get wind of them."

"Have you any idea yet what went wrong on the night?" Paul said.

"I've heard several accounts…the most likely being that the guards being paid to help the King changed their minds and decided to talk."

"But why would they, if they'd agreed to help and were being paid?"

"Maybe they were warned that details of the escape were known by the Roundheads and were trying to lessen their punishment," Sir John said. "I also heard that a rope failed, but the King said that must have been an illusion in someone's 'unruly imagination' as he had not even begun climbing down one."

"Has Hammond said anything?" Paul said.

"Not to me, but he told the King that a password was given to the wrong person and a couple of men were arrested and marched off to the guardroom."

"But you don't believe him?"

"It could be the truth. There were certainly two arrests. But he could have invented the part about the password to allay suspicions from the real culprits, again. An ambush was waiting, remember. How did Hammond manage to have men there so quickly if he knew nothing in advance?"

They had been riding at a leisurely pace, but now they broke into a canter as it began to rain quite heavily. Sir John hoped that his king would still be able to bowl later in the day; otherwise he would probably continue sitting, writing page upon page.

"I have some other news," Sir John called out to Paul. "You will probably wonder why I didn't tell you at once, but I am sceptical about it."

"What is it?"

"I heard from a friend in Westminster that arrangements might be made for the King to meet with Parliamentarians so an agreement can be reached between them."

"Surely that's good news? Sir John." They slowed back to a leisurely pace despite the rain.

"Possibly...though I have doubts, even if it's allowed to go ahead. Hammond told the King that he no longer trusts him and, even worse, said he might tell the whole of Parliament not to trust him, either."

"What? How dare he? The King is just trying to regain his rightful position over those who have betrayed him. His enemies are the ones who cannot be trusted...they're the ones who should be locked up!"

"I quite agree—" Sir John began, but Paul's face was contorted with anger as he rode past him and quickened his horse into a gallop before jumping a ditch. He did not slow down until he had rounded part of the field on the other side and crossed back over the ditch to rejoin Sir John.

"Do you feel better now?" Sir John said half reprovingly, but he understood the younger man's lack of experience in controlling his feelings.

"If the meeting does go ahead, do you think the King will be allowed to go to London?" Paul said, but there was still an angry frown creasing his brow.

"I doubt it. It would more likely mean the ministers coming to the Wight." Sir John feared that a meeting between the King and Parliamentarians would be no more successful than previous negotiations from afar. "Then if Parliament's majority of Presbyterians were allowed to make their peace with him, without taking away too much of his power, all well and good. But a meeting might be little more than a further attempt to force the King to sign previously presented, unjust demands. We must never, for one moment, forget about the ever increasing power of the New Model Army. The King might still need our help to escape." They quickened their horses' pace and did not speak or slow down again until they reached the woods at Wootton.

"Have you thought anymore about making our own plans, Sir John?" Paul said as they began looking for the horses.

"Yes, and I think the time has come."

"Will you include Tom?"

"Maybe…maybe not. I have to decide if it will be safer to include him or leave him behind. But three men must be the limit, and no confidantes over the water like Mrs Whorwood."

"Mrs Whorwood? Is she not the woman who tried to find the King a safe place in London…and sent files and aqua fortis to remove the window bar so he wouldn't get stuck again?"

"Yes, she is, but—"

"Surely she would never do anything to harm him?"

"Not knowingly," Sir John said. "She is an ardent Royalist. Her heart is filled with nothing but good towards the King, he has great trust in her, but I fear she may have confided in the wrong person.

"I made a few discreet enquiries about her and a couple of her contacts: the Blacksmith who forged the files in London's Bow Lane, and the astrologer William Lilly whom she—"

"Astrologer?" butted in Paul.

"Yes. It seems he is a most influential astrologer. His pamphlets and almanacs are read by thousands and are rumoured to have a substantial effect on public opinion. If the rumours are just, any political influence must be subtle as both Cavaliers and Roundheads flock to him in these troubled, uncertain times. It seems they confide in him, but others doubt his honour in keeping what he is told to himself. Well, anyway, Mrs Whorwood consulted him." Despite his sadness Sir John smiled. "I know I should not jest whilst we are discussing such a serious subject, but it's just the thought of all those people telling this man their innermost secrets. Mr Lilly must know enough to blackmail half of London!"

"Look! There's Jet," Paul said. The black horse lifted its head and neighed before trotting towards them. Paul dismounted and when the horse reached him it nuzzled his neck. "I doubt if Parchment is far away." Almost as he finished speaking the other horse appeared through the trees. When it reached them, Paul handed its reins to Sir John and clasped Jet's as he remounted the horse that he had arrived on.

"They should be checked over when we arrive back at the stables. Tell the lads to give them extra feed, too."

"Yes, Sir John." They started the journey home slowly and were thankful that it had stopped raining when they left the woods.

During her walks in the countryside, in the weeks prior to her wedding, Anne met and spoke with Sir John Oglander several times. Mostly they talked of the King, but Sir John also showed concern for Anne: "It was love at first sight for my wife, Franck and me. I was fortunate," he said. "So many people, especially those in my position, are expected to enter into arranged marriages without love—the idea being that love will come later." He frowned and stroked his beard. "Do you think you will be happy married to Samuel, Anne?"

She could not answer that question; for, although she had tried not to acknowledge it, it was one that had been tormenting her since the day she had found herself betrothed to him.

"I think I know you well enough to speak my mind," Sir John continued. "Samuel Jarvis is rather an extravagant creature, don't you think?"

"Extravagant, Sir John?"

"He has rather too many servants for the size of Leeward House, he drinks too much and has had far too many women." He smiled kindly on seeing Anne's expression. "I am sorry. The last thing I want to do is upset you, and I know it's not for me to interfere, but I dislike Samuel intensely. I care about you and I would hate you to be unhappy. You do understand?"

Anne nodded her head, but was unable to smile back. She wanted to tell Sir John that she was only betrothed because she had agreed to consider Samuel's proposal of marriage. She also wanted to tell him how confused her feelings were despite her efforts to think positively. And how seeing Paul made her more desperate to be loved, to be caressed and to be comforted…

"Do you really want to marry Samuel?" Sir John's voice startled her. For a few moments, she had almost forgotten he was there.

'No!' she almost said, surprising herself, but she took a deep breath and fought the panic that was threatening to rise up inside her. "I—I have been asking myself that same question time and time again, deep inside here," she said, resting a hand above her bosom. She could not tell him that she had also been asking herself if marriage would help her to stop thinking about Paul. "I have agreed to marry him and I will not try to go back on my word. Whether or not I shall be happy…well, I shall just have to wait and see…and hope."

Sir John looked worried and she knew that he was not convinced, which was hardly surprising when she was still having difficulty convincing herself. But she felt that there was nothing to be gained by burdening him any further with her problems. There was nothing he could do to change them, although she knew that he would be a kind and understanding listener. She quickly changed the subject. "How is the King, Sir John?"

"I am allowed to visit him once a week, and although he is still in good health, he is getting quite aggressive." For a few moments Sir John's expression was so sad that he looked very old. "It must be so humiliating and awful for a king to be treated like a common criminal."

Anne wanted to comfort Sir John, but he continued: "You know about the new bowling green at the castle, of course." She nodded, but it had been more of a statement than a question. For Sir John had told her about it, himself, when work had begun on the conversion of the eastern bailey. "The King spends his afternoons there, when the weather permits. They're about to prepare a building at the south end of the green, so at least he will have somewhere to rest and retire to when the weather is bad.

"Bowling seems to lighten his mood…at least temporarily…I am sure it would help even more if he would trust someone to trim his hair and beard."

"Why won't he?"

"Hammond refuses to let a Royalist use a razor in the castle, and the King has the same qualms about letting a Roundhead near him with one. His hair is almost entirely grey, now, and so untidy. It isn't like him, of course."

Anne had seen the King once, and she had listened to him talk. She remembered him as neat and tidy, but small and stuttering, with a trace of a Scottish accent. She also believed his aloofness to be hiding an underlying shyness. And Uncle Silas had said that if the King lacked sense of political reality, as was sometimes claimed, he was also well-meaning and brave and deeply religious.

Anne's walks helped her to come to terms with her betrothal; the countryside helped her to think more clearly and rarely failed to lift her spirit when it was low. She would compare her situation to the King's, reminding herself how much she had to look forward to in her future. While the poor King knew not what his future held; or more accurately, what his enemies might have in store for him.

She never ceased to marvel at the most beautiful countryside that she had ever seen, where even the birds seemed to sing more cheerfully. And the miserable weather that plagued the Wight— "Scarce three dry days together since early May," Sir John had said—could not spoil its beauty. But when the weather was unsuitable for leisurely walks, Anne would sit with Mary, in Leeward House, working on the two 'special dresses'.

Anne seldom succeeded in persuading Mary to walk with her.

"It's not that I don't like walking with you—I do, but the dresses must come first. There will be plenty of time for me to walk with you, when you are married to Samuel."

"Oh, Mary, please come to the market with me," Anne pleaded, now. It had stopped raining and the sun was shining, and she felt that Mary had been working much too hard on the dresses. "Please…you will strain your eyes."

"All right." Mary smiled. "I need some lace trimming for this, anyway." She put down the dress that she had been working on. "I have the lace I made, but there is not enough, nor the time left to make more." Anne did not need reminding that there was so little time left before she married Samuel; in less than two weeks time she would be his wife.

"I wish you were getting married tomorrow," Mary said as they headed for the town, "then I would have even less time to wait before you come and live with us. Oh, it's so excit—"

"I wish I could do something to help the King," Anne interrupted suddenly, not wanting to hear any more about her marriage, and Mary gasped.

"Think how angry Samuel would be," she said. But Anne knew that her wish could never be granted, anyway: women always had to leave the heroics to the men.

In the market, Anne bought some rye before following Mary to a stall where various trimmings were on display. They chose some lace, and Mary bought two yards, while Anne chose a yard of blue ribbon for her hair.

She was about to follow Mary away from the stall, when she glanced at two women standing next to her. She stood still, opened her little cloth bag and put the ribbon inside. She had not intended to listen to the women's conversation, but was unable to help overhearing what they said. And when one of them started talking about the King she was loath to turn away…

"It's the second time he's tried to escape," the woman continued. "The first time, he got stuck in the window."

"I know," the other woman said jovially. "I couldn't stop laughing when I heard about it." They both began to chuckle.

He was their king, for goodness sake! Anne turned on them angrily. "Have you no respect? How can you be so heartless? Imagine what it must be like for our king to be deprived of his liberty!" She was surprised by her own outburst. Her heart was pounding in her chest as she left them and pushed her way through the shoppers to find Mary.

She knew that her face was flushed. She pressed her lips together, determined not to tell Mary anything. But Mary seemed to sense her mood and remained silent.

Anne began to feel rather foolish, however, as they made their way back to Leeward House; for she knew how unwise it had been to rebuke the two women and so loudly support the King.

"You are very quiet," Mary said at last. "Is anything wrong?"

"No…not really. It was just something I heard in the market. And something I did…I don't want to burden you with it."

"Please tell me…I want to help you."

Anne put her arm round Mary's shoulder. "Thank you, but I did something foolish. I heard two women belittling the King, and I was rude to them."

"Oh!" Mary said.

"There could be repercussions. It was so—"

"I don't expect anything will happen," Mary interrupted reassuringly. "Did the women know you?"

Anne was slow to answer. "I think not."

"There then…and anyway, it would not stop Samuel from marrying you, if that is what's worrying you…he loves you too much and would probably apologize for you."

Anne removed her arm. "I don't want him to apologize for me!" Her vehemence made Mary cringe and Anne looked contrite. "Oh,

Mary, I am so sorry…" her voice tapered away, and they both remained silent for what seemed like an age.

"Perhaps I should go home," Anne said as they approached Leeward House.

"No…please…we are here now. Unless…unless you have changed your mind about being my friend."

"Oh, Mary, I was thinking of you. What friend am I, shouting at you like that?"

"But you *are* my friend, that's what matters. Please stay," Mary said.

"Of course I will."

As they entered the house, Samuel rushed into the hall to greet Anne with a quick kiss on the back of one hand, and then a lingering kiss on the palm of the other. "My darling, you look more beautiful every time I see you," he said. And not for the first time Anne saw passion in his eyes, which was why, even though his behaviour towards her left nothing to be desired, she preferred not to be left alone with him.

There seemed little purpose in telling him about her outburst at the market. Mary had said it would not stop him from marrying her, and on reflection Anne was afraid that she was right! So why shatter the temperate nature he feigned for her benefit and bring his darker side crashing down upon her unnecessarily? He would know soon enough, if anything came of her outburst.

"He loves you so much," Mary said, when Samuel went to ask the servants to bring wine.

"I know he does," Anne said, and Mary was looking at her, waiting. Anne wished she could tell her that she loved Samuel, too, but it would be untrue, and Mary looked disappointed when she changed the subject. "I wish my father could love me a little, too."

"Perhaps he does," Mary said, and Anne tried to believe it might be so.

She even tried to believe it might be so later that day, when she placed food in front of her father and he grunted and then ignored her. She ate with him, as she did most days now, then escaped to the attic to read.

"Oh, no, it's raining again!" Anne said after looking out of a window. She was at Leeward House, helping Mary with the dresses, but neither of them spoke of the incident in the market place.

Then Anne began saying she needed to walk, despite the miserable weather. For Mary's incessant talk about the wedding and her marriage to Samuel began to annoy her. This happened again the next day—and the next...

But despite all her walks, Anne did not see Sir John until the day before her wedding. She was on her way to the market, knowing that it would be her last chance to go there as Miss Anne Jolliffe. She felt a strange sadness, not only for all the times she had left behind, but also for those that would never be. And then she saw Sir John approaching her on horseback.

He reined his horse to a stop and dismounted. "Is everything all right?"

"Y-yes." She managed to smile at him.

"Are you sure?"

"Yes. Yes, but..." she could not put her feelings into words, even for him, so she quickly thought of something else to tell him: "I overheard someone in the market saying that the King had tried to escape for a second time."

"Well, yes, it's true...but is that really why you look so unhappy, Anne?"

She nodded, but knew that Sir John was unconvinced.

He studied her face as he continued: "Royalists are uprising throughout the land and causing the Roundheads a few problems." His lips almost curved into a smile as though the very idea of the Roundheads being unnerved amused him, but he continued in earnest. "It is making them question security. In fact, reinforcements are being sent here at this very moment.

"The bigoted Puritan ideals are becoming increasingly unpopular. As if repressing sport and other pleasures isn't enough, theatres are being pulled down."

Anne gasped. "How awful!" She was aware that stage plays were stopped from taking place, but she was also aware that there were some beautiful theatres and it seemed sinful that they should be destroyed.

"But a treaty between the King and Parliament is now a strong possibility," Sir John said.

"A treaty would be wonderful…but there is something else, Sir John," Anne said. "I want to ask you to do something for me."

"Of course I will, if I can. What is it?"

"Will you come to the church on my wedding day?"

Sir John smiled. "Of course I will. I would have been there anyway."

Chapter 10

Anne awoke with a feeling of gloom on what should have been the happiest morning of her life.

Not wanting to dwell on the reasons for her melancholy, she turned her attention to her beautiful dress, which was hanging from a hook a little way up the roof. She had put it there so that she could look at it as soon as she awoke. Her eyes travelled over the blue silk and bows to Mary's own lace, which she had used to make a beautiful deep collar. The collar was shaped to fit snuggly round the yoke and end in two points just above the waist. Mary had cleverly shaped and gathered the puffed sleeves in just below the elbows, where she had used the lace from the market to make deep cuffs. Anne felt sorry for girls who had to marry in dresses that they already had, especially if they had been repaired several times.

She thought of the Puritans and everything that they had been trying to banish from the land over the last few years. How she hoped that they would never ban lovely clothes! She visualized everyone walking around in drab clothes with plain white collars, and the absurdity of the idea made her smile and she felt her spirits lift.

Mary had worked so hard on the dresses, doing more than her share of both the cutting and the sewing. Soon she would be arriving to help her into her dress, and to add the last stitches. It was comforting to know that she would have one relative whom she loved and could totally rely upon when she was married. In fact, Mary would be like a real sister.

She was dismayed to discover that her wretched father had gone about his work as if it were just an ordinary day. She counted to ten, to calm herself, pulled on her cloak and a shawl to cover her nightgown and her head, then left the cottage to go and find him.

Her gloom returned. She felt as doleful as the weather. The sky was full of dark clouds and the rain was falling steadily. The countryside looked greener than ever, but now it just made her want to cry. She wondered if other brides of arranged marriages felt like this on their wedding day.

Samuel liked to tell folk that she had gladly accepted his proposal, which made her want to tell them that it was a lie. But she knew it was pointless to dwell on such things, now.

She decided to rebuke her father, using a few well chosen words, for leaving her this morning: 'how could you leave me on this day of all days' would be sufficient. Not too harsh; but enough to let him know how much he had upset her. A rueful half-smile pulled at her mouth. She hardly expected him to admire her dress or support her with encouraging conversation, but it would have been nice if he had at least been at home when she awoke.

She found him sitting on a tree stump, staring unseeingly ahead of him and getting drenched. "Father!" she paused—he obviously had not heard her. "Father," she repeated so loud that he could not possibly fail to hear, "what is the matter?" She moved closer to him, the words that she had chosen to rebuke him lain aside by daughterly concern. "Please tell me what is wrong."

"Ay? What...? Oh, 'tis you...I was just remembering my own wedden day. Your mother", it was only the second time that he had referred to her, "was so lovely. Aye, prettiest maiden in the town. I was sich a milksop...thought nothen could part us...death happened t' others and t' wold folk." His eyes rested upon Anne and he was silent for an age, but then he chuckled and continued: "Pinned her nightgown t'gether at the bottom that virst night—said she always did it avore lest some stranger saw her." And with a start Anne realized that she had carelessly let her own nightgown show beneath her cloak, and the front of her cloak was gaping open, too, with the rain seeping through to her skin. She turned away to adjust her clothes.

When she turned back, Walter was wiping his hands beneath his eyes and for a moment he looked embarrassed, leaving her in no doubt that he had been wiping away tears, not just rain.

Perhaps hating her had given him the strength to go on living when her mother had died, she thought. And now her coming to the Wight had rekindled the memories and his grievances against her.

"What d'you want, girl?" he said abruptly as though regretting his weakness, and probably regretting confiding in her, too. But she had seen such love in his eyes as he had talked about her mother.

Anne knew she had just learnt more about her father than in the rest of the time she had been on the Wight. She wanted to put her arms around him and hug and kiss him, and tell him that she loved him, but she dare not; it would only make him angry.

"Father you are soaked—you will catch your death sitting there. And you should not even be here. Have you forgotten it's my wedding day? You must give me away," she said earnestly. Walter looked as though he was about to refuse, and Anne no longer felt like hugging him as she hurriedly continued: "Or perhaps you would rather postpone the wedding until a more convenient time for you?"

Walter did not hurry to answer as he rose from the log and turned his back towards her. "I'll be there…intended be'en there all along."

Anne turned away and began walking back to the cottage. She knew she should believe her father had intended being at the church, but it was difficult. She sighed and wondered what it mattered anyway, so long as he had agreed to be there now.

* * * *

"Oh, Anne you look like a princess…a beautiful princess." Mary clasped her hands together. "Samuel won't be able to keep his eyes from you." Anne's mid-auburn hair hung in a cascade of ringlets, secured round her crown and garlanded with flowers. Her dress complemented her figure so.

The petticoats only just covered her ankles, so they did not touch the floor: "...to stop you tripping at an awkward moment, or your petticoats soaking up the wet if it's raining," Mary had said, when she had begun turning the hem.

"Oh, Anne, this is the most wonderful day of my life," she said now.

"Mary, has—has there never been anyone...?"

Mary shook her head and looked sad. "No, no one at all. Samuel is very protective...but not in such a kind way as Paul has protected Christina." Then her face brightened again. "But I am just happy for you." Anne turned her head away so that Mary could not see her expression. She must try and show more enthusiasm, if only for Mary's sake.

"Now it's your turn to look like a princess," she said more brightly than she felt. She helped Mary put on her special dress, and then she fastened the points for her.

"You will do my hair just like yours?"

"Of course I will," Anne said affectionately. She had the garlands ready and proceeded to sweep Mary's hair up. It was easy to comb her naturally curly hair around a finger to form ringlets, and the pretty loose tendrils that always framed her face needed little attention. Her dress was a lighter blue than Anne's and matched her eyes, making her look enchanting and even more delicate than usual. She had nearly chosen yellow silk, but had changed her mind in favour of the blue, and that had pleased Anne.

Anne's dressing-glass was not big, but she held it low and away at an angle to let Mary see the overall effect.

"Oh! Anne," she breathed, as she looked at her reflection. Then she picked up the little velvet bag of rice that she had brought with her.

Anne balanced her glass so that she could take a last overall glance at herself before they left. Then they went outside and collected herbs, some of which were flowering, and tied them into two neat bunches with velvet ribbon.

"They look really pretty," Mary said, "and so do you…sister-in-law." They both laughed.

People turned to stare at them as they walked the short distance to the church, and some folk even looked at Anne with kindness now; instead of seeing her as an outsider, they had come to regard her as a local girl whom had been raised by relatives over the Solent.

Walter Jolliffe was waiting at the church door, looking awkward, and Anne thanked him for coming, even though she had left him with little choice.

"You will be coming to Leeward House afterwards, won't you, Mr Jolliffe?" Mary said, and Walter just grunted. "I hope I feel hungry by then. I'm too excited to want to eat anything."

"I could not eat anything, either," Anne said, but she was unable to ascribe her lack of hunger to any one emotion that she could name.

Walking down the aisle with her arm linked through her father's felt so right. But she felt strange as she stood by Samuel's side at the altar. Was she really standing before these people, marrying Samuel Jarvis? It seemed unreal. And she was tempted to cry out when Reverend Bushnell asked for anyone who saw reason why they should not marry to say so. She wondered how everyone would react towards her if she did. It would stop the marriage; there was no doubt in her mind about that. But what would it do to her father…and to Mary? She must become Mrs Samuel Jarvis, even if marrying a man she did not love was a mockery to her own ideals and beliefs.

She realized that the Reverend was waiting for her to speak, and her voice when she made her vows was sharpened by uncertainty. This was not how it should be, she thought.

When Reverend Bushnell said that they were now man and wife, the words frightened Anne. She was Mrs Samuel Jarvis, now, and would remain so for the rest of her life. But as Samuel's lips gently touched hers her fear dissolved and she felt a warm glow of security inside her.

It was drizzling with rain when they left the church. Sir John Oglander was one of the first of the congregation to leave after the bridal procession. He greeted Anne warmly and wished the couple well. Samuel snorted and pulled Anne away. She looked back and smiled apologetically at Sir John, who was staring after her with a sad expression on his face.

"Samuel, how could you…on our wedding day? Could you not forget your political assignations just for one day? I would have liked to ask Sir John to come to the house."

There had not been much of a congregation at the service. Despite people's changing attitude towards Anne, there were still many who did not regard her as one of them. Perhaps if there had been more of a gathering outside the church, she would not have noticed the lonely figure lurking under the archway beneath the town hall, watching. She shivered as she saw him move out of view; for she knew instinctively that he was the rider that had so nearly injured her on Sir John's estate. The same rider who had been watching her in her dream. But there the similarity to her dream ended. For now she realized that the stranger was not watching her, at all: he was watching Mary.

Samuel smiled at Anne and lifted her nightgown up and off and dropped it to the floor. His breathing quickened with excitement as his eyes travelled over her naked body. "Oh, Anne, I need you so much. You are so beautiful."

Anne slowly raised her eyes to Samuel's own nakedness and felt the blood rush to her face. She had thought things would move a little less quickly; that they would kiss and cuddle and wear nightclothes at least until their mood became more intimate.

She turned and walked to the bed, to where the drapes were pulled aside, giving herself time to recover from her embarrassment. But Samuel moved close behind her and swung her round to face him. He kept one hand on her arm, while his other reached out for her breasts. But she hated the rough way that he was handling them, and she tried to pull away. His eyes seemed bigger than usual, and they were gleaming unnaturally in the candlelight. His breathing had quickened to such an extent that he was almost panting. He pushed her backwards onto the bed.

"No…wait…please…" she begged.

"Wait for what?" his voice shook with emotion. He took a deep breath, which was unsteady, like the breathing of someone who had been sobbing, and Anne struggled to move away from him. He grabbed her impatiently and lifted her onto the bed so that her head rested upon the pillow. She was frightened and again tried to struggle away from him, but he clambered on top of her, making it impossible for her to move.

"Please...no...not like this! You are hurting me." He was heavy and writhing about on her as though he wanted his flesh to combine with hers. She prayed silently that it would soon be over.

Suddenly it was as though a demented creature had taken possession of his body. He dug his fingernails into her back as he pulled her against him so hard that she thought her bones would break. Her cries, which were muffled by his flesh, were those of pain as he took her without compassion or regard for her feelings.

"I've been to Hell these past weeks!" he said shakily as he launched into his second attack. His groans of ecstasy and satisfaction smothered her cries, and then she was sobbing into her pillow, feeling bruised and sore and wretched as Samuel snored by her side.

Chapter 11

"No!" Anne moved out of Samuel's reach as he went to grab hold of her. "Please! I—I don't want—"

"Damn you, Anne! You cannot do this to me," Samuel interrupted. He was waiting for her when she came out of the small room adjoining their bedchamber, where she had changed into her nightgown—just as he had been waiting for her every night that week. But unlike the other nights, when he had sighed impatiently and left the bedchamber to console himself with ale, he looked angry.

She went to the dressing table, willing herself to stay calm. She did not want to aggravate his anger, but she could feel his eyes boring into her and wanted to tell him to leave her alone.

She released her hair, letting it fall down ready to be brushed. But her hand was shaking as she lifted the hairbrush from the dressing table and used it to stroke her hair rather than brush it; for grooming was the last thing on her mind as she tried to think of an excuse to leave the chamber. She feared that Samuel would overpower her and force himself upon her again, if she stayed.

"Oh! I have just remembered—" she began as she turned, then she fought to stop her face registering dismay as Samuel moved towards her. The hairbrush fell from her hand onto the rush matting, her shoulders hunched and she absently grasped her nightgown to her with clenched fists; one hand above her bosom, the other below.

Samuel's mouth turned up at the corners, but if he was at all amused it did not reflect in his eyes. "At first I thought perhaps there was a reason."

"There is a reason," she said quickly. "I have been feeling tired…and…and…now I must go down—"

"No, damn you! I thought you were having your—" he stopped and punched a fist into his other hand. "Damn you! Damn you! Damn you!"

"Oh dear!" He had thought it was her time for what some women regarded as the curse.

"Yes, it is 'Oh dear'. I have rights," he said, and Anne blushed guiltily.

But why should she feel guilty? she thought. It was Samuel's own fault she was rejecting him. And as for his rights…it seemed unjust that a man should be entitled to hurt his wife. She wished she had rights.

He was looking down to where her clenched fists still held her nightgown against her, and she instinctively stepped backwards to increase her distance from him.

She wanted to run from the room, but when she looked towards the door, Samuel moved to block it from her view. "There is no escape…I have been much too patient with you." He grabbed her right arm, and she knew that he would hurt her again if she did not say something to stop him…

"You are too rough." It was all that she could think of to say, and while it was the the truth, she doubted if it would be enough to stop him forcing himself upon her.

"What?" He let go of her arm, looking stunned, but he quickly recovered: "You are too rough," he mimicked. "What do you want…a baby's lullaby?"

"Of course not, Samuel. Please don't make this any more difficult. If only you could understand the anguish I have felt…wanting to please you, but fearing you would hurt me again. How will I ever be able to have any love for you if you make me suffer so?"

He spread his fingers and looked down at the back of one hand and then the other, and the thought crossed Anne's mind that it was a strange time to admire his rings.

"It is a sad fact that women suffer."

"You were brutal. You could have been more gentle and at least made it tolerable." She wondered what Samuel would say if she told him what her aunt had once told her. "I might even have—that is…if you had been loving, I might even have found it…satisfactory. Perhaps I would even—" she could not continue and felt her face warming with embarrassment. She lowered her eyes to the floor and wondered if she had said too much already. Samuel was not blessed with the same compassionate and understanding nature as her uncle, and she feared he might think her rude.

He remained quiet for so long that she looked up at his face, but could tell nothing from his expression.

"If you mean you might like it, or even take pleasure from it, I have known women who did so. But they have all been harlots and not women I would ever have considered marrying. I ought to force you onto that bed and put an end to your nonsense." But his voice belied his words, for he sounded unsure of himself.

This was an unexpected change in him, and it was one that Anne found reassuring and she began to relax. "It's not nonsense." She had once found the courage to ask her aunt about her wedding night; it had been so difficult trying to think of a way to ask her without sounding vulgar.

Her aunt had blushed and been silent for what seemed like an age. Then she had turned, so that Anne could not see her face, and told her how, on her wedding night, she had become so aroused by Anne's uncle making love to her that she had been unable to control the spasms and pleasurable sensations within her. She had lain awake the rest of the night, worrying about it, and when her husband awoke the next morning, her anxiety had almost turned into a fever. Her poor young husband had been gripped by concern for her. And so, she had had no option other than to tell him how worried she was because she had lost control of her feelings.

Anne had been eager to hear what he had said, but her aunt had turned to face her and had been silent for several moments with a faraway look in her eyes. Her cheeks were rosy, and she looked almost like a young girl again as she recalled how he had smiled and told her that he knew she had felt pleasure: "God meant us to share our feelings, and to enjoy doing so. It's only wrong when it happens between two people who are not married in God's eyes," he had said.

Anne had been so grateful to her aunt for confiding in her, so that one day she might be spared the same anguish on her own wedding night.

At least now Samuel wore his nightshirt and cap; it had been daunting to find him waiting for her without them those first nights. But he was standing where the candle cast unflattering light on his chubby face, almost making him look grotesque, and she found herself thinking it would be better if he had his face covered, too. The thought made her smile.

"Why are you smiling?"

She wondered what his reaction would be if she told him the truth. "So you would liken me to a harlot if I became affectionate towards my own husband when he was having his way with me. Surely it would be more desirable for me to be happy than left bruised and crying into my pillow?"

Samuel fell silent, again, for what seemed like an age, and then he moved nearer to her. She had already relaxed her hold on her gown, and he took both her hands in his. "I never meant to hurt you anyway, but I seemed to wait such a long time for our first night."

"We have not even known each other a long time."

"Feeling for you as I do, I could not be in the same room with you without wanting to ravish you." He sighed. "I will try to be gentle," he put his hand up and stroked her face, "but that does not mean I am growing weak." He gripped the neck of her nightgown with both hands and ripped it to the waist so that it fell to the floor. Anne gasped, as much from surprise as from shock; for she had made the gown herself and knew the strength of the cloth. There was a glint in his eyes as he put his arms around her.

He kissed her forehead and then the tip of her nose, before pressing his lips gently against hers. His lips felt nice and she found her lips moving in response. His hands, as they caressed her breasts, felt tender and caring and she did not want him to stop.

He was breathing quickly and she sensed that he was having difficulty controlling his lust. But he was controlling it for her, and that pleased her and she slid her arms as far round him as she could.

Lifting her onto the bed, he lowered himself partly onto it, partly on her, and his kisses became more passionate—and so did her responses. His hands and mouth began to roam over her body. It felt so good, Anne found herself making little appreciative sounds. And after he had moved further onto her, she began responding with a need that frightened her for a moment. But the moment was soon lost in the intensity of her emotions. Nothing existed outside the wonderful sensations that were increasing inside her intent on taking over and controlling her body…

Samuel let his breath out in a long satisfied groan, but then he heaved himself from her as though ice cold water had been thrown over him. She cried out in alarm as his hand struck her across the face, twice. Then he pushed her so hard that she fell from the bed.

"Just like a harlot!" he said, scrambling from the bed, and Anne feared he would strike her again.

"W-what have I d-d-done wrong?" she asked weakly. Her lips were trembling.

"You whisper 'Paul' and then ask what you've done wrong!" he said through clenched teeth. "I thought you were so virtuous…clean and pure, as white as snow. Now you disgust me." He turned and marched angrily from the bedchamber.

"I—I did not say—" Anne tried to call after him, but her voice was a croak and barely audible. "I could not have…" she whispered to herself. She was too shocked to cry or move from the floor. She began to shiver uncontrollably. Hugging her legs to her chin she silently prayed to wake-up and find that it had all been a nasty dream. But this was one nightmare that would not go away or be absolved so easily.

"I cannot invite you to my home to make plans for the King," Sir John told Paul. "The soldier the Army has billeted with me comes in at the

most unexpected moments, and he creeps around my home as though
hoping to catch me unawares—at what, I'm not quite sure. I think it's
the Army's way of keeping a close watch on me."

"It's your home—surely you can impose some restrictions?"

Sir John laughed. "That might make the Army angry and cause more
problems than it solves." Sir John was standing with Paul, looking at
the field in front of him. It was sodden and there were pools of water;
even some of the higher fields would become waterlogged if the weather
did not improve soon. Sir John hoped that the hedgerows and ditches
would continue to prevent most of the water reaching the town.

His thoughts returned to his king. "You know, Paul, His Majesty
says he is in no hurry for a meeting on the Wight between him and
Parliamentarians to go ahead. In fact he has been dragging out
negotiations, hoping Fairfax's army will make itself even more
unpopular with Parliament than it already has."

"Most folk probably think of it as Cromwell's Army," Paul said.

Sir John laughed and continued, "Parliament might soon rue the
day it quarrelled with its king!" Despite his optimistic tone of voice,
his fears for his king had been growing daily, and if an escape became
necessary, he feared it would be so much more difficult now: "I did tell
you that the King was moved to the chief officer's quarters at the castle,
of course. And he still holds some hopes of the Scots helping him, as
you know."

"But he might still have to seek refuge abroad if there is no way left
to regain his eminence here," Paul said.

Sir John's shoulders drooped. "I think we all know deep down that
it will probably come to that, now. However willing Parliament is to
reach an agreement, it will be the Army he will need saving from."

Sir John had believed that Oliver Cromwell's influence and ideals
were made temperate by conflicts that raged inside him and prevented
him being a great threat to the King. In fact, Sir John had hoped that he
might, in the end, come round to helping him. But now rumours had
reached him that Cromwell's illusions of being at one with The
Almighty and doing His work were overcoming those conflicts and
his conscience. And they were making him a more treacherous force

against the King than many whom had long been regarded as dangerous extremists.

Sir John had told Paul how Cromwell had been mainly responsible for the Royalists' defeat in the North after the Scots crossed the border the previous month.

"From what I have heard since, the Roundheads had under half the number of men fighting for the King," Sir John had said.

"Perhaps they were hoping to die martyrs."

"Cromwell was reported by some to have been like a man possessed. I believe he has always been a foolhardy—"

"Take the hardy off and I will agree wholeheartedly," Paul had interrupted and they had both laughed.

But Sir John knew that luck had been with the wretched man. The weather had been appalling, and the Scots inadequately armed and provisioned. Some said that the Scots commander-in-chief, the Duke of Hamilton, was inefficient; whilst others said that he fought well. But either way the King had accepted it as another bad omen.

It seemed ironic to Sir John that the King, crowned and given his powers by God, was a prisoner under pressure to relinquish most of his might, while Cromwell, rising on an illusion of God-given power, was free to harm him.

Paul broke into his thoughts. "Presumably we will need to have horses standing by again if the King needs to escape."

"Yes, of course…but I think the unexpected could prove to be as important as our careful planning."

"But we will have to wait near the castle?"

"No, Paul—that would not be at all unexpected. Troopers will search the countryside around the castle before they search anywhere else. I was considering the tunnel from the castle to the Castle Inn at Castlehold." Paul looked surprised and Sir John continued: "I would have previously opposed such an idea, especially taking His Majesty through that inn."

"Is it really such a very bad place?"

"Apparently its illegal marriages are on the increase, and more thieves and vagabonds have been seeking refuge there than ever before."

"And the authorities do nothing?" Paul said incredulously.

"It has always been outside the jurisdiction of the law."

"I can't imagine the Roundheads caring about jurisdictions!"

"Mmm, well, I expect it will only be a matter of time before they realize what a den of depravity it is and knock it down. Meanwhile, those Roundheads who go there for entertainment have as much reason as anyone to keep quiet."

"Hypocrites!" Paul said. "And what a terrible place to take the King!"

Sir John smiled. "My response, exactly, when I first considered it. But then I began thinking I should know His Majesty better than that and not underestimate him. In fact, I can almost hear him exclaiming what an ingenious way it is of outwitting his enemies. You know, Paul, the King suffered bad health as a child, but he overcame his weaknesses with great courage and determination. We must never underestimate him."

"Supposing the authorities know about the tunnel and capture him?"

"I only know about it because a Royalist friend of a friend escaped through it after being taken to the castle." He chuckled. "Hammond allowed him to roam about the castle unaccompanied whilst awaiting escorts to take him to London. His disappearance right under his very nose must have caused a frantic hue and cry!"

"How did your…friend of a friend find the tunnel entrance?"

"Someone inside the castle led him to it. At first, he feared it was a trick and that the other man intended to shoot him in the back as he tried to escape."

They had been walking slowly, and now Sir John looked across to where two horses were grazing in a higher field.

Paul followed his line of vision. "Have you decided whether to involve Tom, Sir John? He could have the horses ready and waiting…and take them to Castlehold. It would be quite a help to us."

"Decisions on whom to trust could be the most important judgements we will ever have to make. Maybe His Majesty's life will depend upon them."

"You still have doubts concerning Tom?" Paul frowned.

"You don't seem to have any hesitations in proclaiming him worthy of our trust."

"He by his fruits hath shown. What about the injury he received declaring himself a Royalist?"

Sir John stood deep in thought for several moments and then beckoned Paul to follow him and they made their way to the stables in silence.

They found Tom grooming a black stallion and he did not look up until Sir John said: "Tom Fletcher, what would you say if you had a chance to help the King?"

"I would consider it a great honour to serve my king, Sir John. I would give my life, such is the depths of my love for him."

"You see, sir," Paul said when he and Sir John had left the stables, "he is as loyal as I am."

"Nevertheless he is to be told nothing until I decide to tell him."

"No, sir."

Sir John had already decided that it might be safer to have Tom with them than leave him behind. But he did not intend making any hasty decisions on how little Tom might or might not be told when the time came.

Sir John and Paul were now so used to the wet weather that they appeared not to notice as it began raining, again.

"Where will we go after leaving the inn?" Paul said.

"I have not made any final decisions yet, but it would be wise to ride with the King to the south-east coast of the Wight," Sir John said. He knew that the King would be safer in France, at least for a while, if all else failed. "We will need someone with a ship or boat to carry His Majesty across the channel to safety."

Paul scratched his head. "A smuggler, perhaps…?"

"I think you are probably right." Much as Sir John adhored the thought of his king being at the mercy of a scoundrel, he knew that it might be his only chance of escape. "A smuggler would be stealthy by nature, full-witted and used to noiseless manoeuvres at night…but I think at least one of us should accompany the King if he has to flee to France."

Mary asked no questions during the days that followed Samuel's departure from the marital bed, but she was perceivably troubled by Samuel's behaviour towards Anne…and his behaviour towards her, come to that.

She knew that Anne was left to spend her long nights alone, while Samuel slept in the spare bedchamber. He had even had his clothes and anything else that he might need in the night taken there.

"I wish you would talk, or argue, anything to end this terrible silence between you. I love you both so much. I can't bear to see you like this," Mary said at last. But she could have little idea of the extent of Samuel's enmity. And Anne prayed that she would never know its reason.

Anne found it difficult accepting its reason herself; for she could not believe she had whispered 'Paul'. Surely she would not…But then she asked herself why Samuel would lie and accuse her of it if she was innocent; he had lost as much as her, if not more, by abandoning the marital bed. She had no option but to accept the loathsome truth: she had been unfaithful to him in her mind.

Chapter 12

A candle stood burning in its holder on the oak table in the parlour, while Anne sat in the upholstered chair. In a particularly truculent moment, she had wondered if the chair was one of the extravagances for which her father had seemed to think she should be grateful, when he had first told her that Samuel was trying to court her. But she would rather live in a small clay cottage with no comforts at all than spend the rest of her life in a loveless marriage.

The thought made her feel remorseful. It was entirely her own fault if Samuel had stopped loving her. And there was certainly no one else to blame for his loss of respect for her.

But some nights, like tonight, she was reluctant to go to the bedchamber that was now hers alone. For Samuel's bitter accusations, made when he had slapped her and pushed her from their bed, were uppermost in her mind and were worse there. So, yes, she was grateful for the chair, at least until she felt tired enough to go to her bedchamber and sleep; rather than toss about restlessly in the big, lonely bed. She knew she must try to stop associating her bedchamber with odious memories of Samuel's accusations.

She sighed and turned her thoughts to how she should try to soften Samuel's grievance against her. It would be difficult, when every time she looked at him his expression forbade her to try.

Everyone else must be sleeping, she thought, as she rested her head against the high back of the chair. She knew it was pointless fretting over things that she could not change tonight.

She frowned, listening, then took the candle from the table and left the parlour. She had heard a noise. It was probably only the servants, she thought, as she reached the stairs.

But a giggle came from the direction of the front door of the house and Anne gasped in surprise. There was more giggling, and a snort, and she decided that it was unlikely to be servants, after all; servants would go round to their own door, not linger in the front porch.

A woman laughed loudly, and even through the door it sounded coarse and unladylike. Commonsense told Anne that the woman was not alone. Should she call out to them to go away? Or perhaps she should raise the servants.

A sudden roar of laughter made Anne gasp in horror, and she almost dropped the candle. "No!" she said out loud, and her grip tightened on the candle holder. Her other hand was clenched so tightly that her fingernails were digging into her palm. No, it could not be…It was late…and she was overtired, and her estrangement with Samuel was affecting her more than she had realized. She should turn away, call the servants, and then go to her bedchamber.

But more laughter made her move nearer to the door, which, now she saw, was neither locked nor bolted. The key was large and awkward to turn, the bolt often difficult to move, and it was usually left to a manservant to secure the door at night. But tonight it was unlocked, suggesting that someone from the house had either unlocked it, or followed orders for it to be left so.

She shut her eyes for a moment, trying to prepare herself, before reaching for the door handle. It was difficult to turn with one hand, but she was gripping the candle holder with the other as though her life might depend upon it.

She let out a strangled cry as a body fell inside, pushing the door back as far as it would go and almost knocking her over.

"Samuel," she said in little more than a whisper. He must have been resting against the door, but she barely heard his foul curses as her eyes rested upon the woman who had stumbled in behind him. Anne only just managed to move out of the way in time as the woman lost her balance and landed sprawled across Samuel. They reeked of ale. The woman appeared to be amused by her own unladylike entrance, and her coarse laughter was all that was needed to make the tears brim over the lower lids of Anne's eyes. She sniffed and swallowed, determined not to let more tears flow.

"Samuel!" her voice shook with emotion, now. "Samuel...how could you do this?" He refused to look at her. But the woman, who was now lying with her back propped up against his chest, with her petticoats twisted beneath her and her garters showing, stared up at her with an insolent expression on her face.

Anne glared at her. "Have you no sense of shame?" The woman was a well endowed wench of about 30 years old. The low cut bodice of her red gown looked loose and dishevelled. Her pink cheeks were flattering, but Anne suspected that the colour was produced with a little conchineal or the like. The shawl, which was essential for modesty's sake, had fallen to the ground outside the door.

They struggled to stand up. Anne felt sick with disgust and wanted to turn away; but she knew she must try to stop them going to Samuel's bed.

"Please don't do this," she said, moving towards Samuel. "Please, send this...this woman away and we can talk about it in the morning."

Samuel moved towards the stairs, pushing Anne out of his way, but then he stopped and turned, and his eyes travelled over her, narrowing in appraisal. "You can join us if you like, whore. There's room for you both in my bed, tonight." He put an arm out to her and she stepped backwards instinctively.

How could he insult her so? She doubted that the drink was wholly to blame: his speech was hardly slurred and he seemed more in control than his harlot. He must have wholeheartedly meant to insult her. How dare he? And he had said 'tonight' as if he had shared his bed with whores before. But surely she would have heard them...It was more likely that he was just trying to provoke her.

"How much are you paying your harlot for her services?" she asked scornfully and held her head high, then she turned away sharply so that they would not see the tears glistening in her eyes. She was just in time to see a servant scurrying out of sight, probably on her way to tell the others what she had just witnessed.

She went to her bedchamber and stood, feeling cold, alone and miserable. What little spirit she had found to throw scorn on Samuel and his whore had crumbled and the tears were now sliding down her cheeks.

Perhaps she should have ignored Samuel's foreboding expression, days ago, and at least begged him to try to forgive her; then things might not have come to this.

She had let the hand holding the candle carelessly fall to her side, with the flame dangerously close to her petticoats. Melted tallow had dripped onto her clothes and was hardening. She raised her hand, knowing that she could have set herself alight, but she was too traumatized by Samuel's adultery to feel alarmed by her own carelessness. She fingered the hardening tallow; it was too soon to scrape it off. But the motion and thought hardly registered in her mind.

How could she possibly sleep, tonight, now? She did not even want to be alone. She needed to talk to Mary. She left her room and went along the landing towards Mary's bedchamber.

She had stopped sobbing, but sounds of gratification coming from Samuel's bedchamber made her eyes fill with tears of frustration. She went to his door and, hammering her fist against the wood, shouted: "Adulterer!"

There was silence, followed by vulgar laughter from inside the room.

Then a door opened below. Oh, no, the servants, again! Anne thought and, raising her petticoats with her free hand so that she would not trip over, hurried to Mary's bedchamber. Going inside, without knocking, she closed the door behind her and stood against it, listening, but she heard no more sounds coming from below.

She crept across the bedchamber and almost tripped over Mary's cloak, which had been dropped in a heap on the floor—it was unlike Mary to be so untidy.

When she had put the candle down on the little table, she hesitated before pulling the drapes aside; it seemed mean to disturb Mary…but then she knew Mary would want her to—

"Oh!" Anne said. "Why didn't you say something to let me know you were awake?" Mary was sitting up in bed, with the bedclothes drawn up to her chin.

"I wondered who it was," Mary said sheepishly and looked away, uncomfortably. "I heard you shouting."

"Oh, Mary, I am sorry for making so much noise."

"It's all right, really," Mary hastened to reassure her. "I wasn't…that is I was…" She looked flustered and lost for words for a few moments. "But what's happened? You look dreadful. Are you ill?" She kept the bedclothes drawn up to her chin.

"No, I'm not ill." Anne pulled the drapes further aside to let in more candlelight. "But I do feel terrible. I needed to talk to you. You are like a real sister to me. Oh, Mary, Samuel has a…a harlot…whore—I want to call her so many names—in his bed." A sob caught in her throat.

Mary's eyes opened wide with shock, but then she said: "You must be mistaken, he would never do that now he's married to you—he loves you too much."

"I was there when they came in…fell in, that is, reeking of ale. I pleaded with Samuel to send the woman away, but he's taken her to his bedchamber…and I—I heard them…just now," she finished in an almost inaudible whisper.

Mary looked devastated. "Oh, Anne, I am so sorry." Her eyes filled with tears. "How could he do this to you?"

"It's unforgivable behaviour even if I am partly to blame." Anne sat down on the bed.

"Oh, Anne, how can you possibly think you are at all to blame? I know Samuel has been ignoring you and making you sleep alone. I don't understand him sometimes, even if he is my twin brother."

Anne shook her head. "You know not—" she stopped and began to weep, and the next moment Mary had let go of the bedclothes and was kneeling on the bed with her arms around her.

"I'm making you cry, too," Anne said at last, hearing Mary's sniffs and wiping the remainder of her own tears away with her hands. "And I have kept you awake quite long enough." She stood up to leave.

"If only I could do something to help you! Please don't feel you have to go," Mary said.

Anne turned back to look at her. "You *have* helped me. I feel better just talking to you. I know I shall have to try and talk to Samuel, even if…you're still wearing your day clothes." It was a mere observation; for she was too preoccupied with her own problems to be surprised.

"What? Oh!" It was obvious, even in the candlelight, that Mary's cheeks had turned crimson. "Yes…so I am…how silly." She moved from the bed and rummaged under the bedcovers for her nightgown.

Anne yawned and went to the door. "Well, good night, Mary…sleep well."

Anne followed Samuel out of Leeward House the next morning. "Please, wait. We must talk." He ignored her and she knew she must stop him before he reached the stables. "Samuel, please!" She was having difficulty keeping pace with him. He turned his head to look at her with his foreboding expression and kept walking.

But this time she had no intention of turning away: "Please talk to me…I know I have hurt you, but you have committed adultery. What you did last night was loathsome. Don't ever bring any more women home." She had not heard his harlot leave that morning, and it was obvious to Anne that he had already been drinking.

He stopped walking and turned. "I will bring home as many damn women as I like—it's my house."

"It's my home, too," Anne said, "and you have no right to bring a harlot into it."

"No right? No right! I have every right to bring as many women home as I want. It's a husband's right to do exactly as he pleases in his own home, and at least this 'harlot' didn't breathe another man's name when we were—"

"Samuel!" Anne looked around her, fearful that someone might hear. "Please don't shout or they will hear you in the stables."

"If I want to shout, I will shout, and you surely can't think my sin is as wicked as yours?"

"Is it not true then that many Puritans believe adultery should be punishable by death?"

"What? I can't help what some people think…but a man has a pestilence inside him that eats away his soul if he has no woman to gratify it. A woman has a duty to one man. It seems quite clear to me that you agreed to marry me for my wealth and my position, and all the time you have been doing it with Paul Miller."

"How dare you? And I have seen nothing to suggest that you have a *position.*" Anne fought to control her anger. "And Paul Miller has never even kissed me—he despises me. You begged me to marry you despite knowing I didn't love you. How could you say such wicked things?

"I know I hurt you, Samuel, but you have punished me tenfold. We took vows, and we should at least try to uphold them. What of our future if we do not?" She knew that she might find it difficult to like him at all now, let alone honour him, but she would welcome the chance to try. The alternatives were too awful to contemplate, and they had the rest of their lives to get through. Samuel spat on the ground and walked away.

Mary was waiting for Anne when she arrived back at the house. "You went after Samuel, did you not?" she said, with hope in her voice. "What did he say?" Anne could only shake her head despondently.

"Oh, dear, do try to make things right with him," Mary begged. "I know it was despicable of him to bring that woman home—but he does love you…I know he does."

Mary's behaviour puzzled Anne: sometimes she looked so sad, which was quite understandable in the circumstances, but then her face would change and she would have a faraway look in her eyes, a delicate pink glow would brighten her normally pale cheeks and the corners of her mouth would turn up into a smile.

Chapter 13

Anne was on her way home from the market with Mary when she met Sir John for the first time since her wedding day. After greeting them, Sir John studied Anne for a few moments with a sad expression on his face, and she wondered how much gossip had reached him concerning Samuel's behaviour.

Anne's disturbing memories of Samuel's accusations had faded now, leaving his betrayal uppermost in her mind. But he continued to stop her attempts to mend the rift between them by fiercely blaming her for everything that had happened. Nevertheless, she knew that it would be dishonourable to discuss it with anyone outside the family; even Sir John.

"I sent a basket of fruit to Leeward House after the wedding," Sir John was saying now, "but it was sent back to me."

"Oh! Samuel never told me. I am sorry...I—"

"Perhaps Samuel knew nothing about it," Mary said. "I wonder why it was sent back."

Oh, Mary, honestly, Anne thought, remembering Samuel's behaviour towards Sir John outside the church after the service. It was so obvious that Samuel had sent the fruit back and, anyway, no one else would have done such a thing. But she knew it was unjust to feel impatient with Mary.

"I have only mentioned it so you know I do still think about you," Sir John said, smiling at Anne, then he continued on his way.

Anne resisted the urge to tell Mary that it must have been Samuel who turned the fruit away, and that she thought he was despicable to spurn Sir John's kind gesture.

"I never even asked him about the King," she said instead.

Samuel was coming home drunk from the alehouses every night. Sometimes, especially if he was extra late, Anne would be unable to sleep, listening for sounds of him bringing another whore into their home. But he was always alone.

Tonight, he was already home in bed, but Anne was still finding it difficult to sleep; the night was hot and oppressive. Then it began pouring with rain, and this was soon accompanied by thunder and lightning. Anne sighed as she left her bed and lit her candle. She would not sleep now. Besides, Mary was so nervous of storms, she would prefer not to be alone.

Going along the landing to Mary's bedchamber, she tapped lightly upon the door, but all she heard as she entered the room was a ripple of thunder.

"Mary, it's me," she said, remembering the last time she had entered Mary's bedchamber in the middle of the night. But Mary did not answer, and Anne thought she must still be asleep. But on checking inside the drapes she found the bed to be empty.

If Mary had gone downstairs before the storm began, perhaps to fetch a drink of water, she might be crouching down there now, too frightened to leave. Anne left the bedchamber and hurried down the stairs.

But Mary was not there. Then hearing a sound like a window closing, she went to investigate.

"Mary!" Anne put her hand to her mouth too late to stifle her voice on seeing Mary's wet cloak.

They both stood in silence for a moment, outside the room that Mary had just left. But no sounds could be heard of anyone coming to see what was happening.

There was another flash of lightning and Anne saw that Mary was shaking, but the thunder was delayed until they reached her bedchamber.

"It's going away," Mary said with relief as they went inside and closed the door. "I was so frightened outside…the dark made it seem—"

"Where on earth have you been?"

"Oh, Anne, you won't tell Samuel, will you? I have met someone…Oh, Anne, I have met someone so charming!" She clasped her hands together in childlike excitement.

"But why are you meeting him in the middle of the night?"

"Please promise me you won't tell Samuel," Mary interrupted urgently. "He has always been so protective. I am sure he would forbid me to see Ed—this man—especially when I must refuse to disclose his name. And you know what he's like now…he would probably banish me to my bedchamber for a fortnight!"

"No, I'll not tell him…but I feel I should be angry with you for meeting this man in the night. I can't help wondering if he has sinister intentions, or if there is some reason he should not be courting you." Her brow was furrowed with anxiety and Mary hastened to reassure her.

"He's not married or anything. And he would never do anything to hurt me…he loves me. He tells me how much he loves me every time we meet. I'm really sorry I can't tell you his name, but he is on a secret mission and has asked me not to tell anyone…well not yet, anyway."

Far from feeling reassured, Anne wanted to beg her not to meet the man again unless he called at the house first to formally introduce himself. "You cannot even tell *me* his name?"

"I promised him. And anyway, you don't know him."

"Then what possible harm could it do if you told me his name?"

Mary's anguish showed on her face as she struggled with her conscience, and Anne was distressed at having caused the gentle girl so much anxiety. There was a strained silence between them until Mary said: "His name is Edmund. I don't know his surname." Her bottom lip began to tremble and she bowed her head and wept.

"Oh, Mary, please don't cry." Anne put the candle down on the little table and put her arms around her. "I am so sorry I have upset you." She held her until her tears subsided.

Mary sat on the bed and wiped her eyes. "I so wanted to tell you, but I doubt if I should have…I have broken my promise."

"Only to me," Anne said carefully, sitting down beside her, "and we are sisters-in-law and friends."

"I think Edmund would be very angry if he knew."

"Well he doesn't know."

"No, but I feel I should tell him—it would be more honest. I love him and cannot bear to deceive him."

"You're right, it would be more honest to tell him, but it might also worry him. He doesn't know me or what I might do. But surely you trust me?"

"You know I do."

"Then let it stay a secret. I'm sure if Edmund loves you he would understand your reasons for not telling him."

Mary looked doubtful. "I love him so much, you know, Anne. He makes me feel so wonderful. When I'm with him I cannot think of anything except him."

"I know how much you must love him." Anne knew that Mary must be besotted with Edmund to deceive her brother so, and to deceive her, come to that. She wished she knew this Edmund, but from what Mary had told her, it was unlikely that she would have a chance to meet him for some time.

"We had better go to bed," Anne said now the storm had gone. She lit Mary's candle from her own and forced a smile, but her heart was far from light.

"It seems firm enough," Paul said to Sir John. They had been checking fences that might have loosened in the ground due to the storm rain beating down on the already sodden earth.

Sir John was looking pensive. "I think we should have a look at that tunnel."

Paul stared at him. "What…now?"

"There is no time like now. It would be foolhardy to make plans to take our king through a tunnel we have never even seen," Sir John said, and they mounted their horses. "We'll collect swords from the house, just in case we need them."

"Is there not a place under your coach for hiding arms?" Paul said, and Sir John smiled.

"Yes, I told you about that, myself, did I not? But wearing swords is hardly likely to raise an eyebrow. It's not as if we have never been seen wearing them before, and we could be going to a tournament."

"I really meant if we take extra arms to the tunnel."

Sir John stroked his beard. "We will only need extra arms for His Majesty—those arrangements can be made later. But now will be a perfect time to inspect the tunnel after all that heavy rain. We need to know the worst that could happen down there."

On reaching Nunwell House, they dismounted and tethered their horses before going inside. Sir John's unwelcome guest appeared to be out. "Don't say anything that might incriminate us in case he suddenly jumps up and surprises us," Sir John said, laughing. But they did not speak again until they were wearing scabbards and swords and had left the house.

"To outwit my cunning guest I must, at all times, act as if my house's walls have ears in them," Sir John said as they rode away. "When we reach the inn, I'll need you to cause a diversion to take everyone's attention away from the fireplace where the entrance to the tunnel is hidden."

"Yes, Sir John."

But when they reached the Inn and went inside, their task proved easier than they had expected. An attractive woman was dancing provocatively on a tabletop, lifting her skirts just high enough to torment the men, and all eyes were turned in her direction.

Several men had drunk too much ale and were jostling each other to get nearer to the table, while a piper played a lively tune.

Paul stood mesmerised and Sir John had to tap his arm twice in order to rescue his attention.

As another diversion was obviously unnecessary, Sir John quietly told him to follow and, taking a candle that was helping to brighten the interior of the inn, made for the inglenook fireplace. Paul followed obediently, and once inside the fireplace, they were out of view of the other occupants of the inn.

"Where's the tunnel?" Paul said.

"I understand the old entrance under the fireplace was sealed because it was feared it might be too easily found." After looking around, he looked above him and pointed to a high sooty ledge, where the back stone wall receded at least three feet. "It's the only place the entrance could be. It looks too high to be accessible to one man on his own. Though, of course, anyone escaping from the castle would come the other way. But how do they climb down?" He stroked his beard.

"Perhaps they use a rope," Paul said.

"And leave it dangling for all to see? Otherwise it would mean at least one other person being up there."

"Perhaps you pull one end through a ring and have two ends dangling so that you can pull it out."

Sir John's laughter lines deepened into silent mirth. "Imagine escaping death by fleeing the castle in a hurry without a rope and then breaking your neck getting down here…no, there must be…ah!" He was looking more closely at the back wall. "Look there." He pointed at two sooty indents where the wall had been chipped away at some time in the past, just enough to make footholds—the lower slightly right of the other.

Sir John put his right booted foot into the lower foothold and heaved himself far enough from the ground to place the candle on the ledge.

"The ledge drops down, leaving a ridge at the front to hold on to," he told Paul when he landed back down.

He wasted no time in climbing back up and grabbing hold of the ridge and placing his left foot in the other foothold to heave himself higher. Grabbing hold of a bar, which was fixed a few inches back, he struggled to pull himself right onto the ledge, and then sat rubbing his knee; he had banged it quite hard on the wall.

"I am really getting much too old for this," he said as Paul joined him.

"No, not you, Sir John."

"Thank goodness the King will be coming from the other direction, which, hopefully, will be easier."

They saw, now, that there was a hole low in the back, sooty wall, which was big enough for a man to crawl through. Sir John held the candle inside it and saw that it was like a burrow, with room to crawl a few feet forward. The other end appeared to be blocked. Then the candle flame blew towards Sir John and almost went out.

"Ingenious," Sir John said. "It appears to be blocked, and if for any reason someone climbed up here without knowing about the tunnel, they might still go away unenlightened!"

But Sir John knew that the entrance to the tunnel must be there, and a draught from somewhere inside the hole had affected the candle. He crawled inside, moving the candle out of his way and along with him, protecting the flame as best he could, and Paul followed.

"Whoops," Sir John said when they had crawled a little way in. "There's nothing in front. I nearly pushed the candle over the edge." He eased himself forward and peered down. He was at one side of a flight of steep, narrow stone steps, which went down from right to left between him and a wall. It was that wall that had appeared to be blocking the way.

"There's a narrow ledge from half way across below us." He had already moved his legs round and down onto it. The ceiling was higher here, anyway, and he was able to stand and walk along the ledge to the top step.

Paul was soon close behind him and followed him down the steps, which widened and curved round. And Sir John warned him to stoop to avoid hitting his head as they went beneath the area across which they had just crawled.

When they reached the bottom of the steps, they found several small wooden torches on the ground, and they took one and lit it from the candle.

The entrance to the tunnel was below the uppermost steps, and they had to stoop again to step inside. Paul led the way, now, and as the ground sloped down away from the inn they were gradually able to unbend until they were standing upright.

But as they went deeper into the tunnel they found themselves wading through filthy shallow water. In places the tunnel had been strengthened with timber, but there were other places that did not look safe.

Paul wrinkled his nose. "It smells foetid…and look at the water leaking in."

"We're below ground level now," Sir John said.

Water was dripping from above, but most was running down the sides of the tunnel. Several large rats—most were black—ran over their feet, squeaking, their fur glistening with water and clinging to their bodies. Two stopped and began to fight.

"The grey of the species now settled on our shores is battling for supremacy. They are not as different from us as we might imagine," Sir John said.

"The Roundheads are rats, aren't they, Sir John?" They both laughed, despite the stale air and smell of decay, mostly caused by the rotting carcasses of dead rats, making conditions in the tunnel even murkier than they could have imagined. Sir John stopped to rub his knee, but then changed his mind on finding the flesh tender and sore to his touch.

Paul stopped to wait for Sir John. "Is someone following us?" He frowned back down the tunnel. "I thought I heard a noise."

"Probably just the rats," Sir John said. Everything sounded loud in the confines of the tunnel, including their own voices, and the water plopping down from above had a ghostly ring. The water soon grew calf deep and several rats swam past them.

"Pardon, sir?" Paul stopped and turned, but Sir John shook his head and rested a finger down his lips to warn him to be quiet.

"It wasn't me," he whispered. "Someone else is here." They stood still, listening to the voices, which soon became clear enough to understand.

"…and Cromwell now seems to be virulent enough in casting aspersions on him, but he is still too slow in taking action against him," a voice said. Whoever was down there was obviously moving towards them, but they were in front of them, not behind.

"He could just be waiting for the right moment," a second voice said.

"I think they are referring to Cromwell being too slow to harm our king," Sir John said quietly.

"What are they doing in here?"

Sir John was looking grim. "I wish I knew...and I wish I could have heard more. They are obviously against the King." He was frightened for his king, and angry. "Wait!" he called after Paul, who was hurrying down the tunnel in the direction of the men. Reluctantly Paul stopped and waited for Sir John to catch up with him.

"We must stop them," Paul said.

"Yes, but getting ourselves killed won't stop anything."

"There they are!" Paul handed the torch to Sir John and drew his sword. Sir John was relieved to see that there were only two men: one was carrying a candle; the other drew his sword.

"Who are you?" the man holding the candle demanded to know. "And why are you trespassing?"

"I was just about to ask you the same question," Sir John said. "Hammond will be grateful to us for telling him about you. Perhaps you are thinking of taking it upon yourselves to harm our king."

The two men did not deny it. "I doubt if you have any more right to be here than we do. How are you going to explain that to Hammond?" the man with the candle said.

The other man narrowed his eyes. "You're obviously Royalists...and planning to rescue the King, I wouldn't mind wagering!" His face was contorted with hatred as he rushed forward brandishing his sword, but there was little room to fight and Paul being lighter and younger soon knocked the other man's sword to the ground.

"If anything happens to our king we will know whom to find and kill. I will never forget your face," Paul said, pushing the other man against the side of the tunnel.

"And neither will I," Sir John said. He looked from one face to the other of the two men. "I will never forget either of your faces. And you can warn anyone who might have been thinking of joining you what will happen to them if they so much as look at the King."

Two things were clear to Sir John now: he could no longer consider the tunnel for an escape; and Hammond had to be alerted. For these men might still try to kill the King. He would have to tell Hammond about the tunnel, and then he would have no alternative but to admit that he had been in it, too.

Chapter 14

Anne leaned over and snuffed out her candle. Then she pulled undone the velvet ribbon that held the heavy drape up enough to let in candlelight until she was ready to sleep.

But on hearing the door of her bedchamber open as she was about to lie down, she stopped and frowned. "Is that you, Mary?" The door shut. "Mary?" She jumped as the bed drapes were wrenched aside, letting in light from another candle now standing next to hers.

"Samuel!" He stood staring down at her without speaking. "Oh, Samuel, say you are going to stop punishing me, at last." He remained silent and she began to feel uneasy. "Please…" she prompted him, but still he did not speak. She could not keep the anxiety out of her voice as she continued: "If you stop punishing me we can start again…please say something!"

Her eyes opened wide with dismay as he fumbled with his breeches. "Please…we must talk…" She wanted to flee from the bedchamber, but knew that he could easily overpower her. She patted the quilt and her voice trembled as she said: "Please sit down and talk to me…please, Samuel." He reached out towards her and she grasped the bedclothes against her with both hands. He wrenched them free. "No!" But he was clambering onto the bed and he sat with his legs astride her.

Panic rose up inside her and she fought to push his hands from her as they moved down from her shoulders. "No, please, not like this. I don't want—"

"Yes you do. You want it. All whores want it." His speech was slurred and he reeked of ale. Panic made her struggle despite knowing that it was futile.

"No…you're wrong…I hate it like this. I'm not a whore. I'm your wife," she said quickly, but then realized that he was no longer listening.

"Damn wench!" he said eventually as he stumbled from the bed.

Anne was weeping and felt wretched, even though he had not been as brutal as on that first night. Perhaps he had taken her earlier criticism to heart. But resentment was growing inside her at having been made to feel so powerless against him. And he had called her a whore, but she doubted that he had ever forced himself upon one.

And what an effort it must have been for him to return to his own room instead of falling asleep by her side. An effort, she felt sure, meant to leave her without doubt that he had only wanted to be with her long enough to satisfy his lust. Perhaps he had been unable to find a harlot tonight, she thought in disgust.

She no longer felt guilty at having driven him away. He was the one who should feel guilty and apologize to her. But it was several days before he even spoke to her again.

"If a treaty is reached between the King and Parliament, we could all be on the same side soon." Samuel drank his ale noisily and slammed his tankard down on the second tier of the beautiful carved oak buffet. He was in a strange mood, but not drunk.

Anne glared at him. "And I thought you had followed me in here to beg forgiveness!"

"What? You expect me to apologize for bringing women home after you—"

"Yes, I do! But I really meant for coming to my bedchamber and…" her voice tailed away. His expression was blank. He obviously did not even remember coming to her bed. She wanted to remind him—to shout at him, even. But how could she put into words what she felt that he had done to her? And he was her husband and would say that he had rights.

Perhaps it would be easier to face him in the future, anyway, if the memory remained missing from his mind, so she changed the subject. "What…what was it you were you saying?"

"Parliament is anxious to mend the rift with the King, and members will be meeting him on the Wight for a treaty. That means to reach an agreement with each other. Soon we will all be on the same side."

"You don't need to explain it to me as though I were stupid. Anyway, I can't see the Army being so agreeable."

"Have you been talking to damn Oglander again? How could you listen to someone who has been imprisoned so many times for spreading scandal to benefit a king nobody wants?"

Anne shook her head. "Sir John was imprisoned two…or three times, I think, not many times, and it was just for saying what many folks think. People do want the King, but most are too frightened to say so. Folk who want to harm him will say anything to—"

"*We* don't want to hurt him. We just want to keep him in his place." Samuel poured himself another tankard of ale.

"And where is his place, Samuel?"

"The King wants even more power than his predecessors, my dear, but everyone else wants him to have less."

"That's nonsense!" Uncle Silas had told her that Parliament had been covertly shrinking monarchy power since Queen Elizabeth's reign. "The King is only trying to regain what is rightfully his."

Sir John had told her that an ever increasing number of people wanted the King returned to power now, on almost any terms; for they realized that the alternative to the King's rule was a far more daunting prospect. But he had also told her that the New Model Army had gained far too much power and might be difficult to control.

"So it's nonsense is it?" There was irony in Samuel's voice and she looked at him in surprise. She had expected more of an outburst from him. He gulped more ale. "We could both be on the same side sooner than you think." His eyes narrowed and wandered from her shoes of black reversed leather over her petticoats and finally came to rest on the pointed lace-collar and perfectly fitted red bodice, which complemented her figure. "Yes, it is about time we buried our differences." His eyes lifted to her face, now, and he moved towards her. He reached out and traced her lips with his forefinger and then traced the centre of her chin. She backed away from him before his finger could go any further. His other hand still held the tankard and he swigged more ale.

She was unnerved and felt apprehensive lest he should try to regain some semblance of a marriage.

Since the night that he had returned to the marriage bed and forced himself upon her she had stopped praying for a reconciliation. Her life was comfortable, if not exciting. And when she thought of the love that was sadly lacking in her life, or a cloud engulfed her heart, she would remind herself of her good fortune in living at Leeward House and having Mary as a sister-in-law and friend.

She moved away as Samuel stepped towards her again, and he roared with laughter. "Is my little wife scared of me? There is no need to be. I can be very gen-gentle and loving."

But Anne did not need to worry. Samuel had refilled his tankard again and the ale was having its effect. He flopped down in his favourite chair, slopping ale over himself.

"Of course there are Royalists who will have to be dealt with in a suitable manner," he drawled, and his mouth twisted into a wry smile and he continued: "Oh, yes, we will soon rid ourselves of the Paul M-illers."

Anne starred at him in horror. "But, Samuel, you said we would all be on the same side. That includes Paul Miller, and...*everyone*." Samuel now slurped more ale down his chin than went into his mouth.

"Life would be better for us if the filth-filth swine were dead. Then you could stop—" His mouth pursed with aggression. "Two filthy swines...and one my own wife. You back away from me, but not from Miller. You're a wh-ore!" He seemed to find new energy as he left the chair and moved as if to strike her, but she sidestepped him and he stumbled and almost fell over. "Damn whore!"

"There is nothing at all between Paul Miller and me—he doesn't even like me..." Anne's voice tailed away. She knew from experience that it would be useless trying to reason with Samuel. She turned and fled from the room. She might not want to mend the rift in her marriage, but it hurt so to be called a whore.

There was an ache in her heart and she was near to tears as she climbed the stairs. It was not always easy to count her blessings.

"Anne," Mary was standing at the top of the stairs, "I have been waiting to talk to you." There was a desperate edge to her voice.

Anne would have liked to be alone for a while. Her own problems had become too distressing to talk about, even to Mary, and she barely managed a wan smile before following her into her bedchamber. But very much out of character, Mary seemed too preoccupied with her own problems to notice Anne's distress.

"Why did you not come down to the parlour?" Anne would have welcomed the interruption during Samuel's disparaging accusations.

"It—it's too private. I didn't want Samuel to hear. Oh, Anne, I am frightened. I—I think I am ill." It was only then that Anne noticed Mary's pallid, drawn face above her linen and lace collar, and saw the fear in her gentle blue eyes. "You know what we all have every month. My mother was alive when mine first started and she told me that all women have bleeding until they get quite old…or at least a lot older than me. But…well…I'm not old at all, but mine has stopped. And—and I've been feeling sick every morning, and now today I have been sick three times. I feel as though something is happening to me."

All the colour had drained from Anne's face. "Did your mother tell you anything else…about the bleeding, I mean? Did she tell you why it happens?"

Mary shook her head miserably and Anne took her gently by the arm. "Have you done anything with Edmund…I mean anything besides kiss and cuddle?"

"Oh, yes, we experience such ecstasy, Anne. Edmund says it's all right. He says he would never let anything terrible happen to me. He says all people who love each other do it. You must have experienced it with Samuel, and I have seen animals doing it but I never realized it felt like that."

"Oh, Mary, you have seen animals giving birth too, have you not?

Did you not realize that the one leads to the other?" Anne held Mary's hand and spoke softly: "Mary, you are going to have a child," and then almost to herself she finished, "but Edmund made you think nothing could happen."

Mary swayed slightly. "N-no—Edmund said…Me, have a child? But, but I'm not married. Oh—oh…I must be very wicked!" She sank down onto the bed, her arms hanging limply at her sides, her head bowed, and for a moment she looked as though she was going to faint.

"Oh, Mary, how dreadful!" Anne's voice shook with emotion. She found herself hating this Edmund for taking advantage of Mary's naive and trusting nature.

"There! You despise me." Tears rolled down Mary's face and she lifted her hands to her cheeks as though trying to hide her shame.

Anne was horrified. "How could you think such a thing? I love you like my own sister and I could not bear to see any harm come to you. I only meant it is dreadful for *you*. I ought to be angry with you for thinking—" she did not finish but put her arms around Mary, who was still weeping, while her own eyes were moist.

"Please don't tell Samuel," Mary said when her tears were all shed.

"He will have to know."

"Yes, but not yet. And I don't want the servants to suspect anything, yet, either. Oh, Anne, I do love Edmund so very much, I could die for him. And he loves me. All will be well. I just know it will."

"Oh Mary, I do hope so."

"You could not help but like Edmund if you knew him. And we love each other, so what could possibly go wrong?"

What indeed, Anne thought, but tried to smile at Mary to hide her own anxiety. Her heart was heavy for Mary—her own problems temporarily forgotten.

"Why do you think Edmund told you it was all right when he made love to you?" Anne asked.

Mary seemed unable to answer and her face creased with anguish.

"I am so sorry," Anne said, "but I'm only trying to warn you that Edmund might not be as perfect as you imagine. Just remember there will always be a place for you and the child at Leeward House should things not turn out well for you."

"Oh, Anne, thank you, but that won't be necessary. Edmund said he would meet me tonight. I have not seen him for four days…nights. I'll tell him about the baby…everything will be all right. We'll be married and be a family."

That afternoon, Anne pleaded with Mary to go for a walk with her. "You look so pale, and the sun's shining—we've had so little dry weather it would be a shame to stay in the house."

"I don't know…" Mary's eyes were red and it was obvious that she had been crying. Anne did not think it would be good for her to stay in her room any longer and mope.

"Well I'm going and I should like a friend to talk to while I'm walking. Perhaps someone will even be able to tell me if there will be a September fair this year. But they might be friendlier if you're with me, seeing as you are a local girl."

"Of course I shall come with you, then—if you need me," Mary said. Anne wanted to cry out loud at the injustice of a trusting and obliging girl like Mary being deceived so unmercifully by Edmund.

After they had left Leeward House, they walked to the nearest field and Anne climbed over a stile. But when she looked back she was alarmed by Mary's languidness as she struggled to follow. "Oh, I am sorry…I should not have climbed over."

"I'm all right," Mary said breathlessly and Anne reached out to help her step down from the stile.

They stood for a few moments while Mary recovered.

"Look at that beautiful falcon," Anne said and Mary managed a wan smile. She looked so childlike standing there that Anne's heart lunged with pity as she tried to interest her in the sheep in the field, and in the birds and the wild flowers.

Mary responded slightly, but then she began to feel sick and they sat on the grass.

"I am sorry," Mary said. "I'm not very good company."

"Yes you are, and I am so glad you are with me, but I don't think we ought to go very far."

"I'm not as strong as you," Mary said.

"The sick feelings will soon pass and then you will be fine." Anne prayed that her words would come true, for Mary seemed so frail.

A woman was coming along the footpath and, when she reached them, Mary asked her if she knew anything about the September fair.

The woman shook her head. "All I knows is the authorities are getting meaner. If there's a fayre and theyn gets wind o' it, I don't know what'll happen." She walked away.

"I hope we meet someone else."

"Oh, Mary!" Anne stood up and helped her to her feet, then put her arms around her and hugged her. "Please forget about the fair. You're always so kind and thoughtful, even when you feel unwell. I hope Edmund realizes what a wonderful wife and mother you will make, but I shall miss you so much."

Tears slid down Mary's face and she began to weep uncontrollably.

"Please don't cry." Anne took one of Mary's hands in hers and she was shocked by how cold it was. "You know I shall always be here for you if you need me. And I know you will visit me."

"I have this awful feeling," Mary said.

"Are you in pain?" Anne asked anxiously.

"No…no, nothing like that. I have this terrible feeling that something bad is going to happen to me. I don't know what…just something…"

Anne hugged her again. "Nothing is going to happen to you—I won't let it. You're probably feeling melancholy because of the baby. You cannot go and meet Edmund alone tonight."

"Oh, please don't try to stop me, I must go. I shall be perfectly safe. Edmund is meeting me quite near the house and he will look after me wherever he takes me."

"Well, be careful," Anne said, reluctantly, knowing that she had to let her go.

Talking about Edmund seemed to have lightened Mary's mood and she smiled. "Tomorrow I'll tell you everything Edmund says."

"One thing I must insist upon is no climbing through the window."

"What else can I do?"

"You will go through the door."

"Oh, Anne, it's so noisy—someone will hear."

That night, Mary tapped lightly on Anne's door. Anne picked up her candle and joined Mary and they both went down to the larder. Anne smiled at Mary to reassure her. Then, handing her the candle, she found a piece of muslin and rubbed it in the pot of rendered meat fat.

Her heart was pounding when she reached the locked front door of the house; she was anxious lest she made a noise and let Mary down.

She wiped the cloth over the bolt, taking care not to make it rattle. Removing the key, she greased the working part before replacing it. She turned it in the lock. Then slowly sliding the bolt back, she spread the fat so that all the sliding parts were greased.

The door still made a noise as she opened it, but it was so much quieter than before. She greased the hinges, just to make sure, and then, beckoning to Mary to join her, wiped away the surplus fat.

"You are clever," Mary whispered as they stepped outside the door.

"No. When I was a child I used to watch Uncle Silas greasing parts of the church door, 'so that visitors would not disturb God' he said.

"Do be careful. I wish I could come with you. I'm so worried at having to let you go alone." She kissed Mary on the cheek and took the candle from her, then stood watching as she walked away.

Please let it be all right, she prayed silently as she went back inside and closed the door without locking it. She was so worried about Mary that she was hardly aware of creeping back up to her bedchamber.

Twice she prayed to God, once by her bed and once in it, asking Him to keep Mary safe and let her be happily married to Edmund. But when she tried to sleep fears regarding Mary's future forced their way into her mind.

She did not want to let the black thoughts control her. She must be strong…like Mary. She thought of the way Mary had found the strength to ask the woman about the September fair despite her obvious malady.

Anne had only suggested asking if the fair would go ahead as a way of persuading Mary to walk with her. But she was sure that the stallholders would pray that their efforts would escape the intemperate authorities and pass as being little more than the town market: respectable and necessary.

At least the September fair, unlike the one in May, would not be associated with the May Day festivities, which had the Puritans' wholehearted condemnation. But Mary had told her that both fairs last year had been stopped almost as soon as they had started. Mary had also told her that in recent years, some of the more worthy wares had been replaced by cheap trinkets at both fairs, which would be held against them by the Puritans.

Even so, Anne hoped that she would have the chance to at least browse with Mary, if Mary felt strong enough to attend…She squeezed her eyes tightly shut for a few moments. It was impossible to escape the dark thoughts for long.

She shuddered just thinking about the scorn that could befall Mary if Edmund chose not to marry her. And she knew that the poor little baby would be referred to as a bastard even before it was born. And if Edmund did marry her, would he make her a good husband? But all she knew about him was that he crept around in the night like a furtive ship and had taken advantage of Mary's innocent nature. "Oh please let it be all right," she prayed aloud.

The stairs creaked and she wondered if it was Mary back from her meeting with Edmund. But then she realized she was listening too intently. It was just one of those night sounds that she had heard many times before when everyone was silent.

She wanted to sleep and escape her troubled thoughts, if only for a while. But she tossed and turned, drifting in and out of a restless sleep until at last morning came.

She did not take the usual care with her appearance, but hurriedly dressed, then removed the rags from her curls and fastened her hair in place. Then glancing at herself in her dressing glass, she was vaguely aware of looking reasonably tidy.

But her thoughts were with Mary. Would she find her happy or crying in her bedchamber? Uneasiness stirred somewhere inside her, telling her that Mary would have come to her bedchamber by now, bursting with excitement, if she were about to be wed.

Hurrying to Mary's bedchamber, Anne knocked gently on the door, and then knocked harder. Then softly she called Mary's name as she opened the door and went inside. The drapes were pulled across, but Mary was not there and the bed appeared not to have been slept in. An icy blast touched Anne's heart and she shivered.

She went downstairs, but there was no sign of Mary there, either, and she thought of the last time she had searched the house for her and found her coming out of a room in her wet cloak. But now the servants were arguing because the front door had been left unlocked and unbolted all night.

Mary had not come home. But she would not have stayed with Edmund all night, of that Anne was certain. Her thoughts were slowed down by icy fear. Perhaps Edmund had upset her and made her too miserable to come home, but where else would she go?

Chapter 15

Anne stared out of the window of her bedchamber. She wanted to go and search for Mary, but where would she look? She felt so helpless not even knowing where to find Edmund. Oh, Mary, please come home, she prayed silently, I am so worried about you. If you don't return soon, I shall have to report you missing to the constables. But what can I say to them?

If it was revealed that Mary had been meeting a man in the night, they might decide that she had run away with him and refuse to search for her.

Would they think differently if she told them that Mary was with child? But she could not betray Mary by disclosing her condition, anyway. Oh how she prayed that she would soon be wed!

Samuel came in at that moment, banging the door behind him, and she left her bedchamber. She knew that the servants must be thinking it was strange that they had not seen Mary that morning, and she was thankful that servants did not ask questions.

"Lazy dogs," Samuel spat, when he saw Anne coming down the stairs. "What do I pay them for? Sitting on tree trunks, discush-cussing how much ale they can sup?" He wobbled and almost fell over. "Well now they can discuss it 'til they've supped the Wight dry and found shome other id-ot to pay them!" He stumbled to the upholstered chair, where he would spend the next two or three hours snoring blissfully.

"Oh, Samuel! Why did you have to get so drunk this morning of all mornings?" Anne knew that it would be useless trying to tell him about Mary. It would be useless trying to tell him anything; for he was already half asleep and would grunt at her irritably if she disturbed him.

There was only one person whom she could ask for help. She put on her cloak and left the house. Oh, please be home, Sir John, she prayed silently.

Royalists on the Wight were becoming restless and saying that nothing was being done to help their king. Sir John was alarmed by rumours that some were making plans of their own to help him escape. He knew he would have to hold an urgent meeting, but Nunwell House was no longer a suitable meeting place, with his Roundhead guest roaming around it at unpredictable hours.

The owner of a manor house, south of the town, was away on the mainland, but Sir John made arrangements with a member of his family to use the great hall of the manor…

As Sir John greeted his fellow Royalists and led them inside the manor, he prayed that he would be able to persuade those concerned not to continue making escape plans, at least until the talks between Parliament and the King were under way.

When everyone was seated on the chairs and benches in the hall, Sir John waited for the talking to stop before he began: "First of all I must thank you all for coming. I understand that some of you have become disheartened by what might appear to be lack of progress to free our king." Angry voices filled the room. "You do know about the proposed meeting between the King and Parliament, don't you?"

"Just because Parliamentarians are coming here doesn't mean the proposals will be any less demeaning than those already presented to him," one Royalist said angrily.

Sir John held his hand up to quieten the noise so that he could continue quickly and dispel the disquiet: "No, of course not, but we must at least give the talks our support, even if we believe alternative arrangements might finally be necessary.

"We, that is Paul Miller and myself, did consider an escape route from the castle, but then I heard that the King was to be allowed to live in Newport while the talks are in progress." Sir John saw surprised faces and waited for excited voices to quieten.

"The tunnel was not suitable, anyway. Nevertheless, I'm glad we decided to inspect it because—"

"What tunnel?" one man said, and another enlightened him before Sir John could continue:

"It must have been an act of God while we were in there we overheard enemies of the King plotting against him."

There were gasps from several of the men, then their voices raised in anger, and Sir John waited until they were quiet again. "I was able to warn Hammond about the plot and men have been arrested." There was a murmur of approval. "The tunnel has been blocked now." Sir John smiled. "I thought I might be arrested, too, as I was unable to give a very convincing reason for being in the tunnel."

"At least you would have been in the right place to help the King escape," one man said.

Sir John laughed. "If I thought Hammond was foolish enough to imprison me near the King I would fall down on my knees and beg them to arrest me." He looked serious again. "But they would more likely send me away from the Wight, like before, then I would have no chance of helping him at all.

"But my main reason for bringing you here together today is to ask you not to make plans that the Derby House committee or the authorities here might hear about, as it could jeopardise the King's release from the castle or even the treaty itself."

Everyone began talking loudly. Sir John knew that it would not help to voice the nagging doubts within him, but he could not stop other Royalists in the room from voicing theirs.

"What about the Army? It could step in if the talks appear to be moving in favour of the King!"

Sir John did not look to see who had spoken but focused his eyes upon those in the middle of the room; he did not want to look into the face of the Royalist who had voiced his own worst fear. "Hope and pray, and be ready to make plans, quickly, to help the King if all else fails." There was so much he could add, but not if he meant to make those concerned realize how important it was to be patient. "Just remember we must do *nothing* to jeopardise the King being allowed to live outside the castle during the talks or stop them even starting." He hoped this last reminder might deter even the most restless of Royalists from ignoring his advice.

Most of the men were looking at him, waiting for him to continue, and his sense of humour came through as he attempted to lighten the atmosphere in the room: "Of course there is an increasing number of people throughout the country who want to see the King restored to power. What a pity that they cannot all join the Army!

"Finally, I must apologize for the absence of ale, but as you know this is not my home."

Sir John felt sad that he had to make plans that did not involve anyone here except Paul; and while he knew that he had no alternative, with the King's wellbeing and maybe even his life depending upon discretion, he hated deceiving them.

He still had not decided if it would be safer to involve Tom Fletcher in their plans than to exclude him, but if involved he would not be told anything until the day of the escape.

Sir John and Paul took a slow, peaceful ride back to Nunwell House.

Their peace was shattered as a servant rushed out of the house to meet them. She looked angry and red in the face, but she tried to compose herself as she addressed Sir John: "Mrs Jarvis is here and wants to talk to you. She was leaving when I said you weren't here, but your Roundhead insisted she stay. Shall I tell her it's inconvenient, now, Sir John?"

"No—no, I'll see Mrs Jarvis." The servant marched back inside.

"*My* Roundhead seems to have upset her," Sir John told Paul with a rueful smile before following her.

Anne rose and hurried towards him as he entered the room. "Oh, Sir John, thank goodness...it's Mary—she's missing!"

"Now, now." Sir John took Anne gently by the arm and led her back to a chair. "How long has she been gone?"

"Since last night, I think, but there's so much more to tell. She's been meeting someone in the night who's supposed to be on a mission and keeping his identity quiet. All I know is his Christian name is Edmund. I'm the only person who knows of his liaisons with Mary, and—oh, Sir John, the most awful thing has happened, she's going to have his child...I'm so worried about her." She stopped to draw breath and, realizing that she had been gabbling, forced herself to talk more slowly. "She didn't know she was with child. She thought she was ill. And then when she did know, she was so ashamed...But she's so sure Edmund will marry her. Oh, Sir John, I have an awful feeling about him," her voice softened, "but Mary loves him so very, very much and she is so trusting. Edmund told her it was all right to...to let him..."

"Oh dear, poor Mary," Sir John said, saving Anne the embarrassment of explaining. He stroked his beard thoughtfully, a worried frown upon his brow. "I hope she is safe," there was a doubtful note in his voice and Anne looked at him sharply, but he continued: "We ought to notify the constables."

"Will we have to tell them about...the baby?"

"I hope not. Mary will have enough problems to contend with later if this Edmund fellow doesn't marry her. But we must tell them she's missing." His voice became gentler as though trying to soften his words. "She could be lying somewhere, hurt." His eyes filled with compassion. "I could never condone depravity, but when a trusting and naïve girl like Mary finds herself with child, she deserves love and understanding. I hope Samuel will try to be understanding and—"

"Oh, Sir John," Anne interrupted, "Samuel loves Mary deeply. She told me how protective he has always been towards her...surely that would not change?"

Sir John smiled at her reassuringly. "Let's hope that Mary and Edmund will soon be married."

He was still wearing his cloak and he turned towards the door. "Come along, I meant to see the constables about some stolen documents, but that no longer seems important."

Neither constable wanted to start a search for Mary right away. "If you don't even know when she went missing, she could have left the house early after making her bed." This made Anne more distressed;

for she feared that she might have to explain in detail how she knew that Mary had been missing all night.

But Sir John saved her from having to disclose anything: "I believe she was in a somewhat delicate state and certainly has not slept in her bed." He looked at Anne for confirmation and she nodded. "She could even have a fever, or be too ill to remember where she lives."

The constables seemed satisfied that this was reason enough to look for her today. Not doing today what could be left until tomorrow was an unspoken custom on the Wight. For unless a deed was profitable or connected with the Church, it was invariably left until the morrow.

Sir John helped the constables gather together a search party, which divided into groups. Anne found herself in charge of one group, but no one seemed cold towards her now; she was one of the Brading folk concerned for the safety of her dear sister-in-law.

Anne and her party went down to Dirty Lane—which was little more than a muddy track—across fields and down lanes and footpaths, past Little Hardingshute and across Peakyclose Copse.

"Peakyclose Copse!" one of the party remarked. "Shows you're not from here abouts. We call it Piggyclose Copse."

"I'm sorry," Anne murmured, not knowing why she felt she must apologize. But she was too preoccupied with her conflicting feelings to care much for reasoning. She so wanted to find Mary; but she wanted to find her safe and well; not here in a ditch.

Gentle drizzle became heavy rain and soaked the group to the skin as they relentlessly carried on their search. Tendrils of dripping wet hair clung to Anne's face and neck, but she barely noticed, so intense were her thoughts of Mary; thoughts that were beginning to take a sinister turn. For she had known all along, deep down inside her, that Mary would never have worried her like this if she had been in a position to come home. But she was no longer able to confine that knowledge to the depths of her mind, and it was now uppermost in her thoughts.

They combed Broadley Copse and part of the Nunwell Estate, before going to Nunwell House where Sir John had arranged for ale and soup and hunks of fresh bread and creamy cheese to be provided.

It was with mixed feelings that Anne went home to bed. At least

Mary had not been found dead. But she lay for hours, unable to sleep, fearing what the impending next day might bring. Finally she managed to drift out of her wakefulness, but only into a restless sleep…

She dreamed she was in church, with the sound of sobbing and mournful wailing echoing all around her—it was several moments before she realized that it was coming from her. She began to walk down the aisle, but it seemed endless. But then it became shorter, and she saw that there was a coffin in front of the altar and she knew instinctively that Mary was inside.

She turned and found herself face to face with the evil stranger, and his eyes bore into hers. She wanted to escape from him. But his horse appeared from nowhere, its mane flying from side to side as it twisted and turned before rearing up and whinnying into the air, just like the last time. But Anne knew that this horse was not the one that had almost trampled upon her. This horse was the biggest she had ever seen, and it was black. And Anne knew without any doubt that this was the horse of death.

* * * *

Anne opened her eyes and wondered why someone was shouting outside in the street at such an early hour. It was barely dawn. A cock crowed in the distance and she yawned and closed her eyes about to fall back to sleep. But then her eyes opened wide and her face took on a frightened expression as the words that were being shouted began to register in her mind. She sat up wide awake in the half-light. "No…no, please…no…" she said, clambering from the bed and grabbing the drapes as she almost lost her balance. Fear made her giddy and breathless, slowing her as she stumbled down the stairs. For the voice was shouting that the body of a young woman had been pulled out of the sea.

Anne was hardly aware that she was still wearing her nightgown as she left Leeward House and forced her legs to move in the direction of the harbour. Someone began weeping hysterically, but Anne did not hear, nor see the pitying faces in doorways and on the street. She was vaguely aware of someone putting a cloak around her shoulders, which she gripped with one hand at her throat, but the only sounds that she heard as she forced herself on were those of her own heartbeat echoing in her head.

She seemed to be moving so slowly; an image of the endless aisle of her dream flashed in her mind, but this was far worse than any nightmare, for she knew that it was real.

A crowd had already gathered in the harbour. People moved aside to let her through to where the body had been removed from a fishing vessel and lay covered on the ground.

She stood staring down at the blanket that covered the body, her fear still making her movements slow as she bent to lift a corner with a cold trembling hand. "No!" Instinct had told her that it would be Mary, yet deep down inside her she had prayed that it would not be her. She fell to her knees by Mary's side. A murmur went round the crowd, but Anne barely heard it, so intense was her heartache as she bowed her head over Mary's still body. She lifted one of Mary's cold, cold hands and desperately tried to rub life back into it. Then, realizing the futility of what she was doing, she lay her head on Mary's stomach and wept until she could weep no more.

When she lifted her head, nearly everyone had gone, respectfully leaving her to mourn her dead sister-in-law, alone. Only one figure remained, standing a few feet away from her. Her eyes were still misty with tears and she was unable to make out the features of the lone, rigid, silent man.

Suddenly, as though something gave way inside him, he hurried forward and went down on his knees too, trying to hold back his tears.

"Samuel!" Anne put out a hand to touch his arm and he clung to her, burying his head in her hair.

"Don't stop the tears," she said hoarsely. "There's no one here but you and me." She knew that Samuel would consider it unmanly to cry, but her voice was all that was needed to release his tears, and he sobbed until she felt his heart must break if he did not stop. He continued to cling to her and she felt a deep stirring pity for him despite her own grief.

Mary's body was removed from the harbour and brought home to Leeward House. It was confirmed that she had drowned. And Anne felt closer to Samuel than she had ever felt before. All their differences and grievances were lain aside as they united in their grief.

Then when Anne felt that she needed to be alone, she went to her bedchamber. She pulled back the drapes that enclosed her bed. The action was habitual; but it was something that she normally did after she left her bed in the morning.

Being alone did not help at all. Sitting on the bed, she began to shiver, but felt empty inside as well as cold and miserable. She had failed Mary. Why, oh why had she let her meet Edmund alone? She should have gone with her, or stopped her from meeting him at all.

She had no idea how long she had been sitting there when Samuel came into her bedchamber. He did not knock before entering, but it no longer mattered.

He stood looking at her for several moments, then he came to her and pulled her up into his arms and they held each other tightly.

She found herself clutching him with a desperate need. And pressing her face against his, it seemed so natural that his lips should seek hers. She had such a desire within her: she wanted to feel his flesh comforting her flesh; his body against hers, and she responded to his kisses with urgency.

He was not rough, now, and in desperation she gave way to all the emotions that had been building up inside her. Only later, was her misery tinged with self-loathing for having quenched her desire so passionately while Mary lay dead in the house.

Samuel fell asleep by her side, but when she awoke in the morning she was alone. She wondered if he had left because he had felt disgusted with himself. Or, perhaps, being Samuel, he had just felt disgusted with her.

She was surprised but thankful that she had slept so well. Now, at least, she would have the strength to talk to the constables; for she believed Mary must have been murdered.

But trying to convince the constables that Mary's death was suspicious proved futile: "There is no evidence. And Oglander said that your sister-in-law could have had a fever when she disappeared. She must have been delirious and fell into the sea after wandering down to the quay. It was established that she drowned." But Anne would not let it rest.

"Oh, Samuel, surely you could convince them," she said when she arrived back at Leeward House. "They will not listen to me."

"I'll try, if you really think she was murdered. You are sure she was meeting someone?"

"Of course I am...oh, Samuel, you may as well know she had been meeting him at night. He told her not to reveal his name to anyone, because he was here on a secret mission."

"She told you that she met someone at night, yet you didn't tell me?"

"She asked me not to tell you. She never wanted to deceive you, but she thought you would stop her meeting him and she was in love."

His eyes narrowed. "Then she would still be alive if it weren't for you."

"Please don't say that. It's a wicked thing to say."

"Damn you! You could have stopped her."

"No—no, I could not stop her from going...Oh, Samuel, she- She was with child. I had to let her meet him to tell him."

"What? I will kill him!" He thumped his fist down so hard on the buffet that it made him wince with pain.

"It would be better to leave it to the constables. But I did persuade Mary to tell me his name. She only knew his Christian name was Edmund. Perhaps it would be all right to tell them you thought she was going to see someone called Edmund, but don't tell them anything else."

Samuel stood staring at her with an unfathomable expression on his face, but then he thumped his hand against the door frame three times before leaving the room.

She breathed a sigh of relief that he had gone. At least now he would be on his way to speak to the constables and insist that they find the man who killed Mary and arrest him.

The rest of the day seemed long and arduous, and several times

Anne gave way to grief and sobbed. She had hoped that Samuel would hurry home after he had spoken with the constables, but she soon began to think she should have known better. He had obviously not spared a thought for the anguish she would be suffering while awaiting his return.

He finally arrived home in the late afternoon. "What did they say?" she asked anxiously, meeting him outside the door.

"What? What did who say?" Samuel yawned, and she followed him inside.

"Oh, Samuel, for goodness sake! What did the constables say?" She went with him to the parlour, where he went straight towards the upholstered chair.

But Anne was determined to keep him awake and make him tell her all she wanted to know. She stood in front of the chair, blocking his way: she would sit in it if necessary.

He grunted. "I haven't talked to them." He tried to push her out of the way so that he could sit down.

"What? Your own twin sister was murdered…or left to die."

"That's your a-ssumption."

"It's not an assumption. She had arranged to meet Edmund close to the house, so how did she drown in the sea? You were angry enough with the man who made her with child to want to kill him, this morning."

"Out of my way," Samuel said, nastily, pushing her again. He was dribbling down his clothes, and she wondered how on earth she could have wanted him so much the day before. He was wobbling about and she could hear the ale that he had supped slopping around in his stomach, and she felt disgusted as she moved to let him sit down.

"Your attitude towards Mary's death has changed completely since this morning. I just cannot understand you. I took it for granted that you went to see the constables. I should have known better than to take anything for granted where you're concerned. How could you betray Mary like this…your own twin sister?" She racked her brain to remember everything they had said to each other before he had left that morning. "Are you protecting someone?"

"That is a prop-p-posterous thing t'say."

She did not want to stay in the room with him one moment longer. She left and went to be with Mary in the small room where she lay ready to go to the cemetery. There was an open Bible, with a candle throwing soft light across its open pages, on the table. The brown leather boots that Mary had been wearing when she had died were by the side of her coffin, and Anne picked one up. It was so tiny; everything about Mary had been dainty. Now she was gone. A tear slid down her cheek and she stood clutching the boot against her with both hands.

As she bent to replace it on the floor, she saw that the other boot had something inside. It appeared to be a small piece of parchment, which bore faint traces of reddish-brown writing. How strange, she thought, lifting the boot to take a closer look. Mary must have managed to push the parchment inside her boot before she died, but why?

Something Sir John had said about lost documents stirred in the depths of her mind. She could not recall what he had said, as she had been too worried about Mary to listen properly.

She doubted that there could be any connection between this and the lost documents, but she wanted to show it to Sir John, nevertheless. She decided not to try to remove the damp parchment.

She went to fetch her cloak and slung it around her, and holding the boot tightly against her made her way to Nunwell House.

"Anne, come inside," Sir John sounded surprised to see her. "I have been thinking a lot about you and what you must be suffering." She handed him the boot without saying anything.

He was frowning as he carefully removed the small piece of parchment. It fell apart in his hands. "This is from one of my stolen documents. You can see what's left of the words that were written in blood."

"We must tell the constables," Anne said.

"Anne," Sir John said softly, "have you thought how unpleasant this could become? Of course Edmund must be responsible for Mary's death, even if he did not actually kill her, but nothing can bring her back, and if Samuel refuses to believe you, I doubt if the constables will, either.

"If you decide to talk to the constables again, I will do all I can to help. But have you considered the possibility that Mary's reputation could suffer and her condition be revealed?"

"No…I don't want anything like that to happen. I want people to remember her with love."

On her way back to Leeward House, Anne thought over what Sir John had said and her mind was in a turmoil. Part of her could understand Sir John's reasoning, while the rest wanted to see Edmund punished. After much deliberation, she decided to talk to Samuel about it.

The next morning, she arose extra early, hoping to catch Samuel while he was still sober enough to listen to her.

He was in his study. She knocked and entered in time to see him hurriedly closing a compartment. "Samuel—"

"Don't you ever come in here again," he said. "Is a man not entitled to any privacy in his own home?" He seemed so angry she feared that he would strike her, but then he just pushed her out into the hall and closed the door. And when she did manage to show him Mary's boot, later, he shrugged and turned away.

"Perhaps Edmund stole Sir John's writing and killed Mary too," she said. "The parchment could prove something."

"What could it prove?" Samuel said, but Anne did not know.

"Your own twin sister must have been murdered by Edmund, but you no longer seem to care," she said with a tremour in her voice.

Samuel's face always looked red these days, but now his cheeks darkened with anger.

"I'm sorry…I should not have said that," Anne said before leaving the parlour.

"If you cared about Mary, you would stop telling the constables you think she was murdered," Samuel called after her. "If they start asking questions, they will almost certainly insist on her being more thoroughly examined." Anne was shocked into silence. Deep inside her, she had known all along that Sir John was right. Now Samuel's bluntness had made it clear why she must let Mary rest in peace and stop trying to bring Edmund to justice.

Chapter 16

"Now at last the talks are underway I can't wait for the outcome," Paul said.

Sir John stroked his beard. "We don't really have a choice." He turned to look at Paul and lowered his voice. "All we can do is continue hoping and praying that the talks will lead to the King's release without the loss of too much of his power. I think I shall continue whispering from habit when my unwelcome Roundhead leaves. He went out a short while ago and I pray he stays away for several hours!"

He lifted his voice a little. "At least the King has Firebrace back in his service now, and we must be thankful that he has a semblance of freedom whilst he's living in Hopkins' house."

Like Sir John, Sir William Hopkins had had his home plundered by Roundheads. He kept a lower profile than Sir John, but regularly corresponded with the King. Sir John knew that letters were smuggled back and forth by servants—like the letters between the King and his beloved Queen Henrietta Maria, whose Roman Catholic faith was used by her husband's enemies as another weapon against him. Rumours were rife that her influence encouraged popish design and would destroy future English political and religious independence. But Sir John knew that she had written pleading with her husband not to resist reaching an agreement with the rebels for the sake of the episcopal organisation of the English Church. In fact, the King had said, she could not distinguish between what she regarded as only two different forms of heresy.

"This is the King's room," Sir John gestured towards the inside of a tapestry covered oak-panelled bedchamber, "where His Majesty slept when he visited me in happier times and on the night before they stopped him leaving the castle. The bed will be aired and the door always open, ready." They stepped inside the room and stood staring at the bed as though hoping that the King would materialize before them.

"Hopkins is naturally happy to have the King live in his home in Newport while the talks are taking place. The King has given his word not to try and escape…and anyway, he knows that an escape would be foolish while there is still any chance at all of him being restored to his throne."

"But what chance is there with so many radicals?"

"The radicals are actually in the minority, Paul. But they make themselves heard above all others and, sadly, those with no thoughts either way are being forced to sign their treasonous petitions against the King."

"That's outrageous."

"Yes, it is. The Levellers, along with other radicals, fanatics, extremists…call them what you will are determined to rid us of our monarchy. These adversaries say there's no reason to have a king or the Lords anymore. And I cannot help but think that as far as the extremists in the Army are concerned, the treaty is a sham," Sir John's voice caught in his throat.

"The King is particularly worried about Prince Charles' future and says he would rather die now than sign away all his powers and leave his heir with no prospects of becoming anything but a puppet king."

"We can't let him die," Paul said vehemently.

"Of course not. We must be ready to help him at once if the Army intervenes," Sir John said. "But even Cromwell is now saying the King cannot be trusted."

"The audacity…they twist everything to suit themselves. If the King had been able to trust his Parliament and—"

"With hindsight, Parliament realizes how foolish it was to oppose its king."

They left the room and both fell silent with their own thoughts until they were right outside. Then Sir John continued on a lighter note: "The negotiations have certainly brought a lot of extra colour and activity to Newport. It is thronging with soldiers and Royalists and the principals of the treaty, and you should hear the carriages rattling along the street, Paul—I have never seen the like.

"The bowling green on St George's Down has come to life and revived all its pre-war activities. If only all this were to celebrate the release of our king...

"Have you made the arrangements for a boat?"

"Yes, Sir John, I have found someone who can be ready at very short notice."

"And he can be relied upon to remain silent?"

"Yes, I believe him to have been sincere when he expressed his sympathies to me."

"I hope so! And you are absolutely sure he can be there if and when we need him?"

"Oh, yes. He is a retired smuggler who only uses his boat for local fishing now."

"A reformed character. We must hope that his wits have not retired too, but it's the answer to a prayer. I abhorred the thought of our king travelling with a practising rogue."

Anne watched Samuel pour more ale into his tankard. She needed to talk to him about Sir John's stolen parchments. While the piece of parchment in Mary's boot made her think Edmund must be connected with the theft, she had a feeling that Samuel was involved, too.

She kept remembering how he had shouted at her for entering his study when she had seen him closing the compartment in his desk. Had he just been overreacting and behaving like a child whose secret hiding place had been discovered—he might well feel proud of the compartment, which blended into the carved woodwork and became hidden when it was shut—or was he in possession of something that he had been anxious not to let her see?

He slurped his ale and smacked his lips, ignoring the liquid running down his chin, but Anne was staring at his eyes: they had grown more like those of the swine in the time that she had known him. She remembered the unfathomable way that they had stared back at her when she revealed that someone called Edmund was the father of Mary's unborn child.

"Samuel," she ventured, trying to sound calm. "Do you remember me telling you that some of Sir John Oglander's writing had been stolen?"

"Yes, and do you remember me telling you to keep away from Oglander?"

Anne sighed and tried again: "Sir John hopes to leave his writing, giving accounts of the times and news of everyday events, for people to read in the future…to give them an insight into how we lived today. He even writes in blood when he's very moved…but his writing is hardly likely to benefit the Roundheads."

Samuel roared with taunting laughter. "Is that what he told you? You are so gullible." He spat. "Why tell me, anyway—did he say I'd stolen them? And why is he so concerned about a few parchments if he has nothing to hide?"

"Did I say he was very concerned?" she said, and Samuel stepped towards her. When he reached her she took a step backwards, but he moved with her. He was clenching his chubby hands together so tightly that they were beginning to look bloodless. Then, leaning forward so that his face was almost touching hers, he grabbed her by the shoulders and she winced.

"Stay away from Oglander." His face was contorted with hatred. "Do you hear? Stay away from him!"

Anger rose up inside Anne and she tried to push his hands from her. "Leave me alone."

"What?" His eyes narrowed. But then, perhaps recognizing the resistance in hers and realizing that he would never be able to browbeat her into obeying him, he released her and continued in an amiable voice: "He would hardly tell you if his writing held evidence of plans to help the King escape, now would he, my dear?"

And you would be unlikely to tell me if you had Sir John's stolen parchments in your desk, she thought. But what if Sir John had inadvertently written something that could incriminate him…and maybe incriminate Paul, too? Oh, she fervently hoped not! A feeling of nausea swept over her. She closed her eyes and clenched her fists, and Samuel roared with scornful laughter.

"So," he said, "my little wife cares what happens to the fiend. And perhaps she thinks her lover, Paul Miller, is mentioned in the stolen parchments, too." His tone was mocking and Anne, knowing it was useless to argue with him or tell him again that Paul was not her lover, turned and hurried from the room. She went to her bedchamber and sat quietly allowing her fraught emotions to settle. But she could not stop her mind from dwelling on Sir John's writing. In fact, she felt strangely fretful. She seemed to be inflicted with a malady these days that was affecting her emotions. Maybe she needed a herbal concoction.

For two days Anne yearned to take a look to see if Sir John's parchments were in Samuel's desk. Now Samuel had gone to collect rents and she would be able to do so without worrying that he might return and catch her. For Mary had told her that collecting rents was a job he did with such enthusiasm that nothing would make him leave the task half done.

She put her hand to her head. Maybe she should give way to the sick feeling inside her and lie down instead, but then she would continue to fret. She went to collect Samuel's keys from his bedchamber, and found them clipped onto the frame of the bed, behind the heavy velvet valance. She sighed, thinking Samuel lacked originality: he had kept them in the same place in *their* bedchamber when he had been sleeping with her. But then, he had been comparatively sober and invariably carried them with him in the day.

She tried not to think about the vows she had made at the altar to honour and obey him. Samuel was cruel…and disloyal: she suspected that Mary's reputation was not the only reason for his change of mind about seeking revenge for her death. For the more she considered it, the more convinced she became that he had stopped bothering after she had told him Edmund's name. She unclipped the large key ring from the bed and hurried to Samuel's study.

Once inside, she quickly looked at the keys on the ring: six were large, but four looked small enough to fit the lock in the desk. Her hands were shaking as she tried first one and then another, but neither key would turn in the lock. She tried the third but that would not even go right in. "Thank goodness!" she said aloud as she turned the final small key in the lock: how typical that it should be the last key tried!

It seemed to take an age to find the tiny lever that opened the hidden compartment; for it was cleverly embodied in wood, shaped to fit in with the carving.

She put her hand inside the compartment and pulled out the parchments. There were six, but not one of them was Sir John's. However, a signature on one letter worried her.

Her aunt and uncle had taught her that it was depraved to read other people's letters without their permission. She hesitated and closed her eyes, praying for forgiveness, before she began to read…

She felt chilled with dismay as she put the letter back with the other parchments and returned them all to the compartment. And when everything was back as she had found it, she fetched her cloak and hurried from the house.

She shivered just thinking about the letter. The beauty around her, the sheep and the singing of the birds could do nothing to lighten her spirit now.

She breathed a sigh of relief on finding Sir John home. "I—" she began and hesitated, wondering how to explain her intrusion into Samuel's desk. "I thought Samuel might have your stolen parchments in his desk…and…and…well, I looked…" her cheeks flushed hot and she knew they must be red, "I was worried."

"Come inside and sit down." Sir John led her into the parlour, and she followed his gesture to a chair.

"Oh, Sir John, your parchments weren't there, but I found a letter from Oliver Cromwell himself." She waited for Sir John to speak, praying that he would understand.

"Don't worry." He smiled kindly at her. "I know you would not have looked in Samuel's desk unless you felt it was imperative to do so. Please continue."

"It said that a visitor has been on the Wight for several weeks…no months, I think it said, but now he's been instructed to gather evidence against you and…Miller, and anyone else he thinks might try to help the King. He is to report back to Oliver Cromwell personally, and he hopes you and…Miller will receive the ultimate punishment with the King!"

Sir John looked alarmed. "Did you notice a date on the letter?"

"Yes, it was nearly three weeks ago."

"It's the King I fear for most, of course. The letter adds conviction to the rumours that Cromwell's illusions of being chosen by God for great work are developing into a fanaticism and overpowering his reservations against harming the King. Any agreement between the King and Parliament could prove worthless if Cromwell refuses to honour it."

Sir John thought about the disturbing letter from Oliver Cromwell on his way to Hopkins' House to visit the King that afternoon.

The King had given orders for Sir John to join him as soon as he arrived. He was in session with the Bishop of London and other advisers, but he broke away from them to welcome his most trusted visitor and friend.

"Thththe commissioners have gone somewhere with Hammond. They are probably using my bowling green while I am left to think about the tttterrible thing that they are doing to me," he said. He was pacing the floor and he beckoned to Sir John to sit down. "I am at my wits' end, not knowing how to satisfy the commissioners without abandoning episcccopacy."

He looked at the other men in the room. "These gentlemen are advising me, but responsibility for the answers I give to the proposed concessions will fall upon me in the end." He turned and addressed his advisers: "I think we should break now." And after they had left the room he turned back to Sir John. "I ttold you last week that I had replied to the first proposals presented to me and agreed not to punish Parliamentttarians and their supporters for anything they did in the war. But I also told you that I was unable to agree to the phrase that said Parliament had found it necessary to undertake a war in their just and lawful defence.

"But now I have been forced to accept the whole as it stands— though I made the condition that it is not binding until I have read all the proposals and final agreements have been reached."

"I am truly sorry, Sire." What faint, inadequate words they sounded in the circumstances, Sir John thought. But he was angry; not only because his king had been forced to allow those traitors who had betrayed him to escape any form of punishment, but because he had been made to vindicate them of any blame for fighting against him.

"You know that I would give my life for Your Majesty if I thought it would help."

The King touched Sir John on the shoulder. "And I would trust my life to you." He sank down onto his knees to pray and Sir John joined him. And it was with a heavy heart that Sir John left Sir William Hopkins' house accompanied by Firebrace.

"Sir, you already know that the commissioners are becoming impatient with the King and have accused him of deliberately spinning out negotiations," Firebrace said. "But there are some in the Army who are becoming increasingly determined that His Majesty shall be brought to trial and, I can hardly bear to utter the word, 'executed'."

Sir John suddenly looked old and shattered and seemed to decrease in size as his shoulders drooped. "Such an act of treason would be an assassination…it is unlawful to kill the King."

"Inspiration for some of the petitions being drawn up against a treaty come from the Army Levellers and other extremists, but there is probably a good deal of animosity being drummed up towards the King in the Army in general," Fibrace said.

"It is really no more than I suspected, deep down, though I prayed for better news." Sir John did not feel that there was anything to be gained by mentioning the letter that Anne had read; in fact he feared that passing on any information in it or regarding it might endanger her. "You will let me know of any further developments?"

"Of course, Sir John," Firebrace said. Sir John bade him farewell and, with a heavy heart, made his way back to his horse.

So deeply troubled was he by the King's distress, and by what Fibrace had confirmed in his mind, that he hardly registered what was happening around him as he led his horse forward ready to mount him. His hand tightened on the rein and he pulled his horse's head back sharply as a carriage rattled by. "Sorry, boy," he said, for almost leading him into its path.

* * * *

Sir John became increasingly aware of the King's weakening spirit, especially after the news reached him that Oliver Cromwell had crossed the Tweed, and that Berwick and Carlisle had surrendered.

When the King agreed to give Parliament full control of the Militia, and appeared to be relenting over other concessions, too, Sir John tried to voice his concerns to him.

King Charles waved his hand up at him. "I must appear to be gggoing along with them—without signing away all my powers—then maybe I shall be able to persuade them to let me return to London to finalise the concessions. But I have told Hopkins to start making plans for my escape…just in case…and I know you would be the first to help if it became necessary."

"Of course, but I have ideas in mind and was hoping to keep them quiet. Might I ask how many people will be involved in these new plans?"

"All my confidants and others whom I trust."

Oh, no, not again! Sir John thought. Holding a meeting would not help, this time. He knew it was natural for the King to continue to think about escaping, but another bungled attempt could put an end to any plans he made with Paul.

But the King would not listen as Sir John tried to voice his concerns.

Concerns that proved founded. For, several days later, the dreaded news reached Sir John that the Derby House committee had received details of an impending escape of the King, and that they had sent all the information back to Hammond. The only gleam of optimism that flickered in Sir John's mind came with the realization that the King's enemies on the Wight no longer had enough faith in Robert Hammond to pass information directly to him.

He knew he could have done nothing more to stop the information reaching Hammond, or the Derby House committee, come to that. But he was anxious to know if this untimely sequence of events would hinder his own plans.

Worse was to follow, however, when on the last day of the time limit set for the treaty, bells, including Brading Church's, could be heard from various areas of Sir John's estate.

"What is happening," Sir John asked a servant back at Nunwell House.

"Haven't you heard, Sir John? Bells are tolling everywhere. The King's agreed to all church proposals." Sir John was horrified, and he rode to Newport as fast as his horse could carry him. He had thought the King would stand firm against the worst of the demands. Did this mean that he was weakening in his response to all the proposals, including the ones that would make him 'no king' and take away all his hopes for his heir?

When Sir John arrived at Hopkins' house, he tethered his horse and went to the door and insisted on seeing the King. And once with the King, he fell to his knees. "Your Majesty, please say it is not true that you have agreed to all the church proposals."

"The reports are wrong," King Charles told him. "There has been no full agreement on either the church or other proposals. And the treaty has been extended, but I fear to no avail—they will never agggree to let me go to London. I am more certain about that now than I have ever been about anything…and now they seem to be following me when I leave the house."

He looked back to make sure that no one was following them as they left the house for a leisurely stroll, then he whispered that he was nearly ready to escape. "Probably on Thursday if all goes well," he said excitedly—it was so pleasing to Sir John to see his king's spirit rise as he spoke. How he wished that he did not have to be the bearer of bad news!

"May I speak freely, Sire," Sir John said.

"Of course," King Charles replied. "I always value your opinions."

Sir John shook his head. "It is bad news I am afraid. Someone has sent a letter warning us that the members of Parliament who belong to the committee that meets at Derby House have details of your coming escape."

"It happens every time," King Charles said despondently.

What Sir John did not tell him was that the letter also contained a warning that the Army and Parliament had almost reached an agreement to get rid of him. He saw no purpose in alarming the King now, especially as he had not verified the information.

"Please don't despair, Sire. I am planning to help you escape," Sir John ventured, "but with your Majesty's consent, I would prefer to keep this just between you and me and the very few people who will be helping. It will involve walking outside, like today, and then riding away to a small boat, which will take you to France.

"It is unfortunate that France is too preoccupied at this time and cannot directly help you, Sire. Do not look round, I think we are being followed."

"At least now I know that they are following me bbbbbecause of news of the escape. Perhaps they will hound me for a few days, then when I make no attempt to escape, leave me alone. I shall, of course, tell Hopkins to abandon the plans."

Sir John wished he could try to reassure his king, but he had difficulty believing the Roundheads might stop following him in a few days. But at least he was able to leave without having taken away all his king's hope.

His own hopes were in danger of fading, however, as he made his way to Carisbrooke Castle. Arriving at the Governor's quarters in the Castle, he wasted no time with polite formalities: "Is it true that the Army intends to bring the King to justice? And that he is to be locked up again and that Parliament and the Army have agreed to get rid of him?"

"I've heard nothing about Parliament reaching an agreement with the Army," Hammond said. "But, yes, the Army Commissioners are putting pressure on me to restrain his Majesty again, but have no fear, I will not be his gaoler a second time. Though you must understand, I am in a very difficult position and my first duty is always to the Army."

"But is it true that the Army is impatient to have the King tried and convicted, and to get rid of him?" Sir John persisted. "Please, I must know the truth."

Robert Hammond looked away uncomfortably. "You really have no right to question me like this. I could have you arrested...but there will probably be a trial if the treaty is unsuccessful—I can tell you no more."

"Is the King in any immediate danger?"

"I think not...now leave before I have to order your removal or your arrest." Sir John had a feeling that Hammond was not being completely honest with him but had no option but to leave.

Hammond was seeing him from the premises when the sound of shouting reached them from the pathway below. A Parliamentary Commissioner was hurrying towards the castle, and when he reached Hammond he shouted breathlessly: "Dozens of Royalists jumped us from behind." Blood was dripping from a wound on his forehead.

Hammond wasted no time in summonsing his men, who stormed down to defend the commissioners. Sir John and Hammond followed, but by the time they reached the scene, most of the attackers had fled. Only one brave or foolish Royalist remained.

"We've heard that our king is to be brought to justice and executed," he said. "You are all guilty of treason. The King was given his powers by the Almighty."

"Arrest this man and lock him in up," Hammond ordered.

The man was grabbed by both arms as one of the commissioners spoke: "If anyone is planning to bring the King to trial it's not us. We have done everything we could to reach an agreement with Charles, and we still hope to—"

"He is not Charles to you. He is His Majesty, the King or King

Charles, and you have no right to take away any of his powers," the Royalist said.

"Take him away," Hammond demanded.

Sir John hurried towards the new prisoner and gripped him warmly by the hand and arm. "Do not despair," he said, but he was filled with foreboding as he went back to the castle to collect his horse. For he knew that Royalists had been executed for less.

Sir John's suspicion that Hammond had not been completely honest with him was confirmed when news reached him that Ireton had drawn up the Army Remonstrance over a month earlier.

"It has now been read out to members of the Commons," Sir John told Paul. "It took over four hours to read and is an evil, treacherous document. It says a treaty is against public interest and should never have been allowed. It claims that the King's war defeat proves God wants him tried and punished. I'm sure I don't need to elaborate as to what they mean by 'punished'. This...this evil document spells out their intentions for a complete programme of constitutional reform. Parliament would set a date for its own dissolution. Can you believe that, Paul? Parliament and the Army criticised the King when he dissolved his Parliament."

"And he had good reason," Paul said. "Parliament should have supported him."

"The only consolation is that the Remonstrance has met with lots of opposition in Parliament. One member declared it to be totally unlawful, others wanted nothing whatsoever to do with it, and at least one other argued that it was reason for an immediate agreement with the King."

"The treaty has been extended for another five days," Sir John told Anne when he saw her. "I think Parliament is anxious for a settlement to stop the Army from starting a revolution.

"But what about you? How are you faring?"

Anne looked away, not wanting Sir John to see the sadness in her eyes. "Oh, I am the same as always," she said. What she did not tell him was that she had been feeling poorly for what seemed like an age. Despite taking infusions of dandelion leaves and of various concoctions, she could not rid herself of the malady inside. Sometimes she wondered if she could be with child, but she dismissed the idea as nonsense. Although she had felt queasy she had not been sick once, and she had had bleeding…though it was a lot less than in the past, but everything she did was such an effort, now.

Chapter 17

"Oh...oh...what is it?" Anne hardly seemed to have closed her eyes when she awoke with a start to find Samuel gripping her by the shoulder. She groaned and he let go of her.

She pulled herself into a sitting position. "Is it morning?" She felt disorientated and put one hand to her head. Samuel had left his ale tankard and candle on her little table and parted the drapes. "What's happening?"

"The treaty is over...it is over, my dear, and the Army doesn't believe the King intends to keep any concessions." Samuel's voice was slurred.

"It's not morning, is it? It's the middle of the night...is it not? Oh Samuel!"

"All they need to do now is to make Parliament accept the Remonsh-strance demanding that the King is brought to trial. It's wonderful news." He clapped his hands together.

"Most people will be devastated by the news," Anne said flatly. "So much rested upon an agreement between the King and his Parliament, but was it really necessary to wake me?" She yawned. "You could have told me in the morning."

"I won't spoil such good news by chash-chastising you for listening to Oglander's tit-tattle, but how could I wait until morning when the new beginning is nigh?

"At long last, we will be rid of the King, the mighty bish-sops will be brought down and it will only be a matter of time before humble beings like myself will find places in Parliament and—and we will help to lead the people to a new and—"

"So you want to be in Parliament…or preach." Anne yawned again.

"No, no, no!" Samuel laughed and swayed around precariously. "That's not it at all. Folks can find salvation with God without biship-shops and other high officials. Most people are against high rituals and church courts that have their roots in the Roman Caf-cath'lic Church."

"How do you know that?" she said languidly, but he did not answer. "How do you know that most people are against high church rituals? My uncle taught me about Henry V111 and his break from Rome and the Pope. But I don't remember him saying that the King asked everyone if they approved or disapproved of what he was doing," she said, and Samuel spat.

"Please don't spit on my floor."

"The King also took unlawful taxes from the people before the wars and—" Samuel stumbled and almost fell on her, "and something must be done to lower taxes and tie-tithes amounting to a tenth of harvests."

"Oh, Samuel, that's how the King's enemies want people to think. Parliament probably outlawed duties on levies and imports to make the King look bad if he had to resort to drastic means to collect money. Though they probably hoped it would lead to him giving into the blackmail that would force him to give Parliamentarians extra power."

Samuel sneered, or came as close to a sneer as was possible with a bellyful of ale. "His conduct was condemned. Blackmail? Sounds like Oglander talk."

"No. My uncle told me that the speaker in the Commons was held down while the King's conduct was condemned. He said if it had happened on a ship it would have been called a mutiny…and he said extra prayers every day when he heard what had happened."

"You foolish, shilly wench!" Samuel's face was almost the colour of beetroot. "Your uncle was biased."

"No, he was not—why would he be? He was always a truthful man who told things as they were. I never knew him to be biased in anything.

He must have been the most unbiased Presbyterian Minister alive…in fact, I don't think he ever condemned anyone."

"Even your uncle would not believe the King intends to keep con-concessions he's made."

Anne was fully awake now and her voice was slowly rising in defence of the King. "If you were taken prisoner by the servants and forced to sign away part of your life to them in order to be released, would you consider the document to be legal once you were free?"

"I'd try to destroy it, but it's not the same."

"No, it's worse. He is the King and it is treason. And he could be forced to betray bishops and other high church officials, and to relinquish most of his own power, too."

Samuel laughed nastily. "I suppose you think he should be allowed to go to London to discuss some of the con-sheshsons, too. It's what he's trying to—"

"That sounds perfectly reasonable to me," Anne said.

"Oh!" He clenched his fists so hard that his knuckles went white. "Can't you see? It's a trick. An'thing could happen once he was allowed a footing in London."

"A rightful footing. The Army is not giving the King a chance."

"The Army has given him lots of chances. They even gave him another chance to agree to their 'Heads of Pro-poposals' before making their final decision…they knew he would never agree to it, but it gave people a chance to see that they were doing ever'thing possible to—"

"And you accuse the King of trickery. The Army seems to be full of tricks. What else could you call giving the King ultimatums when they knew he could not possibly agree to them? You seem to think it's all right for the Army leaders to plot against the King, but not for the King to plot for his own survival. How fair is that? And anyway, you seem to be overlooking one important matter: the Army is supposed to obey the King, not the other way round."

"You think you know s'much, but you know nothing. Cromwell and Ireton tried to make peace with him. In fact, Ireton said that Democ-cracy as being agreed and writ-titten by the Lever-lellers could lead to dictatorship." Anne looked at him questioningly.

177

"I can't really agree of course. It's freedom the Lev-llers want; not chains, and I would be very willing to serve them."

"Oh, Samuel, is there anything you would not do to get what you want? Do stop stumbling up and down. You are making me dizzy."

He went to the door and yelled out for a servant to bring him more ale.

"Samuel, it is the middle of the night. It's unkind to wake the servants. I doubt if they can hear you, anyway."

He ignored her and shouted even louder for someone to come and fetch his tankard.

Anne sighed and forced herself to leave the bed. She stood still for a moment, feeling dizzy, but then she snatched the tankard from Samuel's hand. "Stop bellowing—I'll get your ale." She picked up the lighted candle that he had put on her table and was about to light her own candle to leave with him, but then she changed her mind and left him in the dark.

A manservant met her at the bottom of the stairs. He was half dressed and dishevelled. "I thought I heard—"

"I am so sorry that you have been disturbed," Anne said, and wondered what Samuel would say if he knew that she had apologized to a servant. "Please go back to bed." The servant nodded his head and went back through the door that led to the servants' rooms, and she heard voices raised for a few moments.

She went and filled Samuel's tankard with ale. Her legs felt heavy as she went back up the stairs and took the ale to her bedchamber. Samuel snatched his tankard without a word of thanks. She was tempted to remind him that she was not a servant and would welcome a word of appreciation, but she decided against doing so—it would only anger him, and anyway, she felt breathless and again wondered what could be ailing her.

Samuel swigged all the ale in one go and slammed the tankard back down on her table. Some of the liquid had run down his chin to join the dried patches on his wide, filthy lace collar. There was always a stench of stale ale mixed with his body sweat these days.

Anne placed the candle on the table, but then picked it up again and lit her own candle by placing the wicks together. Then she held Samuel's candle out to him.

"Now take that and go!"

Samuel took it from her, but slammed it back down on the table. She sighed loudly and returned to her bed and sat with her knees drawn up to her bosom, her arms round her legs.

Samuel picked up one of her stockings from the end of the bed and clutched it tightly as he held it to his nose. He closed his eyes for a few moments and inhaled.

He was still clasping the stocking tightly as he continued: "As if anyone would be foo-lish enough to let the King go back to London where he could settle with Parl-liliament at the Army's expense."

"Oh, Samuel, for goodness sake! Please go to bed. The Army just wants to save its own skin and gain all the King's power for itself." She took a deep breath. "And if the King did not intend to keep any promises he made, he would have agreed to everything to give a good impression. It would not matter what he agreed to if he was not sincere. Now please, please go to bed...I am very tired."

Samuel laughed again. But this time the sight of the distorted drunken leer, which accompanied the sound, turned Anne's stomach and she reached. He flopped down on her bed.

"Please go to your own bed and let me sleep."

"I'm glad I came to your room. I have 'roused you and your cheeks are pink." He put a hand out and touched her face. "You've been looking pale," she was amazed that he had noticed, "but now you look so beautiful, my dear." His hand moved down and rested upon her nightgown, not far above her breasts. She hugged her knees to her more tightly and winced as a pain shot through her stomach.

Samuel leaned over and landed a sloppy wet kiss on her lips. She knew how cruel it would be to stop her own husband showing her affection. But she felt ill and feared that he might try to force himself upon her. So when his free hand moved to her leg, she scrambled from the bed and fled to the door, where she stood shaking and regaining her breath.

"It's all right," he said. "I'm not going t' force myself on you, though

I have the right as your husband. Your face!" He laughed. "You thought I wassh going to get on top of you. But after last time I'm sh-prised you're not tearing my clothes."

"Samuel! It…it wasn't like that."

"I reminded you what it was like to be made love to by a real man, not a boy like Paul Mill-iller…and you were like a wh-whore let loose from a nunnery."

"Samuel! How could you say such vile things?"

"You can't stop me imagin-ining I'm making love to you." His voice was becoming more slurred. "I can do what I like…I don't have to ask you. Nor do I have t-to explain my beliefs to you…the King deserves to die."

"Oh, Samuel…" she spread her hands in a helpless gesture. There had been so much bloodshed during the two outbreaks of civil war. Would it never end?

She would never believe that the King was a bad man, though his enemies wanted everyone to think so. Why could those making trouble for him not leave him alone and stop trying to destroy the great love and respect that was still felt for him by his loyal subjects?

Samuel yawned and was looking sleepy. "I will kill your lover Paul Miller, my-myself…" his voice tailed off.

Anne was stunned for a few moments. Kill…kill Paul? What was he talking about? She felt as though she might faint, so she sat on the bed, bent her head down and took several deep breaths to stop it happening.

She lifted her head. "What do you mean, you will kill Paul Miller yourself?" she asked slowly. Samuel did not answer and when she turned to look at him she saw that he had fallen asleep.

She felt wretched but knew she would not sleep if she did not warn Paul. She thought about Samuel's hatred of him. It had never occurred to her until now that Samuel might actually try to kill him. She must go to Paul at once, to put her own mind at rest, even if it meant suffering more of Paul's unkindness.

She pulled her cloak about her to hide her nightgown and made her way down the stairs, trying not to make a sound.

Her limbs ached and she was fighting the malady inside her as she tried to hurry in the direction of Paul's cottage. She prayed that he would be there. Oh, but he must be…at this late…or early hour. At least she had only to go through the grounds of her own home to reach him, which made her feel safe.

Her insides began to feel heavy as she reached the far side of the orchard, and she had to stop to catch her breath. There was a tight pulling sensation in her tummy and she gasped as a sharp pain made her bend forward for a few moments. Cramp, she thought, forcing herself to continue on her way.

When she reached the cottage she was gasping for breath as she hammered upon the door, calling Paul's name; but her voice was not as loud as she had expected, and her effort made her feel so weak and dizzy that her knees buckled beneath her. Pain gripped her stomach, again, and it was even worse than last time. Something she had eaten must have made her ill…given her colic. It must be almost as painful as giving birth…She gasped. Oh, no…Surely she was not…oh, God, no! Please don't let it be that, she cried silently inside herself. But suddenly she knew that she had been right when she had wondered if she could be with child. A baby had started developing inside her and now it was leaving her body after only a few weeks and must be either dead or dying…oh God!

It must have happened that night—when Samuel and she had 'comforted' each other, after Mary had been found dead. One life had been taken, another created inside her. But now that life was at an end, too. Was this her punishment for making love so passionately whilst Mary lay dead in the house? She had no time to ask herself more questions as another wave of pain took hold of her and she groaned loudly. If only she had not rushed here—if only she had known…

"Anne!"

"Oh, Paul!" Two strong arms were lifting her, and holding her: Paul's arms. She snuggled her head against his chest, and he carried her to his bed. She did not want him to put her down, but when he did, she found that the bed was still warm from his body. She wanted to be swallowed up by his masculine scent. But she must not forget why she had come…

181

"Paul," she called softly and he was at her side. "Oh, Paul, Samuel said that the King deserves to die, and—and then he said he would be killing you, himself." She could say no more as the pain gripped her tummy again.

Knowing that the tiny form inside her had either lost or was losing its life was almost more than she could bear.

"Paul!" He was still by her side and he held her and spoke to her tenderly.

Please do not let the change in Paul be an illusion, she thought, for I love him and want him to be kind to me, always. It did not seem strange that she should be thinking about her love for Paul whilst she was suffering such a loss; for somehow, although she knew not why, the one seemed so entwined with the other.

The pains in her tummy had subsided, but not the pain in her heart, and she became conscious of tears rolling down her face onto her hair and the bed.

She was aware of a terrible emptiness despite the fact that she had not known until that night that she was with child. How could she have failed to realize that a wonderful beginning was taking place inside her? She should have been able to cherish every moment; to love the tiny being that was her son or daughter.

Paul was stroking her forehead and her hair. "Go to sleep now," he said, and his voice sounded so gentle. She sighed and closed her eyes.

When she awoke it was light, and Paul was sitting by the bed, holding her hand. She felt so much better.

"I—" Paul hesitated as though wondering if he should continue, "I buried…it."

"Thank you," was all she could think of to say. Had she called out in her sleep? Or had she been dreaming? She could remember calling out and telling Paul how much she loved him.

He let go of her hand and, leaning over, kissed her gently on the lips. It felt so tender, so wonderful. She wanted to put her arms around him…but it would not be right—and he might think her a licentious woman.

"If only things could be different," he said softly. She closed her eyes again, and when she opened them he was gone. Perhaps she had been dreaming.

But now she could hear voices. Paul came back with Sir John following behind him. When Sir John reached the bed he stood looking down at her with a concerned expression on his face.

"I do hope you are feeling a little better now. I'm so sorry…it must have been awful for you," he said gently. "You are looking very flushed. Someone should tell Samuel." But when she shook her head, he said no more.

Paul had already dressed and, after pulling on his breeches and boots, he came and bent over her. "Are you all right, my love?"

Anne wondered if he realized what he had said, and Sir John looked at him sharply. She nodded her head. He had said 'my love'. For a few moments she had a warm glow inside her, despite everything, because she knew that he no longer hated her.

"Anne," Paul said, "we have to go. The King's life is in danger. I hate leaving you like this, but I'll send Christina to sit with you."

Anne wanted to protest. She would rather be alone than have Christina with her. But Paul and Sir John had already left.

Anne had almost drifted back to sleep when Christina stormed through the door. Anne closed her eyes and pretended to be asleep, praying that the angry girl would not vent her temper out upon her in some way.

Christina did not touch Anne, but attacked the rush matting on the floor, kicking it several times. Anne kept her eyes shut and turned over so that the dust would not make her sneeze.

"You're not asleep. Harlot!" Christina kicked the bed. It jarred Anne's tummy and made her wince. She wondered if Paul had stopped to explain why she was in his bed.

"I am not a harlot. I was taken ill," Anne said as she turned back to face Christina. "I'm still unwell and I need to sleep." She closed her eyes, hoping that Christina would be satisfied with her explanation.

"Why are you in Paul's bed?" Christina snarled.

"I was taken ill outside here."

"How convenient for you." Christina pulled Paul's only chair as far away from the bed as possible before sitting on it. Thankfully, she did not say another word, but sat pouting with her arms crossed.

Anne drifted into a restless sleep and awoke to find herself crying into the pillow. As her eyes cleared a little, she glanced around the cottage. Christina appeared to have deserted her, and in a short while, when the girl did not return, Anne breathed a sigh of relief.

But then she began to wonder if she should return to Leeward House. When Paul came back he would be tired and would need his bed. He could not have slept much, if at all, since she had collapsed outside.

And what about Samuel? Would he accuse her of having been with Paul? Ironically, he would be right this time, of course, even if it was not in the way that Samuel meant. But what would Samuel do to her when she returned? Her head swam a little as she sat up, and her tummy hurt, but she knew she must leave Paul's hut now: it would not be right to stay any longer.

As she walked slowly to the door, she prayed that the servants would not see her when she reached her home.

But of course they did. Perhaps they would not realize she had been gone so long. "I had a disturbed night…I need a long sleep, now," she said and put all her strength into walking past them without showing discomfort.

She breathed a sigh of relief as she closed her bedchamber door and leant against it. At least Samuel had not seen her and might think she had slept in another room in Leeward House.

Chapter 18

After sending Christina to his hut to stay with Anne, Paul caught up with Sir John, who was on his way back to his stables to collect the horses.

"I told Tom to have four horses saddled, one for himself," Sir John said. "When we reach Newport, we must first tell your captain to have his boat ready."

Paul nodded but seemed preoccupied with his own thoughts. "Christina was most unreasonable when I asked her to sit with Anne."

"Perhaps she is jealous."

"Jealous? Jealous of what? I have known her most of my life...she is almost like a sister."

"Mmm. She might seem like a sister to you, but does she think of you as being like a brother, especially since she became aware of Anne?"

"Anne?"

"Yes, Anne."

"But...up until now I have not even been friendly towards her." Paul sounded sad and Sir John looked at him sharply. Paul swallowed awkwardly and looked away.

"Never forget that Anne is a married woman, Paul." There was no reproach in Sir John's voice, only concern.

"How could I possibly forget? Samuel made accusations against me in public once. If he had not been so drunk I would have challenged him, but as it was no one believed him."

"Perhaps Christina did," Sir John said.

They arrived at his stables, and another voice took his attention: "Sir John, I must go to the Smithy—my horse is lame."

"Tom Fletcher, you will have to leave him behind and ride one of the others. It's essential that you are waiting with the horses when the King leaves his lodgings."

"I could never trust any other horse the way I trust Flaming Arrow, Sir John," Tom said, with a downcast expression.

"Then perhaps His Majesty should ride him." There was a rueful edge to Sir John's voice.

"It's not that the other horses cannot be trusted, sir. Flaming Arrow and I have formed a bond. We almost know what the other is thinking. And besides, I shall be there long before the King is ready to leave."

"Why did you not check your horse's hoofs earlier in the day? This oversight seems remiss...I thought you were, at least, methodical."

"Well, sir, if you will excuse my blunt speaking..." he hesitated and Sir John nodded, "but how could I possibly know we would be rescuing the King today? You didn't tell me until you wanted the horses saddled."

Sir John sighed, not feeling completely placated by Tom's answer: "Let me see this hoof."

"Yes, sir." Tom led him to the horse and lifted its right front foot backwards and up so that Sir John could see the underneath.

"No you certainly cannot ride him. It looks as though something has forced its way under the shoe. I must order you to ride a different horse—for the King's sake."

"Sir John, you know I would normally obey without question, it's my duty, but I had a dream and it has made me fear for the King's safety if I ride another horse...and even the King's horse would move much faster tethered to Flaming Arrow."

A semblance of amusement crossed Sir John's face. "He would not have much choice if he was tethered to Flaming Arrow."

"No, sir...of course not, sir."

Sir John sighed and was tempted to leave Tom behind, but his earlier suspicions regarding the lad's honesty made him wonder if it would be wise. But dare he ignore what Tom had told him? If the lad had had a warning dream, at the least it might affect his performance and put the whole mission in jeopardy if he was forced to ride another horse. 'Omens' of impending doom had even affected the King's morale.

For the King's sake, Sir John wished he had never set eyes upon the lad. "Very well, you may go to the Smithy," he said reluctantly. "Paul and I have someone to see, anyway, but I shall expect you to be in the trees north of the King's lodgings when we arrive there or I will send someone to find you. Is that understood?"

"Yes, Sir John. I give my word I'll be there." Tom mounted the horse upon which the King would ride and reached over to grab hold of Flaming Arrow's reins.

As he rode away, Paul was looking at Sir John with a frown upon his brow. "You still have doubts about him, Sir John?"

Sir John did not want to try to explain how he felt, and anyway, he could not wholly justify his doubts. "When we arrive in Newport, it might be best if you see your retired smuggler whilst I go to the King's lodgings—we need to know just how well he's being guarded."

Their journey was unhindered until they were within half a mile of Newport and came upon a group of men by an open gate of a field. Some where fighting while others were spurring them on by calling them names and shouting obscenities and jeering. Clearly their tempers were raised.

Sir John rode as close as was possible without his horse knocking any of the men. "Stop this at once," he shouted sternly and most of the men stopped and turned to look at him. "Why are you fighting?"

"Hav'ee not heerd, sir?" one young man said. "The Army es killing the King and taken o'er the country. They be going to kill Royalist and thern families. My brother and father both fought wi' the Royalists in the war."

"I am Sir John Oglander of Brading, and I'm as well informed as anyone, but I doubt very much if you or your relatives are in any danger.

Alas, the same cannot be said about our king." He waited, hoping that the men would disperse.

"Blackguard!" someone shouted, and two men began to punch another. Paul jumped down from his horse and grabbed one of the attackers by the arm.

"His brothers be in the Army. We don't want noo truck wi' he," the man said, trying to shake Paul off.

"Stop this!" Sir John said as the punched man fell down under a renewed assault by his other attacker.

"We den't want no one here wi' brothers in the Army!" someone shouted, and men raised their arms, waving their fists in the air, shouting more obscenities.

"Have you forgotten, already, that brother fought against brother during the war?" Sir John shouted. He dismounted and helped the attacked man to his feet. "Can you walk?"

The young man nodded. But he winced as he moved one foot in front of the other. None of the other men moved at first, but then two came to help him, and he thanked Sir John before leaving, propped up between the men. The group dispersed, and Sir John remounted his horse.

"I fear they are right about the Army taking over the country. We can do little to stop that, but we can do our damndest for our king!"

"Maybe we should have asked those men to come to the King's lodgings and demand his release…and there must be hundreds of others who would join them," Paul said.

"The Army would probably kill some of them as examples to others and lock the King straight back in Carisbrooke Castle." Sir John knew that other Royalists would have heard how the Army was preventing the treaty from reaching a satisfactory conclusion. Some of them would be visiting the King, too. "You know what I must do if we cannot manage to smuggle the King out amongst his visitors?"

"Yes, sir, but I wish you would let me be the one to take the King's place."

"I know more about his ways and habits, and I might find it easier to fool the guards, at least for a while." Despite keeping up the pretence that he meant to take the King's place only as a last resort, he felt now that it would be the only way: someone needed to to be in the room to make sounds and to do whatever was necessary to make the guards believe the King was still a prisoner…at least until he had had time to leave the Wight.

He felt sad, and a little frightened, knowing that he would probably be executed for taking the King's place and allowing him to escape. But if it was a choice between his own life and that of his king, he had no choice at all.

When Sir John reached the King's lodgings, he was dismayed to find musketeers outside the door and at the windows. And when he went inside the house he was searched.

"Where's Hammond?" he demanded to know.

"Hammond isn't here," a sentry told him.

"Then where is he?"

"He has been taken to Army headquarters at Windsor for refusing to lock the King back in Carisbrooke Castle."

"That was brave of him," Sir John said. He knew Robert Hammond would not have found it easy to disobey orders. The sentry's eyes bore into him, but he was allowed to enter the King's room.

"Sire!" Sir John fell to his knees and the King took both his hands in his for a moment.

"This will probably be the last time you will ever see me." He turned to the others in the room. "The last time I shall ever see any of you."

"Samuel! Wake up, damn you!" Tom shook him. "Wake up!" This was no time for niceties. Fetching a slop-pail, which was nearly half full of dirty water, he emptied it over Samuel.

"What the—" Samuel jumped out of his chair, eyes glazed, his mind not fully back from his sleep, but then a blazing fury took hold of him.

Tom, fearing he might strike him, spoke quickly: "Listen for God's sake! Oglander and Miller are about to help the King escape. Now is the chance you've been waiting for. You can foil the escape and kill Miller. What alternative would you have but to shoot a traitor whilst he was trying to get away?"

"What the hell are we waiting for then?" Samuel surged into action. "I suppose I've got to saddle my own horse…I fired the stable lads yesterday."

"I have taken the liberty of saddling your horse for you," Tom interrupted. "It's ready and waiting, so hurry."

Tom had his own reasons for involving Samuel. The ageing King and Sir John he could manage, but three was almost a pack, especially when the third was a resolute young man like Paul Miller. But this was the mission that would gain Tom recognition, at last.

Edmund would want to know why he had involved Samuel instead of him. He would not even have to lie, well not really, but just tell him that he had been told nothing until the day, and then everything had happened so quickly. If Edmund suspected Tom of not wanting to involve him, and of wanting to take the credit for himself, he would punish him severely.

Tom did not wholly trust Samuel Jarvis, of course; the man was totally lacking in graces and manners. Nevertheless he would serve his purpose.

"If I allow you to kill Miller, you must promise me not to disclose my involvement if anything goes wrong," Tom said, and Samuel nodded. "And I trust you will keep in mind the consequences of breaking a promise," he added, then, as Samuel finished dressing, he left and rode away.

"Leave that horse and attend to Flaming Arrow," Tom demanded on arriving at the blacksmith's. "I'm in a hurry…come on…it's a matter of life and death!"

"We will not let you die, Sire," Sir John said. "Please let us help you. If you don't escape now, I fear it will be too late." Sir John felt a tight lump in his throat as he looked at the gaunt face of his king. Instead of the great leader, who had conquered the weak constitution he had been blessed with as a child and grown strong and brave to meet the demands of his position, and who had tried to hold sway against the rebel Parliamentarians that had sent him toppling, he saw a man defeated and stricken with melancholia.

There were dark shadows under his eyes, and when he spoke, there was resignation in his voice.

"I have given my Parole not to escape."

"Your Parole was with Parliament, not the Army, Sire," Sir John reminded him. A mumble of agreement went round the room. Some faces in the room Sir John recognized; others he did not.

"How long have the soldiers been here, Sire?"

"They arrived here with Colonel Corbett and Captain Merriman from Windsor on Wednesday. And they brought orders from…Fairfax and the Army Council, they said, but it was more likely Cromwell, to have me locked back inside Carisbrooke Castle.

"They are still arguing about it, but I already know what the outcome will be—the New Model Army is powered by extremists who never intended to allow me to continue using those powers bestowed upon me by the Almighty."

Sir John shook his head. "I know not, Sire. But Hammond has refused to imprison you again."

"I know…he has been arrested and his Marshall is so confused by what has happened…he has been all over the place asking questions."

"You must escape now, Sire," Sir John said.

"I gave my par—"

"But the Army is making it impossible for you to keep that promise," Sir John said. "I hope you will pardon me for interrupting you, Sire, but your life is in danger."

"Do you think I do not know it? But at least if I die without signing away my powers, there will still be a chance for Prince Charles…he is the one that matters now. He is the person whom I must think about. He is the future."

"Please, Sire, I beseech you, you must leave now!" There were tears in Sir John's eyes as he spoke. He could hardly believe this was the same man that had previously been so desperate to escape.

"That is impossible. I would be caught, the Army would be furious…and besides, it would put you and my other loyal friends in more danger."

"But Sire—"

191

"No buts—I am sorry, but this is how it must be."

"We pleaded with him, too," a gentleman told Sir John. "What else can we do?"

Sir John half raised his arms and let them fall in a helpless gesture. "We have horses standing by, waiting for His Majesty—and a boat." His voice was flat.

"We have a ship. It could even be used as a decoy," Sir John recognized the voice and looked over at the man, who finished: "if only we could persuade him."

Sir John left the King's lodgings and made his way back to where Paul and Tom were waiting. "There are musketeers outside His Majesty's lodgings, and more sentries at the door of the room where he is being kept a prisoner. But worst of all, he has given his parole not to escape and refuses to break it.

"There are others with him, wanting to help, including the Duke of Richmond and the Earl of Lindsey, but His Majesty says he wants to give Prince Charles a chance of becoming a real king. And he seemed so humble when he said that if he tried to escape again, he would just cause us all harm. He seems so melancholy…I think perhaps he is past caring…or even believes that he deserves to die."

"What?" Paul was astounded. "That's ridiculous. He has only done what any king or queen would have done in his place."

"I quite agree, but he told me something very disturbing, not so long ago, and I think in his melancholia it might be influencing his decision."

"What?" Paul was still looking astounded.

"About eight years ago, the King promised Thomas Wentworth, the Earl of Strafford, that he would not let him go to the gallows when vague and worthless charges were made against him. But in the end the King's promise was worthless. His friend's charges were changed to an Act of Attainder, and—"

"What does that mean?" Paul said.

"It means an act of Parliament sentences a man to death without need for accurate proof. Well, then pressure was brought to bear on the King, and when his queen feared for the safety of their children, he was forced to sign Strafford's death warrant. Believe me, he did everything he could to save Strafford but never forgave himself for letting him be executed."

"Oliver Cromwell wouldn't have fretted over it. He would have said it was an act of God," Paul said. "Why can't folk see the King is the honourable one?"

Sir John sighed. "I dare say a good many people around the country who passed on allegations of illegal government and violations of liberty and property, and of court extravagance and frivolity realize it now.

"I must go back, now, and do what I can to persuade His Majesty to escape. Captain Edward Cooke has a ship waiting. It would be an ideal decoy." He was preoccupied with his own thoughts as he left Tom and Paul.

When he arrived back inside the King's lodgings, he wanted to shout at his king, even shake him by the shoulders to make him agree to escape.

"Please, Sire, I can take your place," he said. "All you need do is wear my top clothes and walk out with your other guests."

King Charles looked at Sir John with tears in his eyes. "It is a wonderful offer, my brave knight, but I am sorry I cannot do as you ask. Now I do not want to hear any more about it."

"But Sire—"

King Charles put up his hand. "That is an order. Now please join me in prayer." He knelt down and everyone else in the room did the same.

"I want to say a special prayer for all my loyal subjects, especially those here with me today," he said.

"Our Father, please bless all those who have stood by me and fought for me and tried to free me from my plight…"

When Sir John rejoined Paul and Tom, sometime later, he looked ashen.

"Nothing would induce the King to escape—nothing! We begged— pleaded again and again with him. I almost argued with him…when we may never see him again." He closed his eyes for a few moments as though asking for forgiveness. "But I think he understood how we felt.

He said a prayer for us and suddenly he sounded…stronger, but still so very sad."

Tom's expression was unfathomable. "What did you mean when you said you may not see him again, sir?"

"When he said his farewells to the commissioners yesterday, he told them that they might never see him again, and he told us the same today.

"The truth is, the King is to be taken to Hurst Castle. He doesn't know, yet. I would tell him if I thought it might spur him to escape, but I am sure it would not. It would only add to his anguish—it's a formidable castle set on a piece of deserted, stinking land, jutting out into the Solent."

Samuel went straight to the place where Tom Fletcher had told him to go; the place where Sir John and Paul were to meet Tom, and where a horse would be awaiting the King.

In Samuel's mind, Paul Miller had become the instigator of all his troubles. He had stolen his wife's affections, and he had caused him to become impotent; Anne need not have worried that he was about to climb on top of her when he had last visited her bedchamber. But it would be so different when Miller was dead. Then he would show her…

He could hear voices. He dismounted and tethered his horse before creeping through the trees. There they were: Tom and Paul Miller. If it was not for that fiend, Miller, Anne would love him, he thought. He raised his pistol and tried to line the sights up with his quarry, but his hands were shaking and he had that damn double vision. Why now, of all times? he thought.

He had wanted to sample the thrill of aiming a pistol at his worst enemy. But he would savour the moment when the time came to pull the trigger. That precious moment when the King arrived as proof that Paul was a traitor. He was sure that his hands would be steady then, and his vision would not fail him when that moment came.

After the shooting, he would help Tom recapture the King. Perhaps the Army would reward him. Samuel had never met Edmund, but he was glad Tom had not involved him; he would probably have tried to claim all the credit for himself. Perhaps Tom would try to claim the credit, but he was a mere boy and Samuel could handle him.

There was Sir John, at last. Samuel's breath caught in his throat. His precious moment was nigh. He was trembling with excitement. But where was the King? Where was the damn King?

He could hear the anguish in Sir John's voice, but he could not hear what he was saying. He moved closer, hidden by the trees, and tried to hear every word.

But those words he did manage to hear turned his excitement to anger: the King had refused to escape. He cannot do this, he thought. How dare he do this to me? And how dare Oglander leave without the King? Samuel raged inside. Miller has to die!

But then Sir John left, saying that he must try harder to persuade the King to escape. Samuel was relieved, but still had difficulty curbing his impatience. Oglander would persuade the King to escape, would he not? Was the King not a rogue, making everyone believe he was being honourable by refusing to escape. And then he would 'reluctantly' change his mind to please his friends, at the last moment? Oh yes! That would keep those fools who supported him believing in his honour. But Oglander had better not return without him again! The King had better escape this time. Miller's death depended upon it…and he had to die.

The belief that Paul Miller must die had now taken over his mind. He moved back to his horse, then paced backwards and forwards in the trees. He began cursing Sir John for not bringing the King back with him. Then he cursed the King for not coming with Sir John. How long would he have to wait? His hands were shaking. He needed a drink of ale…but not as much as he needed Paul Miller dead.

When, at last, Sir John returned, Samuel was so agitated that he could hardly keep still. Still no King? What was Oglander saying? He could not hear a damn word…blast. He moved closer, again, and what he heard made him seethe with anger.

Well, he had no intention of letting Paul Miller escape, now, whatever the blasted King had decided. It was hardly his fault that Oglander had twice failed to bring the King here. And, anyway, no one except Tom Fletcher would know that he was the one who shot Miller. He would be doing his country a service by ridding the Wight of another malignant Royalist. But he must hurry, for they seemed ready to leave...

He lifted his pistol. Damn! His eyes would not obey him and they were making it difficult to aim, and the pistol wobbled as he tried to steady it with both hands. He kept seeing images of two barrels on two figures, but what did it matter? So long as he saw barrels on one or both he could not miss. And with this reasoning he fired and almost cried out with relief as he saw Miller fall to the ground. He felt a surge of pleasure course through his body as he returned to his horse and rode away.

Chapter 19

When Anne awoke it was night. Now she was glad that she had seen the servants and told them that she needed a long sleep. At least no one had disturbed her. And no alarms would have been raised. She yawned and closed her eyes...

When she opened them again, a blackbird was singing its cheerful song somewhere outside. He might be full of the joys of the beginning of a new day, but she knew it would be easier for her to pull the bedclothes over her face and go back to sleep.

She would not surrender to self-pity, she thought, and forced herself to leave her bed. She looked into her dressing mirror and saw a sallow face and dull eyes that she hardly recognized. She would have to make an effort with her appearance if she wanted to avoid further speculation; for the servants would already be conjecturing as to the cause of her deviation from normal behaviour.

She dressed in a decorative gown; she had been considering removing some of the rosettes. But today it was just right for drawing attention away from her sallow face. It had ruffles over the shoulders trimmed with lace, and wide oblique lace around the low neck and cuffs. The sides were drawn up neatly to the waist, which along with the front was adorned by red rosettes. Three red bows were spaced out along the bottom of the gown to match the red petticoats showing at the sides and hem.

It took longer than usual to make her hair look right, and her arms were left aching when she had finished. Finally she pinched both her cheeks to bring colour to them before going downstairs.

"Anne! I have something to tell you," Samuel said excitedly.

"Can it not wait. I—?"

"No, it cannot wait," he interrupted her impatiently. "I was going to tell you yesterday, but I—I lost myself."

You mean you were in a drunken stupor, she thought, but he seemed sober now. It was not always easy to tell, these days: sometimes he drank quite heavily, yet seemed sober, while at other times he was clearly drunken...or perhaps she had become confused by his deepening moods. But there was nothing confusing about the way he fell into a deep ale induced sleep in his chair.

"Oh, all right," she sighed and followed him into the parlour, where he closed the door behind her. But she moved to the middle of the room, while Samuel stayed near the door.

"Well, what is so important...and why are you so excited?" She did not like the way he was watching her from the corner of his eyes. He giggled and almost bounced round to face her. He could hardly keep still, and she began to finger one of the rosettes at the front of her gown nervously. "Oh, Samuel, what on earth is it you have to say?"

"You won't like it," he said, and she was beginning to wish that she had refused to follow him into the room.

"I wish you would stop playing games and just tell me what it is."

"You really won't like it, my dear," he said, and she wanted to leave. He was blocking her way, so she tried to walk round him and he roared with laughter. "Trying to run away from me, my dear? I have something very important to tell you." He let his breath out in a heavy, satisfied sigh and clasped his chubby hands together. "It is done—the fiend is dead." He raised his eyes heavenward as though thanking God.

"W—what fien—I mean who is dead, Samuel?" Anne said nervously.

"Why, *who* do you think, my dear?" he said childishly, hopping from one foot to the other. "Whom do I wish dead more than any other?"

Anne did not answer. Swaying slightly, she closed her eyes for a moment or two, and when she opened them, Samuel had an idiotic smile on his face.

"Cannot guess? Then I'll tell you. Paul Miller is the one who is dead, and I was the one who killed him."

"No!"

His delight at her response was obvious as he continued: "I was summonsed to go after him and Oglander. They were about to help the King escape from his lodgings in Newport. And I shot Paul Miller."

Anne barely heard him laugh. For she felt so light-headed and weak; it was as though a cloud had come down over her and was draining away her strength and consciousness...

She opened her eyes and blinked. Why was she lying on the floor? She struggled to remember what had happened. Samuel was standing over her. He looked blurred at first, but then she saw that he was grinning.

"What...?"

"Can you not remember what I told you, my dear?"

Anne closed her eyes. "Oh, my God!" Perhaps she had been trying not to remember. She pulled herself into a sitting position. "You said you had murdered Paul Miller," her voice was little more than a whisper.

Samuel laughed. "Hardly murdered, my dear. The man was a scoundrel and part of a conspiracy to rescue the King, and we all know that once free of the Wight the King would stop at nothing to regain his position, even if it meant slithering through holes like the worm he really is." He was walking about the room as he spoke. "Paul Miller was just another worm. But he was slithering into my—"

"Stop it!" She had regained a little strength, but her voice was shaky. "It's a lie...and you are so vulgar...and what right have you to pass judgements and kill anyone?" She needed to go back to her bedchamber: she could not stay here on the floor. She struggled to stand up. Samuel had stopped walking about the room now and was watching her.

"Whoops!" he said as she wobbled and put a hand to her head. "You look very pale, my dear. Oh! By the way, I guessed you had joined your lover when a servant told me she heard you leave the house in the night, two…or was it three days ago?" He rubbed his chin and narrowed his eyes as though trying to remember. "Anyway, I told her she must have been mistaken. And I made excuses for you not coming down for meals. I said you were unwell.

"No doubt you warned Miller that I was going to kill him. I'm sure he was impressed. It must have been an act of God that gave me the opportunity to kill him when I did."

"Have you really killed him?"Anne said weakly, but she already knew the answer. He could not feign such excitement, so must be telling her the truth.

"I caught him with horses not far from the King's lodgings. I have important contacts. A messenger came to me and warned me about the escape." He stopped talking for several moments, allowing the tense silence to work on Anne's nerves.

"Yes, I have really killed him. I shot him, dead, dead, dead!" He hopped backwards and forwards again, laughing with glee, and then he took a deep breath and looked at her through narrowed eyes. "I should go and lie down," he said, feigning deep concern. And when she did not respond, he walked towards her and, putting his hand under her elbow, guided her towards the door. "I should go and lie down before you fall down again, my dear. We can continue our talk later."

"Yes, I will go and lie down. I think I shall stay in my bed for a long time, so please don't disturb me." Samuel roared with laughter, and Anne left the room.

Once inside her bedchamber she lay down on her bed fully clothed, not bothering to draw the drapes. She felt exhausted and miserable, and only one thought plagued her mind as she lapsed into sleep: Samuel had killed Paul.

When Anne awoke, her eyes were wet and there was a damp patch on her pillow. She knew she must have been crying in her sleep, but she could not remember dreaming.

She jumped, realizing that she was not alone: Samuel was standing by the door. He sighed heavily, and when he turned towards the bed he had an impatient expression on his face. But it changed to one of relief, when he saw that she was awake.

"What do you want?" she said coldly. "Why are you in my bedchamber?"

"You've been sleeping all day, my dear, and I have so much to tell you. I have been very patient. I could have eaten earlier, without you, but I decided to wait."

"I'm not hungry."

"Oh, but my dear, you must eat!" he said, walking to her bed. "Come along." He took her arm and she rose from the bed. Then he led her out of her bedchamber and down the stairs, stepping down one stair ahead of her all the way and, still clutching her arm, led her into the dining room. He let go of her and they sat in silence until a servant brought in some mutton stew and thick buttered crusty bread.

"I really don't think I can eat this," she said, staring down at her plate when the servant had left the room.

Samuel laughed. "But you must eat it. I have waited for you. And I've drunk hardly any ale, just to please you, my dear. We did not finish our conversation this morning. I could see you needed to lie down and—"

"It seemed finished to me," Anne said, flatly.

"Oh, but my dear, I was going to tell you that I've decided to move back into the marital bed now your lover is dead. In fact, I think I'll tell the servants not to disturb us for a whole day so we can—"

"No! Please...I—I don't think...I mean...I am far from well."

"I shall wait a couple of days then, but you will soon adjust...no, *enjoy* sharing your bed with me again." He rubbed his hands together.

She raised her eyes from her plate and looked at him. "I don't want you back in my bed, ever."

Samuel laughed. "That's better. Your spirit is returning. You still have everything I admire in a woman: boldness, spirit, compassion and softness, and when you get indignant or angry you are quite beautiful, my dear. I'll be very generous and give you three days, but then I will move back."

His sudden praise surprised her. How could he accuse her of

adultery and then tell her how much he admired her? However, she did not feel flattered by his praise and she never wanted him to return to the marital bed.

He burped, and then more wind left his body, making a loud gurgling sound against the seat of his chair. Dribble was running down his chin and she looked away as some of it trickled down his neck.

"You make me feel sick."

Samuel roared with laughter. "Oh, dear. You are angry with me for killing your lover, but he was a very wicked boy. He had to be punished. And when I'm back in your bed I will soon make you forget him." Anne left the table and hurried from the room.

"You haven't eaten your meal. It's no use running away," he called after her. But she went back to her bedchamber and cried until her eyes felt sore.

She was relieved that there was no sign of Samuel the next morning. Perhaps he really did mean to give her three days peace. She had quite expected to find him bubbling over himself again, waiting for her.

She had an overwhelming desire to go to church, though she doubted if she had the strength. She knew that she should try to eat something, so she went to the dining room and forced herself to eat a breakfast of coddled eggs and a little bacon.

She remained sitting for a while, and was surprised how much stronger she felt when she fetched her cloak and left the house.

The sky was full of clouds; but even on a fine day the sun would no longer shine for her if Paul were dead.

Somewhere deep inside her was a glimmer of hope that he was alive, and she was in no hurry to have that hope snuffed out. She was vaguely aware of traders setting out their wares for the market; she had forgotten that it was even a market day. She went into the graveyard.

More than ever, now, Anne thought the gravestones that had sunk to different levels and were crooked and weathered by time were symbolic of life rather than of death: everyone sank to a level, but some sank to lower depths than others. How she prayed that she would awake from a nightmare to find that Samuel had not sunk to the ultimate depth of a murderer!

Oh, Mary, she thought as she knelt down by her grave, I wish you were here. Tears slid down her face.

"Are you all right?" a woman's voice broke into her sadness. She had thought she was alone. She nodded her head and stood up.

"Yes...yes, thank you...I am all right." She could not see the woman's face, for her eyes were still misted by tears. The woman turned and walked away. She must be here visiting a grave of someone she loved, too, Anne thought, and it was comforting to know that the woman's kindness probably came from a deep understanding.

When she knelt at her mother's grave and read the engraving on the stone: 'Ruth Jolliffe, 1604 to 1627' she knew that those words would always bring a lump to her throat. Why had God taken both her mother and Mary so young? If she had asked Uncle Silas, he would have said that God needed them. But she needed them more! She sighed and silently apologized to God for her selfishness.

It was quiet and peaceful inside the church, despite the market outside, and she sat down on the pew nearest to the door. Then she knelt and said a silent prayer, asking God to give her more strength to face whatever the future might hold for her. She asked him to forgive her for loving Paul: if only it were not too late, O Lord, for you to punish me instead of him.

She left the church, having seen neither Reverend Bushnell nor Reverend Newland. But now she felt ready, or as ready as she would ever be, to face hearing confirmation that Paul was dead—so she decided to visit Sir John.

Leaving the church, she felt rain in the air. She glanced towards the traders and their wares, and the raw meat being chopped beneath the town hall. But her glance did not arouse a glimmer of interest inside her; it only kindled the sad thoughts that never again would she be able to come there with Mary and—

"Ouch!" She rubbed her arm and winced with pain. "Christina! I shall have a bruise."

"You deserve a lot more than a bruise. How dare you show your face here?" Folk were beginning to turn and stare at them.

"I have been to church," Anne began quietly, "but everyone is entitled to come here, including me."

"Your Samuel shot Paul Miller," Christina said in a loud voice.

Anne's eyes filled with tears on hearing it, even though she already knew in her heart that it was true. "I know and I—"

"You should be hiding yourself away in shame," Christina shouted and more heads turned their way. "If you had not made Samuel so jealous it wouldn't have happened. Harlot!"

"I am not a harlot. I—"

"Samuel thinks Paul has been making love to you," Christina said. "How do I know? Samuel's drink and indiscretion. You and Paul!" she scoffed, throwing her head backwards and laughing nastily. "But no wonder Samuel thought it the way you've been lusting after my Paul."

"That's a wicked lie," Anne protested. "How dare *you*? I have never lusted after him…or after anyone, come to that, but I am so deeply sorry for what has happened to him."

"You want Paul. Can you deny it?" She put her hands on her hips and stuck out her bosom as she half turned away. "I will make you stay away from him…he is mine."

"What?" Anne struggled to control her emotions. "You said…but…you mean…you mean he is alive? I thought you meant…Oh-oh that's wonderful news. I can hardly believe it!"

"You…wonderful? You thought he was dead? Do you think I'd just be standing here talking to you if Samuel had killed him?"

Anne laughed shakily. "No, of course not. I should have realized you would be killing me! How injured is he?" Christina pressed her lips together tightly and narrowed her eyes. "Please tell me."

"I won't tell you anything. Samuel obviously meant to kill him."

Anne laughed again. "Obviously he is not badly hurt or you would enjoy telling me about it…and blaming me." Christina threw herself at Anne and grabbed hold of her hair.

"Come along, Miss." Neither of them had noticed the two officials pushing their way through the market to reach them on being alerted by

Christina's raised voice. "We don't want any skirmishes here." They took hold of Christina's arms.

"It's her you should be arresting, not me," Christina shouted angrily. But the officials marched her to the meat market, pushing buyers out of their way as they did so, and ordered her to move ahead of them up into the town hall.

The sun had managed to break through the clouds and it was a beautiful day in more ways than one. Paul was alive. For now, at least, it was enough to make Anne forget everything else.

"A man came looking for Mr Jarvis with news of the King," a servant told Anne when she arrived back at Leeward House. "I told him we hadn't seen Mr Jarvis since yesterday, and he said..." she thought for a moment slightly nodding her head as she recalled each word from her memory: "'that's when he should have met me'."

Anne frowned. "And you haven't seen him at all?"

The servant shook her head. "No, Mrs Jarvis. He didn't come home last night—his bed's not been slept in."

Anne had been about to remove her cloak, but now she sighed and left Leeward House, again. What had happened to the blessed man? Was he stupefied with ale and unable to come home, or had he just decided to stay at her father's cottage for the night?

She found her father sitting in his cottage and he grunted when he saw her. She cleared all the crumbs from his table before talking to him.

"Samuel didn't come home last night, and he failed to keep an appointment yesterday. I thought he might have stayed here, or you might know where he is."

"No."

"You haven't any idea at all where he might be?"

"How'd I know?"

"He is your drinking partner."

"I hayn't seen him for weeks," Walter said grumpily. Anne kissed him on the brow on an impulse and left before he had time to protest.

But where was Samuel? Where on earth could he have gone? Did he know that Paul was alive? Had he gone to find him? Please, no...

She tried to think calmly. Was Paul living in his cottage? He was unlikely to be living there if he was too injured to fend for himself...or defend himself, come to that. He would almost certainly be at Nunwell House.

But Sir John would know what to do, anyway, even if it was only to contact the constables.

Chapter 20

Sheep were blocking the road along which the King's coach was being led and the army colonel swore at the shepherd.

"Ah...what bist about here, crousty panch-guts?" the shepherd said, leaning on his crook.

"What...? I command you to move these sheep, at once, in the name of Oliver Cromwell!"

"Who might this woooold rattlemouse Oliver Cromwell be?" the shepherd said, turning his head to look at the youth standing next to him.

The youth shook his head. "Noa...never 'heerd o' fellow. 'E don't own no land 'ereabouts."

"Casn't zee't riddle?" the shepherd said, pointing to the coloured marking on one on the sheep.

The youth nodded. "We only takes orders from—"

The colonel silenced him: "Don't be impertinent! If you don't move these sheep at once I will do it for you."

Several more men appeared from a bridle-path at the side of the road and joined the shepherd and the boy. The group was moving nearer to the King's coach, which was flanked on all sides by troopers on horseback.

"Keep away from there...and get those blasted sheep moving!"

"Them's riggish and can't be rowsed, nor can they be 'urried, sir.

Dedn't ye know Wight sheep are best in—?" the youth stopped talking as more men arrived and joined the shepherd's assembly.

The colonel narrowed his eyes. "What is this?" He ordered the troopers to be ready to fire their weapons. But more men arrived and the crowd jeered at the troopers and their leader before surging towards the coach.

"They're confounded Royalists...get them!" the colonel shouted and the troopers fired at the men. One tried to shoot a youth who was climbing into the coach, but the boy was moving too fast for him and he missed.

The trooper swore and grabbed his powder horn and began to reload. The sheep were fleeing and bleating in protest.

Inside the coach the boy lost no time in addressing the King. "Sire, come wi' us. We—" but the King raised his hand and stopped him from continuing.

"I have given my parole." The King sounded calm. "It is too late, anyway. But I thank you for your loyalty. Now please leave and try to save yourselves—God be with you."

"Oh no, please, Sire," the boy pleaded.

Outside, there were Royalists on the ground, either injured or dead. The rest were stubbornly standing their ground, waiting for their king to join them.

"He refuses to escape," the boy shouted as he left the coach. "I begged, but t'was no good."

"Thee dedn't beg hard enough, you," a man shouted back.

"I ded, honest, I begged and begged, but still t'was no good."

The shepherd and those of his group that were left standing rushed to help the injured men to their feet and support them as they all fled.

"Fire!" the colonel shouted.

"No!" King Charles was leaning out of his coach. He pulled off his plumed hat and threw it so that it spun through the air in an ark. There were gasps when the hat lost height and landed on one of the horse's heads, where it balanced in front of its ears before falling to the ground. Several of the men began to laugh, some nervously, and then most of the others joined in.

"Silence!" the colonel bellowed, and the laughter stopped abruptly. The men were commanded not to make a sound or move 'nor even flex a muscle' then they were reprimanded in crude rhetoric.

The convoy continued on its way along the road in the direction of the coast.

Anne wanted to hurry straight to Nunwell House. But she needed to check Paul's cottage first; for it was possible that his injury was so slight that he was still living there. But deep down inside her she knew that she would be checking to make sure that Samuel had not found him there and killed him.

The fresh air had helped to make her feel stronger, but it was fear that forced her on as she hurried to the cottage. Her legs felt weak when she reached it, and a fleeting image in her mind of the last time she had rapped upon Paul's door accompanied her knock. There was no answer. She knocked harder. Her heart was pounding in her chest and she was shaking as she tried the door and it open.

She exhaled, making a 'phew' sound, then closed her eyes for a moment, relief flooding through her because he was not there. She sat on Paul's chair, and her relief made her laugh weakly at herself for letting such anguish overcome her.

When she felt recovered enough she left the hut; but when she reached the stile, she had difficulty climbing over onto the tree-lined path that she had so often walked along before. But despite her lack of energy, she was not concerned about herself; she was thinking about Mary. Her eyes filled with tears as she remembered their last walk together, when Mary had struggled to follow her across a stile. She had not complained, but that was so typical of Mary, always so kind and so obliging, never wanting to disappoint anyone.

A movement at the side of her vision caught her attention, and she heard leaves crunching on the ground under the trees near the path. Turning her head towards the trees, she inadvertently stopped walking. The birds had stopped singing, and a shiver ran down her spine. She heard a twig snap, but no one was in sight.

A large bird flew out of the trees, squawking, and she wanted to believe the sounds could have been made by the bird foraging for worms, or by a wild animal…but she could not believe it. For the crunching leaves and breaking twig had sounded more like a human pursuing his prey.

She wondered whether to try to run, even though she still felt far from strong. Or should she challenge the person lurking there? Then she remembered Samuel saying that she was bold.

"Who is there?" Her throat felt dry, and her voice cracked under the strain of shouting, and it sounded far from bold, even to her. "Who are you?" Then she gasped. Of course…how silly…how dare he frighten her like this? "Samuel!" she shouted with relief in her voice. "I know you are there." She went towards the trees. "Samuel…where are you?" She could only see two trees with trunks wide enough to hide his girth, and she went to look behind one, then the other, half expecting him to jump out at her, but he was not there.

"Samuel…" Doubts began filtering into her mind. Where was he? How did he elude her so fast or so furtively…and would Samuel hide from her?

She left the trees and hurried away from them, back to the path, and continued on her way. She tried to convince herself that the movement and sounds were made by a child playing, and that she had scared him or her away. But she did not feel safe until she had almost reached Nunwell House.

Thank God! Her relief was well founded this time. For Paul was ahead of her, walking and laughing…and looking wonderful.

Christina was holding his left arm, possessively, while his right arm was bound. So it was his arm that had been injured. She closed her eyes for a moment, trying not to resent Christina's closeness to him. Paul had a right to happiness with an unmarried girl who could make him happy. He was alive, and not badly injured—that was what mattered. But she was unable to control the jealousy that was rising up inside her at the sight of them together. It felt as though a sword were being twisted in her heart.

Christina turned at that moment, as though sensing someone was there, and her eyes blazed with fury when she saw it was Anne.

"Why are you here?" she said through clenched teeth.

Anne drew herself up straight. She would not be intimidated, this time. "I have come to see Sir John because Samuel is missing," she said as matter-of-factly as she could, and then she turned onto the path that led to the main door of Nunwell House.

"Another of your family is missing," Christina said nastily, and Anne saw Paul push her away from him.

Anne hesitated at the door, closing her eyes briefly, praying for help in mentioning Paul without disclosing her love for him.

But the door opened. "Anne—what a pleasant surprise. I saw you from the window." Sir John looked drawn and tired, and she hesitated, but he was waiting for her to speak.

"Samuel didn't come home last night, and a man came to Leeward House looking for him, this morning. He said Samuel failed to keep an appointment with him, yesterday."

Sir John looked grim. "Perhaps he wanted to tell Samuel that the King has been taken by the Army and locked in Hurst Castle across the water. It's a terrible place, standing on a beach full of stinking mud at low tide…always cold, and fog surrounds the place. Even the guards are unable to endure the place for long. Sadly there is nothing we can do for him."

The news made Anne's eye fill with tears, but she knew there was nothing she could say to ease Sir John's anguish. He seemed distant now and she waited for him to return to her.

"I am so sorry to add to your problems at such a sad time, but I'm also worried in case Samuel tries to kill P—Mr Miller, again."

"I don't think you need worry. The last I heard of Samuel he was asleep in someone's barn and too drunk to be woken."

"Oh!"

"I do sympathize. I know your life is not easy…but how remiss of me—do come inside." He stood aside to let her enter.

As she moved past him she heard shouting coming from outside followed by a commotion, and Sir John was frowning as he turned back towards the door and went out.

When Anne reached the door, she saw Paul with his uninjured arm round a man's throat while struggling to force him towards the house. Christina kicked out at the man when he tried to break free. Tom Fletcher was with them, and Christina kicked out at him, too, and grabbed his arm when he tried to help the man.

"What do you want?" Paul was demanding angrily of the man. "He was lurking in the trees with Tom Fletcher," he told Sir John. "They were spying on us."

"Oh!" Anne said again, and Paul and Sir John looked at her. "I—I thought someone was hiding in the trees on my way here."

Her eyes travelled to Paul's injured arm. It was hanging stiffly out of the way of physical contact; it was not even in a sling, but Anne knew that he must be suffering some pain.

The stranger had no option but to face Sir John now, which meant that Anne could see his face, too. Looking at those evil black eyes like pits from hell made her feel as though her blood had turned cold in her veins, and she shivered. They were the same eyes that she had seen when she had almost been trampled down. The same eyes that she had seen in her dreams…

"You would never have caught me if it had not been for this adolescent," the man said, gesturing towards Tom. "I should never have trusted him again. Let go of my arm." His eyes bore into Paul's, but Paul's grip tightened.

A terrible suspicion was growing in Anne's mind; it was so terrible, in fact, that it was almost beyond her belief. Any fear that the evil figure had aroused in her was outweighed by her need to know the truth. She went outside.

She found it difficult to look up into the man's face without shuddering, but she was determined not to let him see her fear. "You nearly rode over me when I first came to Brading…" she said, and he fixed her with a cold evil stare, but she forced herself to continue, "it was near here. And you were watching my sister-in-law, Mary, outside the church after my wedding." His stare did not waver and his face told her nothing at the mention of Mary's name.

"What do you want?" Paul demanded again. The man's eyes turned back to him and bore into him again. But if he imagined that his silence and piercing dark eyes would unnerve Paul and make him look away, he soon found that he was wrong. Paul was as defiant as the other man, holding his stare without a flicker of an eye or a movement of his head.

"All right," Sir John said. "That's enough."

"We followed her," the man spoke at last, pointing a finger at Anne. His voice was as deep and dark as his eyes.

"We realize that, but why?" Sir John said. "And Tom is supposed to be working for me in my stables, tending my horses. So why is he here with you, wearing a sword?"

"There's no need for him to work here now his assignment is over."

"You were right about Tom then, Sir John," Paul said in surprise.

The man continued: "The King is no longer on the Wight and I have all the evidence I need against those who intended helping him escape."

"Then why were you following Anne?" Sir John said, but the man did not answer, and Anne wondered if she should voice her suspicions, but she knew they might sound ridiculous, at least before this frightening entity gave his name.

"Well?"

"I'm curious as to why Samuel Jarvis' wife should still be calling on rogues like you and Miller." It surprised Anne that he even knew whose wife she was...but then, of course, if he had known Mary...

"Jarvis assured me that he had forbidden her to talk to either of you. I shall advise him to punish her severely and to keep her under better control in the future," he said. "I'm leaving the Wight, probably tomorrow, and I hope you and your accomplices will be following me when I've surrendered the proof of your treachery to Oliver Cromwell."

"The treachery you speak of is of little worth compared to the treason against the King committed by you and your Roundhead friends," Sir John said, and the Roundhead's evil eyes stared back at him as he continued: "Where is this 'proof'?"

"The proof is in a guarded place where you will never find it." The Roundhead was struggling to free himself from Paul's grip, but Sir John stepped forward and took the Roundhead's other arm.

"I find it difficult to believe you would entrust anyone with such important documents," Sir John said.

"I would hardly bring them here."

"No? Not even if following Anne was a spur decision?" Sir John said. "And you hardly intended to be caught. Even through your cloak I can see the bulge of parchments—give them to me."

"Certainly not, and if you try to take them I will have you arrested."

"Can you see anyone here waiting to arrest us, Paul?" Sir John said with feigned amusement.

"No, I can't. Perhaps they are hiding in the trees, too."

"Will you free him of the parchments or shall I?"

"I think you should, Sir John, but I'm ready to knock him down if he proves difficult."

"With one arm?" the Roundhead said as Sir John reached inside his cloak and jerkin and pulled out parchments from an inside pocket.

Looking down at the parchments, Sir John released his grip on the Roundhead. But when he looked up again, he narrowed his eyes at him before saying to Paul: "These are forged documents, supposedly written by me, copied in my hand and partly written in blood—as I do on occasions. They contain details of a planned rescue of the King, involving previously convicted and various suspected Royalists, included you and me, of course. I certainly never wrote these and it is mere supposition."

"It is not supposition, the details are correct," the Roundhead said.

Sir John ignored him and was looking at one of the documents as he continued: "There are details of smuggling too, by you, Paul, to raise money to help the King." He looked up. "There are extracts from my stolen documents cleverly incorporated to make these appear authentic." He addressed the Roundhead. "Where are my parchments?"

"I destroyed them."

"Hmm, well I shall keep these in a very safe place. If you try anything like this again, you will only incriminate yourself. Even you would have difficulty explaining two sets of forged documents with almost the same content." He tucked the forgeries inside his own clothes.

"Curse you," the Roundhead said, but there was no passion behind the words; they sounded so ominous in the Roundhead's deep, cold voice that Anne shivered, fearing the curse would cause something terrible to happen to Sir John—but then she silently told herself not to be silly.

"So you were sent to spy on us," Paul said.

"What is your name?" Sir John demanded.

Anne clasped her left fist inside the palm of her right hand. She wanted to know his name, too. But at the same time she dreaded hearing him say it. She felt breathless and unable to look away from his face.

"Edmund," he said.

"Edmund what?" Sir John demanded at the same time as Anne made a sound in her throat. She had known deep inside her that he was going to say Edmund, but actually hearing him and knowing that she was standing with the man whom she so hated and wanted to bring to justice was almost too much to bear. "What is it, Anne?"

"He—he is Edmund—Mary's Edmund."

Sir John looked shocked. "Are you sure?"

"Y-yes…it all makes sense, now, but how could she love *him*?"

"The most evil of men can sometimes be the most charming when they want to impress someone," Sir John said, "or take advantage of them."

Paul said, "This is the Edmund who was seeing Mary. The father of her unborn child." It was more a statement than a question, but Anne answered him, nonetheless.

"Yes, Paul, and he murdered her!" She was surprised by her own outburst; and surprised that her conviction that Edmund had deliberately killed Mary was still so raw and bursting to come out.

She directed her voice at Edmund now: "You fiend! You murdered dear, sweet Mary. She loved you so much, and she trusted you. She would have done anything for you." Tears rolled down her face and Paul released his grip on Edmund's arm and took a step towards her.

"Please don't cry," he said. He moved as if about to comfort her, but then he stopped. Christina went to him and angrily tried to pull him away, but when he refused to move she continued holding onto his uninjured arm possessively.

"It wasn't my fault," Edmund said.

"Not your fault?" Anne's voice shook with emotion. "You murdered her."

"No, I did not murder her," Edmund said without a flicker of humanity in his eyes or voice. "You should be careful what you say. We went to the quay. I told her I was unable to marry her and ordered her not to tell anyone about us. When I showed her Oglander's documents and said they would lead to his execution and put you in the stocks for listening to him and defying your husband, she tried to snatch them from me."

Anne butted in angrily: "It was unlike Mary to snatch anything from anyone. You must have known she was trying to save us from harm…and why did you show them to her and say those things? You must have known it would upset her. And they weren't even genuine."

"That was when I left her," Edmund said loudly, ignoring Anne's outburst. "The tide was up and she must have fallen into the sea. Perhaps she fainted. How do I know what happened?"

Anne gasped. "Even if you didn't kill her or make her fall…or even know she was in difficulty, you killed her by leaving her there alone. You must have realized she was unwell."

"I left, thinking she would go back to Leeward House. How could I know she was so weak. I thought it was only her mind that was feeble."

Despite still lacking strength herself, Anne ran forward with clenched fists and pummelled Edmund on the chest. He grabbed her roughly by the arms and threw her to the ground. Now it was Paul's turn to gasp. He pulled his arm away from Christina and rushed towards Edmund, who went for his sword.

Sir John stepped between them and put a restraining hand on Edmund's wrist before he had time to remove the sword from its scabbard. "We are unarmed. I think we should go into the house and talk."

Paul hurried inside ahead of them and Sir John turned and smiled at Anne, who had left the ground and was sitting on the stump left by a felled tree. "Are you all right?"

"Yes, I am just a little tired, that's all."

"Paul isn't fit to fight, with his bad arm, and I think I am rather old to defend your honour." Sir John spoke calmly and quietly, as if to soothe her troubled mind, but then Paul reappeared with a sword in his left hand and stood 'on guard'.

"No! Please," Anne begged. "Paul, please don't—" she stopped at the sight of Christina's red face. Unlike those times when Anne had seen anger enhance her beauty, this was intense rage and was contorting her features into an ugly expression.

"How could you fight for her honour?" Christina raged. "Honour? She has none!" She grabbed Paul's right arm, and he winced with pain. She let go of him and took a step towards Anne, who was still sitting down. "Now look what you've made me do! You should never have come to the Wight. I hope you die an agonizing death."

Paul looked aghast. "Christina!" Christina had the grace to look contrite, but Anne suspected that it was feigned just for Paul; clearly the girl was having difficulty controlling herself.

"I am sorry, Paul, I would not have hurt your arm—" Christina began.

"You just did...now please stay out of the way," Paul interrupted, and she was glowering down at Anne as she moved aside.

Despite not wanting Paul to fight, Anne watched in wonder as he fought with his left arm. She was struck by his courage and might in holding his own against this ruthless fiend. She could almost feel Paul's pain when his right arm came into combat. She saw Edmund push his body against it deliberately, causing a cry of anguish from Paul, followed by cries of triumph as he began to match Edmund's movements and delivered feint attacks with perfectly timed strokes. Anne was overawed with admiration as he deflected Edmund's threatening blade with his sword in a simple parry. But then as Paul lunged in the final movement, Edmund parried him and lunged back. But Paul was too light on his feet for him and nearly struck him. While

Edmund was recovering from this, Paul delivered his counter-offensive action with superior speed and timing and delivered his final hit. He only pushed the tip of his sword into Edmund's flesh; just far enough to make it clear that he had won. Then he withdrew his sword and stepped back.

Tom had been watching the duellers with a tense expression on his face. Now he leapt towards Paul with his sword and arm extended. He threw the weight of his body forward onto his front leg. Then to save himself falling forward, his rear leg left the ground and swung past his front foot. He had started too far from Paul to hit, but his intervention gave Edmund time to retire and balance his body. Then Tom's quick running steps heralded the return of Edmund from his new starting position.

"No!" Anne cried out, realizing that Paul would stand little chance against two swordsmen, even if he could use both his arms. Sir John tried to wrestle Edmund from behind as he was about to drive his sword into Paul. At least it surprised Edmund and made him drop his sword. Without a curse passing his thin lips he pushed Sir John to the ground and bent to retrieve it. But Tom had taken advantage of the distraction and was almost ready to hit when Paul lunged forward and drove his sword into him.

Tom cried out, and Edmund left his sword where it had fallen and watched Tom fall to the ground.

Anne's first feelings were of relief that it was Tom on the ground, not Paul. But then she began to tremble. It was awful seeing Tom killed…even though Paul had had to do it to save his own life.

Cursing Tom, Edmund sank to his knees and pulled him round into his arms. "You cause me nothing but grief." Edmund was staring down at him with a grieved expression on his face. "Can you never do anything right?" His voice sounded weaker, less cold and less menacing, and Sir John, Anne and Paul looked at each other in surprise.

But he withdrew his arms suddenly, as though regretting his show of weakness, and stood up. His eyes bore into Sir John. "This is your fault for interfering." His voice had regained its former chill.

"No," Sir John said, "it is yours for being dishonourable and continuing to fight after Paul had won and spared your life." He had been looking at Tom as he spoke and now his eyes rested upon Edmund. "What is your surname?"

Suddenly Anne knew what was in Sir John's mind, and why something about Tom had seemed familiar and worried her when she had first seen him.

"What is your surname?" Sir John repeated, when Edmund did not answer, but now his voice was more demanding.

"Fletcher," Edmund said. "The same as his—Tom's. He was my son...my only son. I shall send someone to collect his body." He was looking around at the ground for his sword, but Sir John had picked it up.

"Whoever collects your son's body can collect your sword, too. I think you should leave it here now, or you might be tempted to use it on us," Sir John said, and Edmund left.

"I never wanted to kill Tom," Paul said, downheartedly, and now Anne longed to comfort *him.*

"I know," Sir John said, "but it was his life or yours. We must tell the constables what happened—at least we have witnesses."

"Do you think Edmund will try to avenge Tom's death?"

Sir John fingered his beard. "I hope not. And he knows what to expect if he has any more parchments forged. But he is a powerful enemy and could still tell an incriminating tale. Not quite so damning perhaps, but nevertheless..."

Chapter 21

Christina walked by Paul's side on the way to see the constables, but when she tried to link arms with him he pulled away.

"Please, Paul, I didn't mean to hurt you."

"Just be quiet…please!" he said, and Anne's heart filled with compassion for him. She could see the anguish in his eyes and prayed that he would soon find relief from the distress he must be suffering at having had to kill Tom.

She was walking with Sir John, but they both remained silent with their own thoughts. Sir John had insisted that Anne ate and then rested for a while before they left, and although she had found it difficult to eat anything after what she had witnessed, she did feel stronger now.

But she found it difficult not to keep remembering the way Tom had struggled for breath before he had died: she could not imagine anything so terrible as not being able to breathe. Of course she knew that it could have been worse: how she thanked God that it had not been Paul lying there! Even so, she was sure she would have nightmares.

In all the years that she had lived in her Uncle's parish, she had seen many things. She had seen a few dead folk awaiting burial, and it had been traumatic finding her uncle dead in the vestibule of his church. But this was the first time she had witnessed someone being slain by a sword. Maybe she had been fortunate to have lived so long before seeing her first duel; lots of folk, many younger than she was, must have seen many.

But she was sad also because an evil man like Edmund could love his son, while her father was unable to love her.

Sir John gave a brief account of the duel to the constables, while Anne stood clasping her hands together, wishing it was all over and she could go home. She feared she would give way to inconsolable tears when she tried to give her version of what had happened.

Sir John touched her reassuringly on the shoulder. "You do understand why it was necessary to report the matter quickly?" he said softly, and she nodded. Yes, she understood. If the authorities heard of the shooting before it was reported, they might seize the opportunity to arrest Paul and accuse him of murdering Tom in cold blood. After all, Paul was an ardent Royalist; while the authorities would soon know, if they did not know already, that Tom was Edmund's son and on their side.

They were waiting for her to speak. "It was horrible…" she stopped and swallowed the tears that were threatening to run down her face, "I shall never forget what happened." She closed her eyes for a few moments, willing herself to continue.

"I am sorry, Anne," Sir John said. "Perhaps we should come back tomorrow…at least we have reported it."

"No…it's all right," she said. She must do this for Paul. But it was impossible to keep her voice steady; her bottom lip kept trembling as she struggled to give her version of the events leading up to Tom's death. Her throat felt parched, and she had difficulty swallowing before saying Edmund's name; for she hated the feel of that evil man's name upon her lips. She looked from one constable to the other. Their faces showed no emotion. She concluded by saying:

"Paul Miller was only saving himself from being killed by Tom Fletcher."

"Had the duel anything to do with the King?" Paul was asked.

He looked the constable straight in the eyes as he spoke: "No, sir, I was defending Mrs Jarvis's honour."

The constables looked at each other and one shrugged and raised his eyebrows.

"I suppose you have the same tale to tell?" the other constable said, looking at Christina, and she nodded. "Then I cannot see any just cause to keep you here. You may all leave."

"Do you think they believed us?" Paul said quietly as they left.

"I hope so," Sir John said. "We only told the truth." He turned to Anne. "I'll walk with you to Leeward House. You have been through quite an ordeal."

But Anne had been thinking it might be a long time before she was able to visit her father after Edmund had spoken to Samuel. "I don't want to go home yet. I would like to visit my father," she said, and Sir John insisted on accompanying her there. Not that she objected, for she was thankful for his company, and it warmed her heart to know that he was never too preoccupied to show her compassion or give help when the need arose.

"Thank you…I do appreciate your kindness," she said when they reached her father's cottage.

"Kindness?" Sir John smiled. "It was my pleasure." He turned and left.

Despite her father's unloving attitude towards her, being in the home of her only living flesh and blood relative soothed her mind. She shut herself inside and leant against the door, breathing in the familiar odours of the cottage. It seemed only a short while ago that she had found difficulty calling it her home. But now that she no longer lived in it, she ran to it for sanctuary: how typical of life!

She found her father sitting by the table, with his back towards her, just as she had found him when she had entered the cottage for the very first time. Only now, as she moved to the table where he could see her, she fancied she saw the glimmer of a smile at the corner of his lips.

"I can almost believe you are glad to see me," she said, but he just grunted. Instead of feeling vexed, however, she felt a surge of affection for him. "I'm so glad you're home, Father. It would be nice if you could love me a little. But I think I have forsaken any hopes that it might one day happen."

Walter looked away and she continued: "I might not be able to come here for a long while." Walter looked back sharply. "Tom Fletcher was killed today. I—I don't really want to talk about it, it was awful, but it was a duel...not even planned...not even his duel...it was his father's..." her voice tapered away sadly.

"I heerd Tom's father was killed in t'war," Walter said.

"Tom told lies. And Tom's father followed me to Nunwell and intends telling Samuel I'm involved with active Royalists and that he is to punish me."

"How d'ye think he'll punish thee?"

"Maybe he will put me in the stocks...no, perhaps not, it would be too public. Perhaps he will stop me from leaving the house."

Walter surprised her by laughing. "I canst zee't happening...you're a strong-minded wench—I've ne'er seen the like...except in your mother."

"Am I like her?" Anne asked quickly, fearing that her father would stop talking to her at any moment.

"In many ways...yes. And if thee wast wondering 'bout the books in t'attic—they be hern...I loved her readen to me..." He stopped talking, but she knew by his tilted head and slightly open mouth, together with his pensive expression, that he had not finished and she waited for him to continued: "She tried teachen me...damned if I could be bothered wi't."

"It's so much easier to learn when you are a child," Anne said. "But I could read to you." She began clearing the table. "And I know you are right." He frowned, not understanding, and she continued with spirit: "I will not let Samuel stop me leaving the house. Oh, father, you have cheered me...can we stay like this?"

Walter shook his head. "'twould hay always ben like it if your mother had lived. I loved her so much."

"I know you did." Anne cleared away all the bread and cheese crumbs, fetched water, washed the plates and mugs and wished her father would wash them sometimes.

"Mother would have wanted you to love me, you know..." her voice tailed away. For Walter was resting his head back on the chair, pretending to be asleep, and Anne knew this was his way of dismissing the subject, and her.

She finished the chores and was about to leave when Walter opened his eyes and, completely ignoring her, went to pour himself some ale. She went to him and kissed him on the cheek affectionately before leaving the cottage.

She thought about her visit as she walked home. Her father had shown an interest in what she had said, and he had likened her to her mother. It was reassuring, but she knew it would be foolish to build hopes upon one conversation only to have them shattered next time she visited him—it would be best to accept things as they were and—

Oh no! There was a dapple-grey horse tethered outside Leeward House. How could she have forgotten even for a moment that Edmund was coming here? Tom's death might have hindered his plans for leaving the Wight, but she should not have imagined for one moment that it would hinder his intention of reporting her to Samuel; nor his intention to command that she be punished.

He would be in Samuel's study, now, talking to him about her and making her visit to Nunwell sound as damning as he could. But there was nothing she could do except go to her bedchamber and wait.

She went into the house and lifted her petticoats enough to hurry up the stairs when she reached them. But she jumped on finding Samuel standing outside his study door.

"We've been waiting for you, my dear," he said and, grabbing her by the the arm, hauled her inside his study and closed the door. "I understand you have already met this gentleman," he beckoned towards Edmund Fletcher, who was standing by the wall, his dark, piercing, cold eyes fixed upon her face, "and you know why he is here." He relaxed his grip on her arm. "I have told you to stay away from Oglander and his kind, so why did you defy me?"

Anne wanted to tell them how she had visited Sir John because she felt responsible for Paul's injury. But the shock of being hauled into the study and being in the presence of Edmund Fletcher again, made her babble.

Be bold, she told herself firmly. Be bold. Despite this day being one of the most traumatic in her life, she was not about to let the man who had caused Mary's death intimidate her.

She took a deep breath and, keeping her eyes on Samuel, forced herself to speak slowly: "It was because of what you imagined I was doing with P—Mr Miller that you shot him, so I had to know if—"

"My dear, I think you should be careful what you say," Samuel interrupted. "I was just in the middle of telling this fine gentleman how I shot Miller and stopped him and his Royalist friends from helping the King to escape." He added smugly: "And all on my own."

Anne stared at him in amazement. "I know nothing about an escape."

"I told the band of Royalists I knew exactly what they were doing, and they could hardly deny it, seeing as they had an extra horse with them for the King, and anyway my information came from a reliable source."

"I don't believe you." Anne fought to keep her voice calm and steady. "You shot Paul Miller out of jealousy and hatred, because you imagined I was being unfaithful with him, and this *fine gentleman*," her voice quavered as she lifted her hand towards Edmund, "was responsible for Mary's death, even if he did not murder her."

Samuel laughed. "Please forgive my wife, she has been ill. If I hadn't challenged the band of Royalists and shot Miller when they tried to defy me, Charles could be in France now." Samuel had his thumbs in the top of his breaches with his hands resting on his belly, and he rocked forward and then back and lifted his head high as though smelling the air.

Anne sighed. She doubted if an evil person like Edmund would care why Samuel shot Paul, anyway. She guessed as far as Edmund was concerned, the only good Royalist was a dead one. He probably wished Samuel had killed Paul.

"I can tell you why my wife visited Nunwell. She's friendly with Oglander and believes his Royal banter, but that was not the reason she was there, oh no," resentment was creeping into his voice, "it was Paul Miller she went to see. He's been staying at Nunwell House while his injury heals—is that not correct, my dear?"

"I did not go to see Paul Miller," Anne said, "but if you think you know so much, why ask me?" She doubted if Samuel had expected her to answer; and he probably would have preferred it if she had not done so.

Now he ignored her and continued: "I dare not caress my wife, lest she breathe Paul Miller's name, not mine." Resentment was now controlling his voice. "Paul Miller is her lover."

"That is untrue." Anne turned on Samuel angrily: "You told me to be careful who heard me say you shot Paul out of jealousy, yet now you are ranting like a jealous husband. Perhaps you are the one who should be careful.

"You know, Samuel, you can accuse me of anything you like, but at least I would never fraternize with Mary's killer."

"I thought we stopped all that nonsense."

"It isn't nonsense. He," she said with a slight head gestured towards Edmund, "admitted he was there."

"I said it was an accident," Edmund said indifferently.

Anne ignored him as she continued: "When I said Mary had been seeing an Edmund, who was supposed to be on a secret mission, you must have realized I was talking about him." She glanced at Edmund angrily this time. "That's why you disregarded what I told you and seemed to stop caring…now it all makes sense."

Samuel's face had reddened and he appeared uncomfortable. "Utter nonsense."

"Because of him your own twin sister is dead, yet you stand with him not as an enemy in combat but as his ally against me. I loved Mary like my own sister…like my own flesh and blood. I cannot bear to see you talking together."

"Edmund has told you that Mary's death was an accident."

"A convenient accident." Anne's emotions were in tatters. "Even if Edmund didn't murder her, he left her to die. That's almost the same thing. Edmund used her and then when she was with child, my niece or nephew, he wanted to be rid of them both."

"You must learn to control your fanciful imagination," Samuel said ruefully, raising his eyes to the ceiling, any awkwardness gone.

Anne sank down onto a chair. "I thought you loved Mary as much as I did. How can you betray her like this?"

"Edmund has explained to you what happened to Mary," Samuel said impatiently. "There is no evidence to support your accusations of killing or purposely leaving her to die. And anyway, whatever I did wouldn't bring her back…we must think of the future."

Anne was about to say that Mary had no future, but Edmund's eyes were boring into her. "These silly accusations you are making against me are very dangerous," he said. "Even if they were true, they could never be proven," he smiled at her in a way that made fear grip her body, "but they could bring wrath upon your own head."

She looked at Samuel. Surely he must realize that Edmund was threatening her, but he was avoiding meeting her eyes as he supported Edmund: "And in these times we can't afford to accuse our friends of being criminals and to make enemies of them. We could endanger our lives with such accusations, my dear."

Anne knew that Edmund had been threatening her, but Samuel…? She stared at him with dawning realization: despite wanting to kill Paul to regain her affections, his first love would always be himself. If they were in peril and he could either save himself or her, she would be the one to die. She could not bear to be in the room with either of them one moment longer. She stood up and fled from the room and went to her bedchamber, not caring what punishment the two men had in mind for her.

Samuel and Edmund left the house together. They had probably gone to one of the ale houses now that Edmund no longer needed to hide, Anne conjectured. How she hoped that he would soon leave the Wight! Even with his evil influence gone, it would be difficult remaining civil towards Samuel, but she must try. She must try not to think about Paul; and for Paul's sake and for her own integrity, she must stop listening to her heart.

Was Mary looking down upon them? Did she know of Samuel's treachery? Oh, Mary, I am so sorry, she said silently. But if Mary knew of Samuel's disloyalty in befriending her killer, she also knew how much Anne still missed her and wanted her death avenged.

"Oh, Samuel," Anne said. "What do you want, now? I don't want you in my bedchamber." She was ready to go to sleep and about to lean over to snuff out the candle and release the ribbon that held the drap back.

She closed her eyes for a moment, remembering her pledge to be civil, and then she bit back further unwelcoming words.

Oh, no! He had a belly full of ale, she could hear it rattling, and he was stumbling; he almost tripped over his own feet. He moved towards the bed and swayed over her.

"You shou—you shouldn't've a-accush-ed me of not loving M-Mary. You sshouldn't have—" he sounded broken and gulped, almost in tears, and Anne's forced tolerance dissolved into pity.

Despite his apparent increased capacity to drink heavily without appearing drunk, or at least show no more than the slurred speech that now seemed permanent, he had excelled himself again tonight.

She could not help thinking what a pathetic sight he was with his red face, enlarged veined nose and fat stomach. He was tottering precariously from side to side, while the liquid in his tankard slopped over the top and landed on his bloated belly. He put his candle down on the little table next to hers and, with irony, she saw the flames flicker together briefly as one.

Yes, he was a pathetic sight. He slurped his ale, but most of it ran down his chin. For the second time that day Anne did not want to be in the same room with him. She left her bed and, putting on her cloak and picking up her candle, left the bedchamber. She would rather go and sleep in an unaired bed than stay with him.

"Where y'go-ing?" she heard him say.

Thank God! she thought, when he did not follow her. He would probably flop down…or more likely fall down on her bed and go to sleep.

In the bed, in the spare bedchamber, she burried her face down in the bedclothes; it would take her an age to feel warm, but she was tired and it was not long at all before she slept…

Anne groaned, half asleep; something had disturbed her. What was that? Her eyes flickered open, and she groaned again and then closed them.

What was that crackling sound? Was Samuel in the room? No, he would not crackle, she thought. It must be one of the servants…She turned over, trying to escape the sounds, and was about to snuggle her face back into the bedclothes, but a pungent smell penetrated her senses and she coughed. It smelt like…the word slowly filtered up from the depths of her mind…'smoke'. She sat upright in the darkness. "Fire!" Something was on fire. She left the bed and tried to remember where everything was in the room. Grappling with her cloak, she struggled to pull it about her, and then fumbling about, coughing, lit her candle. Smoke was filtering into the room beneath the door. She clasped her hand over her nose and mouth as she opened it.

A cloud of smoke engulfed her and she pulled her gown up over her mouth and nose and made her way to the top of the staircase. She released the cloak from her mouth only long enough to shout "Fire!" to the servants, between coughs. Then again she shouted: "Fire!"

She listened and could hear voices of servants stirring below. She checked Samuel's bedchamber. But as she feared, it was empty.

She headed for her own bedchamber. "Fire, Samuel. Fire!" she shouted as loudly as her voice would allow, but now affected by the smoke it was no more than a croak. Her throat was uncomfortable when she coughed.

She opened her bedchamber door. "Ouch!" It was hot and a flame leapt out just missing her, while another licked at the top of the doorway. Anne gasped and stepped back in horror, releasing the cloak long enough to call "Samuel!" urgently, straining her throat. Smoke was billowing down the stairway.

What on earth was she to do? She must act quickly or Samuel would burn to death. She tried to call down to the servants, but how could they hear, anyway? Those still in the house were making so much noise. She snuffed out her candle, from habit, and put it down.

Fear gripped her as she forced herself forward. She pulled her cloak higher over her mouth and nose. Oh, God, please help me, she prayed silently as she entered her bedchamber and huddled against the wall, trying to avoid the flames.

As she moved further into the room along the wall, she wanted to turn and run back out. But what of Samuel if she did? He would suffer a horrific death. She had to reach the bed and awaken him. She left the wall. She was almost continually coughing into the cloth. She felt so dizzy that she almost stumbled as she stretched out her hand to try to feel the bed. Her eyes were smarting and sore, and she withdrew her hand sharply as intense heat licked her fingers. The skin was burnt, but the pain dissolved into her other discomforts as she struggled for breath. She had to leave before it was too late. I don't want to die, she thought as pain filled her chest. Her legs gave way beneath her and she fell.

Chapter 22

"Paul…" The word was barely audible, but it was enough to send Paul into raptures of relief.

"Oh, Anne, thank God!" He bent over and buried his face in her hair and kissed her head. "I was afraid you would never wake up."

Anne coughed and it hurt, and Paul helped her to sit upright, then he changed the position of the bolster behind her so that it supported her.

She felt dizzy and her eyes felt sore and were watering. "I can hardly see you." Her voice was barely more than a whisper. She put up her hand and touched Paul's face with her fingers. He was real. She must be awake; for she hurt inside, and she could not remember ever having felt physical pain in a dream.

Paul clasped the hand in his, lifting it to his lips and closing his eyes as he kissed her palm and kept it against his mouth for a few moments. She began coughing and was unable to stop, and Paul leapt from the chair to fetch her a drink of water.

"I'm all right," she managed to say when he returned and handed her the cup. Her other hand was swathed in bandages and she put it to her bosom. "Irritation."

At least the cool liquid soothed her throat. She handed the cup back to Paul and he leaned over and placed it on her table. Then he sat on the bed and held her hand in his. But she frowned, thinking she was really giving Samuel cause to be jealous now, if he was here. She pulled her hand away.

231

She wondered why she was back in her father's cottage, and in his bed, at that, not in the attic. It seemed to be taking an age to remember the simplest things…but then the answer to why she was here filled her mind suddenly: fire! She closed her eyes. Samuel had been in her burning bed…"Samuel?"

Paul sighed and shook his head and spoke softly as though trying to lighten the burden of what he had to tell her. "I think he must have been dead when I arrived. And the ceiling fell in on him as I was carrying you from the room. There was nothing I could do for him."

"Thank you…for saving me." Paul was about to speak, but she continued: "I did try to save Samuel." Her voice was still little more than a whisper; it hurt her to talk at all. And while she knew that she had tried to save Samuel, it took all her concentration to remember anything about it. She could just about remember entering her bedchamber. She put a hand to her brow. "But obviously I failed…he must have suffer—" Another attack of coughing had cut her sentence short, and Paul reached out and picked up the cup from where he had placed it on her little table. This time he held it to her lips.

"I know you tried to save him. You could have been killed…in fact, you did nearly die," he scolded gently. "But I doubt if Samuel suffered. He probably died in his sleep without knowing anything about it."

"Do you really think so?" She remembered the deep sleeps that he seemed to go into these days. "Of course he had been drinking." She began coughing again and Paul held the cup back to her lips.

"Well, there you are then."

But Anne wondered if she might be responsible for what had happened to Samuel, and she struggled to remember more.

"What is it?" Paul said.

"What…? Oh, I think I might have left the candle burning in my bedroom." Paul held the cup back to her lips.

"We can talk about it when you're better, but don't you dare start blaming yourself for what happened. Stop trying to talk, now. All I care about is that you are alive—you gave me such a scare.

"I don't know what woke me but I had this terrible feeling that something was wrong. I went outside and saw the smoke…I ran through the orchard, and then when I saw the flames I thought I might never see you again."

"Aye, I thought same," a shaky voice said, and Paul looked round at the bent, trembling figure. Without saying a word, Paul rose and took the almost empty cup to refill it with water.

"Father," Anne said. She had dabbed the water from her eyes and although they were still smarting, she could just about see that her father was looking down at her anxiously.

"Please sit down," Anne said.

He sat on the chair by the bed, still looking anxious. "When someone knocked and said t'house was burnen, I be that muddle-headed...I found I cared what was happenen to thee, you. Sorry for...well..." his voice caught in his throat. He put out a hand, but hesitated as though not sure what to do. Anne took the hand in hers and it seemed to give him the encouragement that he needed to say simply: "I love you."

"Oh, Father, I love you, too," was all she said now, for she did not want to start herself coughing again, and it was all that was really needed to reassure her father that she still wanted him in her life.

"You should rest now." Paul had returned with the cup, which he had refilled with water, and he placed it on the table. "Your father told me he intends sleeping in the attic until you've recovered." Paul looked at her father and he nodded.

Anne squeezed her father's hand gently before falling back to sleep.

"Colonel Thomas Pride has banished all those who are more likely to make peace with the King from the House of Commons," Sir John said flatly. "He stood outside the Commons with a force of soldiers either arresting or dismissing the majority of members including all the moderate Presbyterians. All that's left now is a handful of radicals!"

Paul turned from where he had been chopping the wood of a fallen tree. "How can they do that? Surely every member has a right to be there?"

"Of course they have, Paul, but Colonel Thomas Pride was acting under instruction from the New Model Army. No one can stop the Army now that it's a law unto itself."

"It should never have been allowed to get like that!" Paul said vehemently.

Sir John shook his head. "I don't know how we could have stopped it happening.

"Colonel Pride and his men are obviously helping make preparations for the King's trial—a trial instigated by treacherous men scorning the law of the land. With the only members left in Parliament being those considered radical enough to find the King guilty of whatever charges might be trumped up against him." He absently fingered his beard, knowing that Paul did not need him to finish. "Leave the rest of the chopping for the woodsman, Paul. We can talk while we inspect the park and farmlands." But distressed as they were by the plight of their king, he knew that it would be difficult to keep their minds on any task.

"I'm so angry that there's nothing we can do," Paul said as he left what he was doing and followed Sir John. "I hate the Roundheads…they've destroyed the King with their wicked lies."

"More exaggerations and distortion than lies."

They had stopped by a field where three horses were grazing, and all three were on their way over to where Sir John and Paul were standing. "I don't think the King would have been given a chance whatever he did. I think I told you about the members of Parliament held down in their chairs to stop them obeying the King."

"Yes, you did, and I was angry then, too."

"There have been some lies too, of course. Like the Parliamentarians claiming Middle Ages Parliamentary Government had had complete rule. And even though it wasn't true it made the King fear gradual loss of his own power until there was nothing left."

"When in reality it was even worse than the gradual loss he foresaw…his power was taken away all at once," Paul said in disgust.

"It seems that way to us, but as far as the King is concerned now, not finalizing concessions means that the power can still pass on to his heir.

"You know, Paul, some folk say the King should have fought back years ago when John Pym was alive. He did so much towards the King's demise and caused those who'd served him to be arrested or driven into exile. But if he had fought back it would only have been turned against him, I'm sure. The Moderates became quite concerned at the methods Pym used to force his views through Parliament."

"You'd think that would have made everyone support the King."

"Many did, but the King's shyness sometimes made him tactless in his remarks and speeches, and some people misjudged him.

"When Parliament was recalled in 1640 the election was based entirely on a 'for or against the King' policy. And in the politicians frame of mind at that time, the King was defeated.

"What on earth are you doing with that piece of fence?" While Sir John had been absently stroking and patting the horses, Paul had been venting his frustration by picking at the bark of one of the branches with which the fence was made. "Please stop before you damage it." Paul picked up an old piece of wood from the ground and began stripping the bark from that instead. "You know of course that the King's enemies are more united by negative aims than by positive ones."

It had not been a question, but Paul nodded. "I wish I could go to London and do something to stop them," he said vehemently as he threw the remainder of the piece of branch that he had been stripping, making Sir John jump. But the corner of Sir John's mouth turned up into a half-smile.

"What...and be locked away again? Believe me, I know how you feel, but relieving your frustration by trying to fight a lone crusade won't help. You will just add your name to the long list of dead Royalists. All we can do now is pray that a miracle will save the King."

Chapter 23

"Christina!" Paul shouted and rode after her. "Where are you going with him?" Edmund turned his cold eyes towards Paul, but Paul ignored him and continued talking to Christina. "You know he killed Mary."

"She knows it's a lie and that you killed my son," Edmund said, and Christina opened her mouth as if to say something, but then had the grace to look ashamed and lower her head.

Edmund took out a pistol and a powder horn as he spoke: "She is coming with me to report your activities to Oliver Cromwell."

"Is this true?" Paul asked, directing his speech at Christina. "After all the years we have known and trusted each other, you would do this...but why?" In contrast to Edmund's chilly tone, his voice shook with emotion.

His words seemed to infuriate Christina and she raised her head. "Yes, I trusted you, but now I intend to do my duty and report traitors like—"

"Oh, Christina!" Paul interrupted. "A traitor is what you will be if you continue with this foolishness. Please come with me instead, and we can talk."

"We have listened to enough of your feeble prattle," Edmund said, then beckoned Christina forward with the pistol, and they both rode away from him.

"Christina, please don't go with him. He is heartless and dangerous," Paul shouted as he rode after them. "Have you not done enough harm, Edmund Fletcher?" Edmund stopped, and so did Christina.

Paul moved nearer to her and reached out to touch her arm. "You cannot trust him. He will hurt you...he may even kill—" He stopped when he saw that Edmund was pointing the pistol at his head. He pulled on his horse's left rein, turned and galloped away. There was nothing more that he could do alone.

He reached Nunwell in full gallop and breathed a sigh of relief on seeing Sir John standing outside the stables.

"I have just seen Christina and Edmund together," Paul shouted, then he reached Sir John and pulled his horse to a sharp stop.

"Christina and Edmund?"

"Yes, she's leaving the Wight with him. I challenged Edmund and he said she was going with him to give evidence against us to Cromwell. I could hardly believe she would betray us like this."

"Perhaps she was being forced."

"No...I don't think so. I asked her why she was betraying us. At first she looked embarrassed, or perhaps it was shame...then she looked me in the face and angrily informed me that she was doing the right thing in helping the Roundheads track down traitors like me. Edmund pointed the pistol at my head, and I left. For the first time in my life I felt I didn't know Christina at all."

While he was talking Sir John beckoned to a stable lad to saddle a horse.

"Jealousy can arouse unpredictable reactions. We had better go after them, anyway, and try to dissuade Christina from leaving the Wight with Edmund."

"I have never done anything to make her believe I felt more than sisterly love for her."

"I know, but we can't control what people feel for us anymore than we can control how we feel about them."

"It may sound irrational in the circumstances, but I still feel concerned for Christina. I can still see the evil look in Edmund's eyes when he looked at her," Paul said.

"I think he *is* evil," Sir John said, "but no, it does not sound irrational. Christina might even have changed her mind about betraying us by now and need rescuing."

"Oh, my God!" Sir John said. "It seems we're too late."

Paul groaned and closed his eyes for a moment. They both dismounted and went down on their knees, trying to stem the blood flow from the side of Christina's neck, where it had been slashed. It could have only happened minutes before, yet already it was too late to save her.

She made a sound in her throat and was struggling to speak. "Fo-for-give— I—stop Edmund telling—"

"Of course we forgive you," Paul said, taking one of her hands in both of his. A gurgled sigh escaped her lips, then her eyes stared unseeingly. Sir John used a thumb and forefinger to close them, and they both bowed their heads over her in prayer.

Sir John stood up, intending to leave Paul there for as long as he needed to say goodbye.

It was only then that Sir John saw the pistol lying in the grass by Christina's feet. He picked it up and followed the bloody trail leading away from Christina's body.

"Paul! I think you had better come and see this." Sir John had mistakenly believed that all the blood was Christina's, but now he had found Edmund where he lay face down in the bracken. And on rolling him over, he found a bloody wound in his chest.

"Do you think Christina shot him?" Paul said.

"Yes, I do." Sir John stared into the bracken before continuing: "I think she was trying to tell us that she had stopped him from going to Cromwell. He probably lashed out at her after she shot him, intent on cutting as near to her throat as possible. We will never know exactly what happened, or how she got Edmund's pistol…though that could not have been too difficult for someone like Christina…but it might be kinder not to think too much about that.

"All we really need to remember is that she shot Edmund to save you. She has saved us both, Paul…from being imprisoned, at least, and saved others too, whom Edmund intended reporting." Paul walked back to Christina's body.

Sir John followed him. "She had no one?" he said gently, trying to ease Paul back into conversation as he stood silently staring down at Christina.

Paul shook his head. "No, she has no one to mourn her or give her a decent burial. As you know, the old couple who found her as a baby and raised her are long since dead. And if the rumours were right and she was left by gypsies, goodness knows where her relatives are!"

Sir John looked doubtful.

"You know, Paul, I cannot imagine gypsies abandoning one of their own. But then who can say? Christina certainly had the looks of a gypsy about her. Well, anyway, she will have a decent burial—I can at least see to that."

Paul nodded. "That is very generous of you, Sir John."

"Oh, I don't know…maybe I am just repaying a debt. With both Tom and Edmund dead our futures look rosier—I only wish that the same could be said about the King's."

"Edmund could have let Christina live," Paul said, suddenly angry. "Killing her served no purpose at all, except revenge: only he would use his dying breath to kill a woman!"

Sir John looked at him intently and then walked away from where Christina lay. He waited for Paul to follow him before he spoke: "You know, Paul, the circumstances surrounding Christina's death will remain as mysterious as those surrounding her birth, but at least she will have us to remember her.

"But what about you, Paul. Or should I say you and Anne?"

Paul looked questioningly at Sir John, and he smiled: "I probably knew you were in love with each other before you knew it yourselves. I know how difficult it has been for you both—you behaved well in the circumstances—but now Anne is free."

Paul had love in his eyes as he answered: "I intend to ask Anne to marry me as soon as a it is respectfully possible."

* * * *

"Of course you must have heard the terrible news!" Paul slammed his fist against the frame of the open door in frustration.

"Yes, I have heard," Sir John's voice reflected the heartache that he felt, "but you had better come in before you break my door."

"How could they do such a thing?" Paul sounded incensed.

"I don't know, Paul. But I do know that only six officers backed Ireton's demands for extreme measures, and the Lords refused to co-operate in the King's trial at all." He turned and ran his forefinger and thumb down his chin and beard before he said: "In the end, it counted for nothing that the extremists calling for the King's head were in the minority. Next to Cromwell and Ireton, I feel most aggrieved with fanatics like the one that had the crowds believing he saw God amongst the soldiers…and likened Moses leading the Israelites out of Egypt to the Army leading the English people out of serfdom by destroying the Monarchy!"

"May they be punished in Hell!" Paul said.

"They well might be," Sir John said. "But they weakened the House of Commons' resolve and made it easier for Cromwell to persuade members to sign the King's death warrant…if persuade is the right word. Not even those left in the Rump all readily supported the warrant. At least one member of the Commons was reported to have been held down and forced to sign away the King's life."

"How could such a warrant be valid if signatures were obtained by force?"

"Everything that has happened to the King has been as unlawful and as sinful as if he had been kidnapped straight from his throne and hanged from a tree," Sir John said. He had prayed that Cromwell would overcome the darker side of his nature and help lessen the pressures being put upon the King. "Rumour had it that Cromwell secretly admired him and even slept in one of his beds in Whitehall. But finally he hardened his heart and let the Devil persuade him he was acting on behalf of God. We failed the King, Paul. We failed him!"

"He trusted you more than anyone else. If you could not persuade him to escape, then no one could. But what will become of us, now? No, not just us…the whole kingdom?"

"There's not much we can do about the Kingdom, I'm afraid, except hope that Prince Charles will soon take his rightful place on the throne." He summonsed a servant to bring ale in two tankards.

When the tankards full of ale arrived, Sir John took one and raised it: "To Charles."

Paul had taken the other tankard and they both raised them high. "To Charles." The tankards clashed together. They drained them before either of them spoke again.

"Is it true that the King was executed only three days after being sentenced?" Paul asked.

"Yes, Paul, it is. It left no room for an appeal or reprieve. Few people knew what was happening until it was too late.

"But the King faced his accusers with bold, straight answers and died like a gentleman…so bravely…he even wore an extra vest in case the cold made him shiver and give the impression that he was afraid. He died with dignity for the sake of his son and heir.

"I'm going to the vicarage, this morning, to see what preparations are being made for a special service. I suggest you tell the workers to leave all but essential duties…you can wait for me at the vicarage later, if you like, but if you're not there I won't wait." When Paul had left, Sir John gave way to silent tears that had been lurking behind his eyes since he had heard what had happened to his king.

* * * *

Anne awoke to the sound of birds singing. It was a beautiful day, and she felt she must be the happiest girl in the world. Only one thing could have made it better: Mary being here, too. She pushed the thought away, determined not to let anything make her sad, on this, her special day. For today was her Wedding Day. Today she was going to marry her beloved Paul and become Mrs Paul Miller.

She still had difficulty believing she would be sharing the rest of her life with her beloved Paul. So much had happened to her, but it no longer mattered: it was all in the depths of her mind, now, like the fading memories of a bad dream.

In the last few months she had been happier than she would have thought possible. She pushed the bedclothes from her.

Jumping up, she twirled round with her new dress in front of her; it was a pretty red dress that she had made especially for the occasion. It was actually much plainer than the one that Mary had made for her marriage to Samuel. But Anne had used colourful ribbon and some brocade to brighten it. She knew that her father considered it an extravagance: she already had nice dresses, he had said. But she wanted to start afresh with this wedding, so the new dress was essential.

"You look lovely," her father said softly, when she eventually emerged from the attic, "like your mother." Anne knew that such an expression of sentiment was not second nature to her father, and she was glad she had been extravagant. She slung her arms around her father's neck and kissed him. She heard his sob, and drawing back she looked at his face and saw tears in his eyes.

"I don't deserve thee—how can I e'er make amends?"

"There's nothing to make amends for. I had a happy childhood. And now I could not wish for a better father. Let's forget the rest. Just go on being my father now," Anne said fondly.

Everyone wanted to see them married: Anne and Paul. They all accepted Anne now. She had no bridesmaids. If Mary had been alive it would have been different, of course. But Mary was not alive, and Anne could not bear to have anyone else.

This wedding was so different from the last one, and Anne could not believe that anyone had ever felt so happy, as she walked down the aisle towards her Paul.

Epilogue

The angelic looking girl with curly, fair hair ran towards her two brothers, laughing. One boy had brown eyes; the other had dark blue like his father.

"Paul, John, Mary, stay with us now," their mother called out to them, and they ran over to be with their parents.

They arrived at St Mary's Church in plenty of time for the service, but the church was soon full, with more people crowding outside its doors. For the service was a long awaited one: special services were being held in churches all over the Kingdom to give thanks for the return of King Charles 11. And in England special prayers were being said for his coronation—he had been crowned King of Scotland after his father's death.

"Sir John would have been so happy today," Anne whispered, and Paul squeezed her hand gently. Sadly Sir John had died five years earlier and had been lain to rest in the Oglander chapel in the church. But two of his sons were sitting near the front of the congregation. Anne hoped that Sir John was at peace with his beloved wife and others of his family that had died.

"He *is* here with us," Paul said, looking towards the Oglander chapel, and for a moment Anne thought she felt his presence.

While Anne and Paul's marriage remained as happy as on the day they were wed—or, if possible, even happier now that they had Mary, Paul and John—they had not stopped praying for Charles 11 to return as King.

And now, with the Lord Protector Oliver Cromwell dead—having died bitter and disillusioned because he had failed to instigate a 'godly commonwealth'—people were gathering everywhere to pray and rejoice because Charles was to be accepted as their king.

Anne knew that some had proclaimed Oliver Cromwell the greatest soldier, while many believed him to be no better than when he was a boy, playing truant from school, breaking down hedges and stealing doves from cots. He had also been reckless and disorderly, and as a Cambridge University student had leapt from a dormitory window onto a horse.

Anne knew that Cromwell had formed his own Parliament in 1653, ousting the rump that had been left by the purge. But then he had found it necessary to dissolved two more uncontrollable Parliaments. Both Anne and Paul hoped it had given him insight into what the King had had to endure, years earlier, when he had been forced to rule alone.

Paul had said that when the republican leaders had been allowed to return to their seats in Parliament, they had wanted to destroy the Lord Protector: for they were outraged at being forced to return to what they referred to as 'an Egyptian bondage'.

Anne knew that Cromwell supporters claimed he had become more tolerant since his Puritan youth. And Paul had said it was true he had mellowed enough with age to believe only those who had murdered, or carried out acts of treason or rebellion should face the death penalty. But Anne, Paul and other clear thinking Royalists would never forget that he was guilty of all three.

On Oliver Cromwell's death, his son Richard had taken over as Lord Protector.

Anne remembered how, seven months later, Paul had hurried home and, with excitement in his voice, told her how army leaders had carried out manoeuvres and forced Richard Cromwell to dissolve his third Protectorate Parliament.

"This could be what we have been waiting for," Paul had said. And the Rump Parliament that Richard's father had ousted had been returned. How they had prayed for King Charles 11! He had tried to reclaim his birthright, with the help of the Scots, a few years before, but had then fled to France...

"I hope no one makes the mistake, ever again, of thinking we don't need a sovereign," Paul whispered. "If they do, they will deserve another Oliver Cromwell and his blessed son!"

Paul was still holding Anne's hand, and he gripped it gently again and they smiled at each other as the service began.